I0760770

Blissful

Monica Shantel

Blissful

monica shantel

Blissful

ISBN 978-1-960696-93-9 (Paperback) ISBN 978-1-960696-00-7 (Hardcover)

Book Cover by Monica Shantel

Illustrations by Monica Shantel

First Edition

For all the girls put into a box.
Be you and ignore the voices on the inside.

Mia Dawson
6/20/23

Dylan Adler
6/20/23

One

WAVES ROLLED BACK AND forth, calling me to the waters.

Mia...

It was almost haunting, as if something or someone else lurked beneath the surface. Maybe a siren. Maybe a mermaid.

Or maybe both.

I'd always had a fascination with the sea before I left, but now that I knew what I was, I had a deeper connection than I'd ever felt before. I was *bred* from the ocean.

While curling my toes in the sand, the fresh breeze blew through my hair. The scent of the ocean mist filled my nose with a wonderful memory.

After I'd asked Mom why she wanted to send me to a school named after mythical sea creatures, she told me the truth about what we were. The academy was a seven-year program for all oceanic creatures, and I had to be ready to handle it all when I turned eighteen. In just less than a month now, I would finally get to see what my tail looked like in the water.

For mermaids and sirens, our tails didn't reveal themselves until our eighteen birthday. It felt as though a part of me was missing and I was more than ready to explore the ocean without limits.

As soon as my much-needed visit to the ocean was over, I headed back home. Everything became all too familiar. Mom had renovated the kitchen since I left, but nothing else had been changed. Including my room.

When I entered my old bedroom, the pink had blinded my eyes. Every inch of it remained my favorite color since I was six.

However, my favorite color had changed. Pink could not be the focal point of my room anymore and I needed to do some serious redecorating.

I tore down the posters and removed everything from my walls. My room appeared so barren, but it was a start for new growth.

Movement flashed behind me, and I turned towards my window to find another straight across from me. The window to Dylan's old bedroom in the house right next door.

I wondered if Dylan remembered me. He was probably gone by now, but it would have been a nice thought if he'd stuck around. Dylan was my best friend during our childhood days. Now those days were far behind us.

Leaning closer, I squinted as someone passed by the window. I swallowed, stepping back. They had a male physique, but it could have easily been someone else.

Until he stopped in front of the window and I almost gasped.

Dylan Adler.

Also known as the boy next door.

I almost pissed my pants when he pulled his shirt off. I immediately pulled my pink curtains closed, knocking into the dresser and falling to the floor.

Seconds passed. Then I heard my name.

"Mia? Mia, are you in there?"

He was calling my name. What did I do? I could only imagine what he grew up to be. Was he the jock or the nerd? But the real question was: could we be friends again?

Afraid to move, I stayed silent until the yelling stopped.

All was back to normal. Or could I call this normal? Hiding from your childhood best friend.

I eventually got off the floor and finished stripping my room of all my childish decor, which took until the sun had set. I threw most of it in bags to donate or put in the attic, whichever felt right.

Thunder boomed outside, causing me to jump. Seconds later, light flashed outside of the small window at the front of the attic.

I dropped the last bag just as the power went out. "Shit," I mumbled. I used the beams along the walls to guide my way back to the hatch before climbing down. "Mom? Dad?" I called out.

"Down here!" Mom yelled.

I pushed the ladder back up until it folded into the ceiling. I hurried downstairs and found my parents and brother pulling out the flashlights.

"Power outage," Mom said. "The lightning must have struck a pole again. It should be out all night so we might as well light some candles and get comfortable."

Christian, my brother, grabbed the keys. "I'll grab the rest of the flashlights from the truck."

"I'll go with you," I said.

We went out to the truck to find the flashlights. "What's

taking so damn long?" my brother joked.

Rolling my eyes, I straightened myself and faced him. It began pouring rain, reminding me that in just a week, I couldn't openly stand in the rain anymore. "I'm not as little as I used to be." And Dad's truck was narrow as hell in the backseat. I turned back around and searched again until I found one. "Got it! We can go now!"

"Mia?"

I froze at the sound of his voice. That wasn't Christian. No, this voice matched the same one who'd been yelling at my bedroom window.

"I'll be inside," Christian said as he snatched the flashlight from me and walked in.

I swallowed my fear, taking my time to look at the boy next door. "Hi, Dylan."

He'd grown so much, and that sounded stupid coming from me. Everyone had grown since I left. Wasn't that what people did? But Dylan had grown taller. We had once been similar in height, but now he stood at almost a whole foot taller. How had this happened?

"I didn't realize you had come home," he said as he rubbed his neck.

"I came home today. I haven't been home for long, really," I said in a quiet voice.

After glancing around the dark street, Dylan smiled just a tad. "Well, since you are home and the power has brought us back to the dark ages, why don't we head inside?"

Why did that make me so anxious? Because it had been seven years. Because my whole world had changed since I last saw him.

"Sure." I forced a smile.

Dylan and I decided to head into my house. We would have stayed downstairs in the living room with my family, but we had too much catching up to do. And with all this lingering awkward tension, we didn't need an audience.

I sat on my bed while Dylan plopped down in the tiny chair in front of my vanity. "I see you grew but your room didn't," he said with a laugh.

My smile formed more genuine. "It has been a while."

Then the dreaded question.

"Where were you for those years?"

"I..." I wasn't sure how to respond. What did I tell him? "I went to an academy."

"Didn't picture you as the academic type."

"It was just a program. Supposed to help my future or something like that. An academy for girls. That's all." Why did I say that? Why were the lies spilling from my lips like a snake's tongue slithering from its mouth?

"You went to an all-girls school?" he asked.

Nodding, I picked at my fingernails. "I did."

He furrowed his brows. "Why? I could never survive with only boys for seven years. You..." His face turned red as he looked at me. "You started to have crushes and date."

"That's true." I nodded. Not entirely. Dating wasn't so easy for me. Everyone knew what I was, and no boy would touch me.

"Were you sneaking out to look at the boys or were you getting eye candy in class already?" Before I could answer, he jumped in to say, "but that's cool if you are! Olivia is into girls, too."

Laughing, I shook my head. "No, Dylan. I like boys. I just didn't date any. But I'm home now and there's a possibility I could find someone here. Maybe. It is senior year. We should make the most of it."

"Fair." He looked at my wall. "It's been so long that I'm surprised you're back."

"Why? Did you not think I was coming back?"

"I assumed you were going to be at that school until you graduated. You'd come back here to see your family for the summer but forget about me. You'd leave again to go to college." He messed with a thread on my comforter.

I shrugged. "It's a seven-year program. Thankfully, I did find a friend there. The school wasn't all that bad." Yeah, except for *Jason*.

Dylan's phone pinged and out of habit, he glanced at the screen. "Oh damn."

"What is it?" I was tempted to peek over, but I let him have his privacy. We weren't friends. *Yet.*

Showing me his screen, he shook his head. "They found a dead body tonight. A boy. Down by the ocean."

Immediately my stomach curled in on itself. Who would do such a thing? But I already knew. "A dead body? Do they know what it looks like? How he died?"

"Nothing. It just says any information is going to be released at a later date. They haven't released any details other than that." Dylan put his phone away.

I swallowed, looking out of my window. "Do you think it was the storm? Or something else?" I stood, leaning against the windowsill with my palms flat against it.

"Something else? Like a shark, or a person? I think maybe he was swimming in the ocean and got caught in the storm. He drowned." Dylan coughed a little. Did he think I was crazy?

"It's possible, sure." But I knew things. I'd never been able to swim far out in the ocean to find out, but sirens did things to boys—horrible things. They tore them apart for dinner. And storms were the perfect ingredient to a dish well-served.

"I think I learned something new about you," he said.

"And what is that?" I asked him, glancing back.

"Crime and mystery intrigue you."

I leaned my shoulder against the window. "You could say that." I pushed away from the glass, grabbing my flashlight. "But I need answers."

Dylan scurried up from the floor. "Whoa, whoa. You're not considering going to a crime scene, are you? In the middle of this storm?"

"Rain doesn't scare me, Dylan." It could be the last time I could walk out in the rain in public. It could be the last time I could *walk* in the rain.

He snickered. "No, but lightning should."

"I'm not afraid of a little lightning. Besides, it's more likely to strike farther away from the storm. Not in it." I shot him a smile before I walked down the hall. I knew my parents wouldn't let me out in this weather, so I headed downstairs and slipped out through the back door. I walked through the gate and jumped when I tried to close it, but instead caught Dylan's foot. "You decided to come?"

"I can't let you go alone."

Alone.

It was now that I realized it would be our first adventure together years after we split apart. My insides warmed at the thought of mending our childhood. Tonight had to be just right.

"If you follow me, we can't tell anyone about this."

"Aren't you about to turn eighteen?"

A fire started at the base of my stomach. "You remember my birthday? After all these years?"

Dylan shrugged, forming a smile. "You think I would forget my best friend's birthday? Highly unlikely. Even if you were gone for so long. Now come, let's go see this crime scene." He took my flashlight and led us to the ocean through the dark.

The flame grew as I followed him to the beach. Police tape blocked it off, but it didn't stop Dylan and I from sneaking past it.

No bodies littered the sand, but I found the blood right where the rocks hit the ocean. "Dylan," I whispered, "I don't think the boy drowned."

"Mia, look at me," Dylan said. When I faced him, he refused to make eye contact with the crimson stain. "Maybe we shouldn't be involved in this."

"Maybe. But I feel an obligation to find his killer."

"Why?"

Because I knew who did this. There were sirens in these waters, waiting and watching for any prey that swam their way. If I were to prove to everyone that I wasn't the monster they feared, I had to solve this boy's murder and bring justice. I had to find these beautiful sirens and expose them for who they really were.

Two

My mind came to an abrupt stop. The world around me seemed to slow down to a complete stop as realization hit me. I couldn't solve a murder, could I?

The first day of senior year wasn't anything that special. Dylan and I walked to school, but we barely talked about what happened a few nights before. We split up and decided to meet up at lunch, and he didn't want to talk about the murder. But I was hellbent on solving this boy's death.

During lunch, I got the courage to tell Dylan my plan until someone else got to him first. She approached him and greeted him with a big smile on her face. He never mentioned a girlfriend.

As much as I acknowledged the ping to my heart, I denied letting it fester. Dylan was bound to find someone else when I left, and that was what I had to accept. If he had a girlfriend, it wasn't my place to swoop in and steal him away for a murder mystery. Even if we had once been best friends and he still lived next door.

I hid behind a corner, shaking my head. I couldn't say

anything about the crime now. That would be too awkward. Maybe I needed to figure it out myself. It was time for me to find my own friends.

The memories Dylan and I shared still resided inside my head as if they had been created just yesterday. We had been so inseparable as children.

"Mia, ignore them," he said.

But his words didn't stop the other kids from laughing at me. They all stood around the dock, watching me in a way that made me queasy.

"I can't. Everyone is staring," I whispered.

There was no way I could move my legs. I loved swimming and I would have happily jumped into the water. However, something happened before I could. I thought maybe I had peed myself, but it was too dark. Instead, blood flowed down the sides, soaking my shorts.

"This is embarrassing." I choked on a cry. "Why me? Why did this happen to me?"

Dylan didn't respond. He grabbed my wrist and dragged me away from the lake and into one of the cabins. "This is normal. School told us this would happen. It's just some blood."

"That's easy for you to say," I shouted. "It didn't happen to you, Dylan! Nothing ever happens to you. You're the perfect child. I've always been odd, and now the whole camp knows I've started my period."

Dylan stayed with me in the cabins for the rest of the day because I'd been too afraid to move. But for that, I always admired him for simply being there.

I swallowed, turning away. There would be a lot of memories to give up letting go of Dylan. I walked in the opposite direction. I sat at a table in the corner, but I had trouble enjoying my food when I could only ponder over the fact that he had a girlfriend I didn't know about. Why wouldn't he? Dylan had always been so caring, and now that we weren't kids, every girl was destined to recognize that.

Taking my mind off him, I decided to focus my energy on the boy from the beach.

Christian sat beside me, nudging my arm. "What's up?"

"Who is Dylan's girlfriend?" I asked.

He lifted his eyebrows. "Girlfriend? He got a girlfriend? This is news to me."

Was Dylan keeping her a secret or what my brother so dense he didn't notice?

"I saw him with a girl. Earlier. She had black hair." What was her name?

He shrugged. "You might have seen him with Olivia."

Olivia? Hadn't he mentioned her?

He had. He told me she was into girls, too.

"Olivia? Is she his best friend?" Girlfriend or best friend, it didn't lessen the tension. The less people I associated with this year, the better. At least that's what I told myself to keep my secret safe.

"He is not obligated to be at your beck and call."

Scoffing, I rolled my eyes. "I know he needed friends while I was gone. I also know that he isn't required to put me first or even be my friend at all. We were friends when we were children, and we might not be able to fully repair that. Maybe he's upset that I left without any explanation, and he's worried I may do it again. He has every right to be upset with me." Or he might have been upset after we entered a crime scene. I wasn't the same Mia who left him behind years ago.

Christian didn't say anything in return.

When lunch ended, we went our separate ways. The last two classes passed by in a rush and by then I found myself walking home alone. Christian had gone to the movies with his friends.

I got home and Mom was cooking up something delicious. "How was your first day?" she asked me.

"Average." I slumped onto the couch and groaned.

"Average? That doesn't sound average to me."

"Dylan has a friend. Or girlfriend. I'm not even sure what she is, but what if she hates me? What if she convinces Dylan that I'm the bad guy? Is it easier to just drop our friendship? We aren't human after all."

Mom paused for a moment. "You grew up to become different people. He doesn't know how to go about that. Olivia and Dylan don't seem to have romantic feelings for each other from what I can tell, and you shouldn't be so quick to assume the worst. She might be the nicest girl ever, especially if Dylan likes her. It'll help ease your worries if you just talk to them."

"In other words, I'm a drama queen and I should just suck it up and hang out with him if I want to."

"Exactly." Mom smiled and offered up some boneless wings smothered in teriyaki sauce.

I took a bite, savoring the flavor. Teriyaki and orange chicken were my two favorite types of chicken. She put the plate of wings down and cleaned up her space while I headed up to my room.

Pushing my curtains to both sides, I looked at the empty room across the side yard. I opened my window just a crack, but he wasn't there.

I frowned and sat on my bed, wishing he would've been

there to realize I was here, and I wanted to see him. Where could he be? With Olivia, of course, and I knew that was the only answer. Were they dating? Truly?

I wanted to laugh and cry and share silly moments together. I wanted my best friend again, but I didn't want to be the girl who came between Dylan and his girlfriend.

As I laid back on my bed, I looked up at my ceiling, wondering how I could introduce myself in a way that wasn't cheesy. Did I say hi? If I said hi, it wasn't cheesy, but it was too simple. Simple was just not going to cut it.

Some noises from the house next door carried through to my room. I ran to the window and peeked out, keeping myself out of view just in case.

Dylan opened his window and pulled off his shirt. "It's a nice day outside, Oli. Let's go do something active."

"I'm required to do everything you want to do?" she asked.

Dylan let out a chuckle and looked back at me, or more specifically, my window. "Hm."

"Hm, what?"

"It looks like she might be home and I wanted you to meet her." Dylan shook his head.

"Are you talking about Mia?" Olivia asked.

She knew my name. He'd told her about *me*.

He nodded. "Yeah. It seems like just yesterday she had to leave for a private school. I don't know why they sent her away. She wasn't a bad kid at all, and they all stayed except for her. It still doesn't make sense to me." He sat down on his bed.

Olivia came closer to the window. "Her window is open."

"What?" Dylan stood and got closer to realize she'd been right. "She must be home. Come on, let me introduce you to her." He looked at Olivia and back at my window.

They both stood in front of his window, looking at me, or what I assumed was them looking at me.

"Mia," Dylan shouted.

I was too nervous to respond. My stomach was doing flips and flops, refusing to settle down. I couldn't be expected to just meet his (girl)friend through a window, right? Of course not. It was absurd.

"You are pathetic." Olivia shook her head and opened their window more. "If she is over there, you need to speak up."

It surprised me that she was so persistent to get him to talk to me. I hadn't expected this of her, and it proved she was not who I judged her to be. My mom was right, and I was always worrying for no good reason.

He glanced at her. "What if she has music on? Then I'm just screaming to the window and that looks weird. The neighbors will assume I'm crazy." Throwing his arm in my direction, he turned away from me.

"Then I say let them. Go knock on the door if that's what it takes. You will never get what you want in life by hiding in your room. We're getting nowhere by standing here," she said with a chuckle.

Dylan grumbled, agreeing.

The two of them closed his window and he put a shirt back on. I watched them walk out of his room and disappear before coming out of the front door. They were headed this way. Shit.

Our doorbell rang and someone answered it. The voices were muffled until I heard my name being called. Completely frozen, I didn't reply. When I heard more voices and footsteps walking up, I jumped onto my bed and put my earbuds in.

I couldn't get my heartbeat to slow down no matter how hard I tried. Why was I this nervous? We had talked just the other night.

When my door opened, my mom stepped in. I looked over and took out an earbud. "Yes?"

"Didn't you hear me calling you?"

I waved my earbud around to let her know I had music blasting in my ears. As if.

She huffed. "Well, Dylan came over to say hi and see if you were home."

I nodded, letting the words fly from my tongue, "Send him in."

Still, I wasn't prepared when the boy I'd grown up with walked into my room with his new friend trailing behind him. If I had just kept my window and curtains closed, this could've been avoided. Yet, part of me was thankful I made that move in the first place.

Dylan stopped, his eyes fixed on me. "Mia."

I sat up, swinging my legs over the side of my bed. "Hey, sorry about today. I got caught up with finding a job."

"That's okay. I want you to meet Olivia." He gestured to her as she stepped forward. "Olivia, this is Mia."

I waved to her, and she nodded in response.

"I wasn't sure if it was okay or not, but I told Olivia about the crime scene we visited. I wanted her to possibly help us solve his murder. More eyes are better." Dylan shrugged as if he hadn't shared something secretive. Hadn't we agreed? Had I not told him to tell nobody about what we did?

I had.

But he did it anyway, and that stung.

You are such a damn drama queen. Drop it and accept the

help. This isn't about you, it's about the boy whose life was ripped from him.

It was about me, though. Because if sirens were the murderers, Dylan would be opened to a whole new world—a world I wasn't ready to bring him into. If I couldn't play my cards right, they would tear his heart out, too.

Three

Rain poured down from the sky as I climbed onto my roof. Pulling my knees up, I admired the neighborhood from here. It seemed peaceful during a time like this. As if a boy hadn't just been murdered a few miles down the road.

"I thought I'd find you up here," Christian said as he climbed up.

"Is it selfish of me to be upset with Dylan because he told Olivia a secret I asked him to keep?" I slightly turned my head his way, but I never made eye contact.

He shrugged. "Depends on the secret."

"What if I told you that telling her could help serve justice for someone? But that telling her also meant Dylan and Olivia could possibly find out about...me. They could find out about sirens and mermaids and all the other creatures living in the ocean. It could put them in danger." I swallowed. "So which is the safer option, Christian? Getting justice for a boy or possibly hurting the entire world of oceanic creatures? What if instead of hurting us, it hurts Dylan and Olivia instead?"

"I can't give you a straight answer if you're going to act so mysterious," he joked.

Keeping my mouth shut, I didn't say anything else on the topic. Instead, I let the rain wash away whatever animosity I had lingering in my veins.

"They aren't dating," my brother started, "Olivia and Dylan. Just in case you were still wondering. They became friends after you left. Olivia moved here and he decided to befriend her. Besides, I doubt she's his type. Unless he's hiding a vagina, Olivia is looking elsewhere romantically."

I chewed the skin off my lip. "I heard. But I couldn't be sure if she only liked girls, or if she was bi. That's not my point, though. Dylan can date whoever he wants. He's his own person." And I needed to stop being such a bitch when it came to him having friends or girlfriends outside of me.

When I looked back over at Dylan's backyard, I saw the soccer goal and soccer ball.

Christian followed my line of sight. "He still plays. He's actually really good."

I tilted my head. "And Olivia? Is that how they met?"

"She doesn't play soccer as far as I know. But she goes to his games." He faced forward. "That's what good friends do."

Good friends—something I wasn't. I'd left Dylan for seven years and now I sat here, pitying myself because he told Olivia our secret. I would be eighteen in just a few days. I needed to begin acting like it.

Thunder boomed, causing me to almost slip. I caught myself as a memory flashed in my eyes.

"It's my first real date, Nat. I'm nervous," I said as I turned to her.

She smiled and fixed my hair. "You'll do great." She grabbed my shoulders, making me face the door. After knocking, she ran around the corner.

I swallowed as blue eyes appeared when the door opened. A smile crept up on his lips, but I missed the hidden smirk at the time. "Mia, come in."

I smiled back and walked into the room, but nothing prepared me for what happened next. A sack was thrown over my head and I was pushed to the ground. I tried to fight back, to kick my feet and pull the burlap sack off. Hands wrapped around my biceps, dragging me somewhere. I started to flail my arms when my head was shoved underwater.

A burning spread along the inside of my lungs, growing into a fire. And when that fire was ready to burn me to ashes, air rushed back in.

I ripped the sack off and gasped for air, about to start crying.

Jason bent down. "Know your fucking place."

As soon as I made it to my dorm, I dropped to the floor and began crying. I never understood why he hated me so much out of all the others. Maybe it was because I pretended to be someone else.

"—and then he told me I was way out of my league."

I looked at Christian, furrowing my brows. "Out of your league?"

He studied my eyes. "You weren't even listening to me, were you?"

"I'm sorry. I got distracted."

He laughed. "By what?"

I wasn't about to tell my little brother that I'd been the victim the whole time. That was humiliating. "Just the rain is all. I'll never be able to sit up here in the rain again. I want to savor this moment."

I LOOKED OUT MY window, peering into his. He entered his room and grabbed something before leaving it again. I sat on my floor, resting my chin on the windowpane. "Dylan, thank you for being my friend," I whispered to myself. I turned around and planted my butt on the carpet with my back against the wall. While scanning my room, I started thinking about some ideas to make this room my own again. I'd grown up now and my room had to grow up with me.

With a deep breath, I felt content.

To humans, I was a freak. To mermaids, I was a freak. But deep down, I was excited to see my real form, and I was scared because this would prove to everyone else that I was just a fish and hiding that fact would not be easy to do. I would not be allowed around water when anyone else was nearby. A huge part of my life was going to change. How did Mom make it work? How did Dad learn to accept her?

Regardless of what was going to happen, I was determined to solve that boy's murder on my own. I wasn't going to drag Dylan into this world. It was far too dangerous. We could be best friends, but not as close as we'd once been. That stung me the most.

I jumped away from the window at the sound of water beating against it. It had begun to pour rain and the wind picked up.

Getting up from the floor, I went downstairs to see if anyone else heard about a hurricane warning or anything else, but nobody was home.

I checked my phone but saw no warning. That was odd.

The winds picked up outside, rattling the house. I rushed to the basement and grabbed the survival kit from the shelf. Maybe it was a bit of an overreaction, but I couldn't be too safe. I was trying my best on my own.

I screamed at the sound of a loud thump upstairs. I hurried up the steps, but the door didn't budge. I cursed under my breath and pushed harder, but it had been blocked or stuck. Either way, I needed a new way out of here.

The rushing of water echoed, and I swallowed, turning back to see water pouring in from the small window to the backyard.

When I approached the window, it broke away from the wall and the water continued at a higher speed. Since I hadn't transformed yet, water was a danger to me. I could drown tonight.

I waded through the knee-deep water and made it to the stairs. I opened the box and looked instead. Flare gun. Flashlights. Water, food, and a radio.

Whistle. Perfect.

I grabbed it from the box, but it slipped from my fingers too quickly, falling between the steps. "Shit!"

Without another thought, I walked into the water now waist-deep and went under the stairs. I lowered my body under the water and searched for the whistle, but nothing came up. I lifted my head above the surface to see that the water had gotten up to my neck. I swam over to the window, pressing my back against the wall. Without any way to signal for help, I needed to find my way out of this. And there was only one way I could get out, and that was through the hole in the wall.

The water rose until all I could do was float. And I floated up until the top of my head hit the ceiling. If I didn't try, I'd be certain to die.

I gulped in air before going under the water and finding the hole. I gripped the sides, falling back as the bricks gave way. Reaching forward again, I felt around the edges until I came across pieces that were firm enough to hold my weight, and then I began to pull myself through. When I had gotten most of the way, I swam to the side and kicked off the wall, away from the hole. My body took a hit as I hit the back of the house, but I was able to sit up and gasp for air. The water didn't get high enough in the backyard.

"Mia!" Mom yelled as she ran around the side.

I coughed and stood, wringing out my hair. "I'm fine. Really. I'm pretty badass," I said with a dry laugh.

Instead of scolding me for my language, she pulled me into her arms and kissed my head. "I was terrified. I couldn't find you anywhere. What happened?"

"I was trying to get the survival kit, but something must have blocked the door. It happened so fast," I whispered in her ear.

Mom grabbed my hand and dragged me to the front, and we went inside. "Are you hurt?"

"No. This storm just came out of nowhere."

"Is she safe?" Dad asked. He saw me with his own eyes and crushed me in his arms.

Mom's voice darkened as the words slithered from her tongue, "It's what happens before the Turning."

I stumbled away from my dad. "What?"

"It's a sign that your transformation is almost here, Mia," she said.

That would imply that I almost died because of my own

ancestry. In other words, I was to blame for this storm. How many people *did* die because of me? I couldn't seem to escape my fate—to escape what I was.

Maybe the flood was fate's way of saying I was supposed to succumb to the execution. What if this storm was a sign for what laid ahead in my future? The thought alone made my stomach clench.

Death. Destruction. Murder.

Dylan could never know about this part of my world. He could not know what I was or would become. If he found out what possibly killed that boy on the beach was the same monster that fueled me, he'd run in terror. I wasn't willing to risk such a thing.

Mom and Dad took me to the living room, away from the windows. The storm lasted all night and early on the next morning, and my guilt lasted just as long if not longer.

The damage had been mostly done on the outside of the homes, although a few had shattered windows and trees shoved into them. How could one single transformation do all of this? It was nature's way of warning the world what was about to be unleashed. Maybe I was the monster everyone at Naiad told me I was. If I was, what was the solution? It had already been woven into my DNA since conception and I couldn't just cut out the bits I didn't want.

Was there a way to remove that part of me and leave me home? Doubtful. Even if there was, the process was certainly excruciating. So what was my option?

Maybe I could steer clear of Dylan altogether and save him the trouble. What would my excuse be? I doubted he'd even believe me or fall for it. My life was too complicated to bring him into it and yet he was the one who shoved his way in the minute he knew I was home.

Now I stood here, caught up in all my own lies. I wasn't going to be the one hurt from this either. No, it would be Dylan who would fall victim to my villainy. My deception would be the death of him.

Four

Olivia pushed Dylan in a playful manner. "You're an ass."

I followed behind them, laughing to myself. They certainly seemed close as friends. I guess growing up alongside each other for six years did that to people.

"But I'm right!" he yelled.

She shook her head and crossed her arms. "You're wrong. Just because Mia proved you wrong doesn't give you the right to be an asshole." She grabbed my hand and pulled me to her. "Us women must stick together."

Dylan grumbled. "You're both against me now."

I glanced at Olivia before facing Dylan again. "At least someone can call you out on your assery. Good friends keep your ego in check."

Olivia laughed. "And we both know your ego needs to be managed by a thousand miles, plus that."

Dylan narrowed his eyes on us. I smiled in return.

Olivia let go of my hand. "We should hang out after school."

Dylan looked at me for my answer.

I scratched the top of my hand and laughed a bit. "I don't think I can today. I have plans. Tomorrow, though."

"Plans? What kind of plans?" Dylan asked.

I bit my lip, to keep from letting anything slip. He didn't remember my birthday after all. I was eighteen today and he had no idea. How could that sting more than I wanted it to?

"Just some plans." I shrugged.

Great lie.

He nodded. "Well, I can't hang out tomorrow because I have soccer practice. Maybe we can all hang out this weekend?"

"Sure." I nodded.

We went our separate ways.

I walked home with Christian after school, but I kept sighing and kicking pebbles. "He doesn't remember my birthday. Did I do something wrong?"

"What? Guys don't remember birthdays. It's not his fault. You've been gone for so long and he may have forgotten." He nudged me.

"It's not that hard to remember a birthday." And he'd already told me he knew when it was. Why did he forget it within the span of a few weeks?

"It is if you're Dylan."

I gasped. "It's sad that you're so right." And he was. It was just like Dylan to remember one minute and forget the next. How convenient for him.

"It runs in the family." He gave me a playful smirk.

We neared the front steps of our home, and I took off my backpack. "My back hurts already."

My brother looked back at me with furrowed brows.

"What kind of books are you carrying in there?"

I shot him a surprised look. "If I told you, you would ask me if the subjects were even real classes." I walked into the house with him and stopped in my tracks when I saw Dylan and Olivia. "What are you two doing here? I thought we were hanging out this weekend."

Isn't the answer so obvious?

Dylan chuckled and looked at my mom. "Does she remember?"

Olivia leaned her weight against Dylan and smiled. "I was told that you are eighteen today. That is so very exciting."

"I mean, I know it's my birthday and all, but I'm still confused." I dropped my backpack by the front door.

Dylan nudged Olivia until she stopped leaning on him. He looked at me. "You thought I forgot. I didn't forget."

I swallowed, nodding my head. "Great. How long are you staying?"

"Mia, that is rude," Dad said.

I looked at Mom, asking her to please chime in. She must have known I was dying to know what my tail looked like. However, Mom didn't get the memo and she just set a cake on the counter in front of Dylan and Olivia. "Cake time."

What I really craved was bath time.

I walked over and looked at the beautiful cake. It was a red velvet cake and it seemed to soften the blow. Just a little, or maybe even a lot. It even had vanilla ice cream in it. Red velvet was its own kind of cake.

Mom put the *1* and *8* candles on the cake and lit them with a lighter.

Everyone sang happy birthday to me while I stared at the candles. The world moved in slow motion as I blew out the flames, smoke drifting into the air.

They all cheered and clapped. I couldn't hear what they were saying. Their voices were muffled as I pictured my tail. It was supposed to be the best day ever and now I was eating cake with people who didn't understand how desperate I was to see my true form.

Mom cut my cake and gave me the first slice. I ate a bite of it and closed my eyes. Heaven was an understatement.

Throughout the night, everyone ate cake and laughed at stupid things like sports and which teams were better. I didn't care about sports. Instead, I sat on the stairs and messed with the bracelet around my wrist.

My brother sat next to me. "How's the party?"

I shrugged and looked at my feet. "I just wanted to go to the ocean and see my tail."

"Can't you see it tomorrow?"

"I waited so long for this moment. When Mom told me what I was, I remember asking why I hadn't grown a tail yet and she said we don't get one until we're eighteen. Sea nymphs don't have to wait until they're eighteen. It's just unfair that we do—that *I* do. The color of my tail is this major question that haunts my mind and the only way to make it go away is to answer it by seeing what color it really is. It's a big deal to me." I rested my elbows on my knees.

"I'm sorry."

I let out a sigh. "It's my birthday. Shouldn't I get to spend it the way I want to?"

He nudged my shoulder with his. "We didn't realize."

"I know. But Mom should have realized. Dylan couldn't have known and it's not his fault, but she knew, and she should have saved me." I wasn't strong enough to end Dylan and I's friendship over this, but I could never tell him the truth. I feared losing him forever.

"Why can't he know?"

"Because being from the sea isn't normal. Not for humans. It's the equivalent of being the nerdy kid in school during the eighties." I leaned my upper body weight onto my elbows.

Christian looked at everyone and watched them all bond over sports. That was something we didn't know too well. We were excluded when sports got involved.

Dad had been a big football player when he was younger, which is why Mom fell in love with him. Their love for football was what pressured Christian into trying out but Christian was just not that type of person. He was an artist. He wasn't an athlete. It took a few years before they accepted that he was going to be his own person and not their version of that.

I stood up. "Tell everyone I went to bed early." I went upstairs and grabbed my pajamas off the floor. I looked at the beads left on my vanity, studying their colors. I wanted to know.

I had to know.

After grabbing a towel from the hallway closet, I went to the bathroom. I locked the door behind me and stripped to nothing but my birthday suit. I ran the bath water and took a deep breath. "This is it, Mia. You finally get to see what it looks like."

I stepped in and sat back, watching the transformation begin. There was some pain—a tingling and stinging kind of pain surging through the nerves of my legs.

It started from my feet as they merged into one. My toes elongated and thinned out as the skin rippled into a slimier texture. A fin formed where my feet had once been while identical fins grew on either side of my thighs.

As my legs fused into one, the skin layered itself with a slimy texture before scales came cutting through the skin and setting on the surface. I gripped the sides of the tub until the scales had all grown in. The transformation continued up my waist before coming to an end, leaving behind a gradual blend with my human skin.

I couldn't take my eyes off my tail. All I could focus on was admiring the colors that blended so seamlessly—vibrant and stunning. I could never have asked for anything better.

Taking a second, I moved my fin in an up and down motion. The dark turquoise shifted to a lighter hue from different angles based on the way the light hit the water.

Gills lined the underside of my breasts, three slits under each, as if I hadn't had enough insecurities already. I hoped seeing my tail would finally help me in some way, but the gills burned that quickly. I'd forgotten we had them, and it only backfired.

I touched the green-shifting scales, eyes glued to every inch. I could only imagine it would be far more beautiful when I got a chance to use it in the ocean. I was desperate to swim in the ocean like the mermaids. Experiencing my tail in action would be innate.

I sat back in the tub and moved it around. I hardly had room, but it would do. It was so surreal having a fishtail. I could control it all by myself and it wasn't just a mermaid blanket or fake tail. It was *mine.* There was no way I could ever wish to be a human now, knowing what I knew about being the creature I was. This was miraculous.

A smile crept up onto my face and grew as wide as it

was allowed, refusing to let me go. I was filled with utter happiness. This was an amazing feeling, and I wasn't willing to feel any other way.

I laid in the bath for hours until my dad knocked on the bathroom door and told me it was time to go to bed. I got out and asked Dad to get Mom.

When Mom knocked, I scooted over and unlocked it. She came in and gasped, bending down. "Mia, it's beautiful."

I used a towel to dry it off until my legs separated and the scales retracted under the surface of my skin. The slimy layer rippled back into the human texture of skin. "I couldn't wait. I wanted to see it so bad." I stood up and grabbed the towel, wrapping it around my body.

Mom gave me a nod, smiling. "I'm proud. I really am proud to see that you've fully transformed."

She followed me to my room, and I changed into my pajamas. I looked at her and sat on my bed. "I'm happy about it. I'm excited to try it out in the ocean."

I could see the worry form in her eyes. "Ocean?"

"Yeah. We're sea creatures. We clearly belong in the ocean. I need space to swim in."

"Mia, we have a pool."

"Yeah, but I want more room than a cement box. What's wrong with the ocean?"

She lifted her chin, asserting her authority. "There are bad sea creatures out there."

I sat back against my mountain of pillows. "I see now. You think they're going to judge me and take advantage of me as a newbie." I crossed my arms behind my head.

"That's not what I said."

"But you were thinking it," I pointed out.

Mom sighed. "Mia, I'm serious. Stay away from the ocean." She closed my door.

I heard a knock and thought she was coming back to apologize but it was just my brother. "What?" I asked in a bored tone.

"What happened to you?" He narrowed his eyes.

"She banned me from the ocean. Can you believe that? The ocean!" I shouted.

Christian shrugged. "I don't know what to tell you."

I sat up and turned to face him. "Can you cover for me while I visit? I'm not going to be able to contain myself. This tail of mine needs to be free. It needs room to do its job and swim."

He put his hands up in defense. "Whoa."

"Please. Tell her I'm with Olivia. Or Dylan."

"And what about them? They need to cover for you as well."

I shrugged. "I'll deal with that. I promise. Just, please... Please cover for me," I pleaded with the puppy dog eyes.

He groaned and swayed his body in a childish manner. "Fine. But don't get caught or I will use it against you for the rest of your life."

"Yes, deal. Thank you." I gave him my best smile.

He left my room, and I snuggled in my bed. Mom might have had good intentions, but she must have known that teenagers loved to rebel. If you told us one thing, we'd do the opposite, and telling us not to do something made us want to do it more. She couldn't keep me from the ocean no matter how hard she tried.

Convincing Olivia and Dylan somehow to agree and say I was with them would be challenging but I needed them to have my back. If anything, I could say I was at his soccer practice. I needed him to agree to this so that my plan was solid.

I could only imagine the feeling of the waves rolling over my skin while the salty water absorbed into my pores. The coolness would be refreshing against the last of the summer heat. I was craving the ocean and my mom had to understand that as a woman who was the same creature I was. I needed her to understand.

I closed my eyes, letting my dreams take over my mind. The sooner I slept, the sooner tomorrow came. The sooner tomorrow came, the sooner I could go to the ocean and be myself. I just had to make sure tomorrow went smoothly and everyone involved in my plan agreed to help cover for me.

If I knew one thing was for sure, it was that Dylan would always be willing to help me out as my best friend. He was not one to betray me and I had to make sure he trusted me enough to know I wasn't having him cover for me while I broke the law. I just wanted to swim. I craved the ocean, and it was not a craving I could suppress, and I certainly wouldn't be willing to.

Five

I HUMMED TO MYSELF, walking back to our house when Christian nudged me. "Still going to disobey Mom?"

"Yep. I plan on it."

"Mind if I join?"

"You can't swim in the ocean and breathe underwater." I looked at him.

"I can still enjoy the ocean like a human being. Most humans like the beach, you know," he said.

I rubbed my nose, wincing at the inflamed, red bump. "Fine. I'll let you come with me."

"Did you talk to Olivia and Dylan about this?"

"Of course. They're going to cover for us. More than anything, Olivia had to convince Dylan because he wanted to know why I needed a cover, but Olivia understands that I don't want to tell him something personal, as a woman."

He nodded and looked at the sidewalk in front of us.

I sighed as the red bump ached. "I have a pimple growing on the side of my nose and it is the most painful experience I've ever dealt with on my face."

Christian laughed, knowing very well that other things could be more painful. "You've never been punched?"

I shrugged. "I mean, yeah. But I'm a drama queen, remember?"

He furrowed his brows. "Wait, you've been punched? Was some girl jealous of you?"

The last thing I wanted was to talk about this subject. "It's in the past. Not everyone liked me."

Christian stopped walking. "Mia."

I slowed and turned to face him. "I don't want to talk about this now. Please, leave it be."

Thankfully, he did. He dropped the subject and that was the end of it.

I wasn't sure if it was the protective brother side of him or if he was just curious about the nature of me being punched, but I didn't want to tell anyone. Natalia knew, but she was now home in her state, away from me. It was in the past and that was where it was going to stay.

Christian and I headed to the ocean and skipped going home. If we dropped by, we would blow our cover of being at Dylan's soccer game.

We dropped our bags in the sand and removed our shoes.

I looked at the water. "Well, here goes nothing."

"Go in. What are you waiting for?"

"For you to shut up." I laughed, scanning the shore for big rocks. I ran over to a few and crouched behind the rocks, stripping off my clothes. I left my bra on because that would be too weird for my brother.

I ran into the water and the salty waves rushed over my toes. I dove under the surface and watched the transformation take place all over again. It was just as mesmerizing but a little less painful this time around.

When the process was complete, I moved my tail in the same direction a whale did, swimming over to the shore where my brother waited. I planted myself in the shallow waters, smiling. "This... This is incredible. The pool just wouldn't have been the same."

"I'm glad it suits you." He sat in the sand.

"Suits me? It is me!" I laughed, flapping my fin around in the blue water where the ocean foam met the sand. "I feel at home. I can't believe Mom wanted me to worry." I shook my head.

He leaned back. "What was your life like when you were away? I mean, you didn't have parents around and that must have been great."

"It was different, for sure. I met a girl named Natalia there. She sees me for who I am and accepts me anyway. There were so many different types of sea creatures and that was interesting, but they always judged me for being the one that refuses to show my true self. I didn't even want to sing. I didn't have music for the mermaids or songs for the sirens. I did what *I* wanted to do. It sucked at times, but Natalia made it better. She made me feel like I mattered." I laid on my back.

"You guys were split up based on your DNA, correct?"

I shook my head. "Somewhat. We had classes based on our heritage so that we would learn about what we were supposed to know about our species. But other than that, we could mingle with whoever we wanted. Natalia was my roommate and that's how we met. Besides, we still had to take required classes for basic schooling so I could go into senior year with the credits I needed."

Christian chuckled, nodding. "What is she?"

"She's a sea nymph. It's quite interesting, what I know about sea nymphs anyway. Everything I learned about was because she taught me." I smiled a bit.

"She sounds great."

"She is. She is such a good friend."

I remembered the fun times we had together, the laughs, and when we would prank people. I couldn't replace the memories she gave me, even if we were over a thousand miles apart.

"I wish things would change so she could be here. It would make life easier. I know I have friends now, but what about someone who understands me? Nobody knows what it's like trying to fit into a world of humans when you're from the ocean. Natalia understands me. She knows what that's like. That was one thing I loved about the academy. There, I was surrounded by people who understood me. I didn't have to worry about hiding a secret or swimming alone. It's tough trying to fit back into a normal life when I'm anything but normal." I looked at my brother for some answers.

He nodded. "I understand. I mean, I don't know what it feels like, but I can imagine."

"Are you something different from normal?"

He shrugged. "We're all different from normal. I'm just trying to help."

I groaned. "It just really sucks."

Christian was quick to change the subject, but I didn't mind. "What do you know about girls?"

"Besides the fact that I am one?" I joked.

He rolled his eyes.

I lifted both eyebrows and sat up. "There's a girl in your life."

"No, there's not. I just think... I think Sabrina is cute."

"Sabrina?" I choked. "As in, the cheerleader? Christian, how do you think you're going to win over a cheerleader? They don't exactly go for guys like you." I gestured to him. Maybe he should have been a football player.

"Guys like me? What does that even mean? I'm not a jock but I like to think I have something going for me. It's not only jocks who are interesting." He shot me a glare.

I looked at the sky. "Whatever you tell yourself to help you sleep at night." I laughed. "But I would argue that you aren't very interesting. You're as boring as they come. You might have to settle for a turtle wife. Maybe somewhere out there a turtle is secretly a woman."

He grumbled. "I tell myself that you're not my biological sister. That seems to cure me from lack of personality."

"How rude."

"You're welcome." He sat forward. "We should probably go. We need to go home soon before Mom realizes we're gone."

"We haven't been here that long. I say we don't go home until I feel like it, and I sure don't feel like it." I yawned, covering my mouth. It was a strange habit I had picked up somewhere, but I wasn't worried about breaking it.

He ran his fingers through his hair. "Sure, whatever you say..."

I scooped some water up and let it wash over my tail. I cleared my throat and said, "The classes were different from public high school. They were...more personal. They pertained to us as sea creatures and the teachers cared about what we were learning."

Although, I couldn't say the same for how they cared when

it came to rivalries between students.

"Natalia, wait up!" I ran like a fish without legs. I caught up and grabbed onto her. "I'm so glad you did this."

"Is that so?"

"He deserves it. He's an ass." I swung my arm around her shoulders.

She put her arm around my shoulders in return. "I still think it would've made more sense if you did it. You are the one he embarrassed after all."

"Exactly. He's going to blame me for what you did anyway." I shrugged and we stopped when the teacher came out of the classroom before us.

"Hi, Mrs. Gofer." I smiled.

She smiled at both of us. "Hello, ladies. What's going on out here? Shouldn't you be at the meeting?" She looked back towards the gymnasium.

Natalia stepped in. "I was helping Mia with her girl problems. She ran out of tampons, and I had to supply her with more."

Mrs. Gofer nodded. "Ah, mother nature really isn't that predictable."

Natalia and I laughed.

"You ladies better get to the meeting."

"We will. Thank you." I waved and walked with Natalia to the gym. I looked inside the window through the door, watching him. "Shall we go in and sit to look less suspicious?"

"We shall." Natalia smiled and grabbed my hand, walking into the gym with me. We sat down in the bleachers, trying not to draw attention to ourselves.

The entire class burst out laughing as a balloon with paint fell onto his head, ruining his precious hair. His eyes went wide as he began scanning the bleachers. They stopped on me. I knew I was going to get blamed, and he would pay me back, but I couldn't stop laughing. His hair would be tinted pink for a long while.

A lot of what happened to me at the academy was something I kept to myself and for a good reason.

"They always excluded me. They told me I would never be one of them," I said in a quiet voice.

"What do you mean? Who?" He sat up more.

"The mermaids. They never included me. They judged me. It's unfair the way it works. I just wanted to be included but they never let me be a part of their group. Natalia was the one who really accepted me. She didn't care if we were different. She will always be the friend I know I can count on. She has a special place in my heart." I wrung out the water from my hair.

My brother understood and got up on his feet. It was time for us to head home before Mom called up Dylan.

As I swam back to the rock where my bottoms were, I dried off and got dressed again. We grabbed our bags and headed home. I made sure my hair was dry before we got in the door. I even took a shower before I ate dinner so Mom wouldn't smell the saltwater on me.

Mom asked us how Dylan did with his soccer practice and we both lied, saying he did well. It wasn't like we had any other choice. What was another lie on top of one we already created?

Once I helped Mom clean up after dinner, I walked up to my room and looked out my window. I waved to Dylan through my window, and he waved back. We both opened our windows for a goodnight conversation.

"Are you going to tell me where you went?"

"I went to the ocean." It was true and he didn't have to be kept in the dark about my love for swimming. He already knew.

"Why can't your mom know?"

"I... I don't know, honestly. Maybe she's afraid of the ocean or something happened in her childhood and now she's projecting that fear onto me. I never expected that she would keep me from the ocean like this, though. I was born to be in the ocean. It's cruel in my eyes. It's like telling a dog not to run. It's mean. The ocean is something I love." I laid my arms on my windowsill, resting my head on top of them.

Dylan chuckled. "So, I'm assuming tomorrow we are all hanging out as you promised."

"Yes. We can do that. What will we do?"

"Whatever we decide we want to do." He shrugged.

I laughed. "Okay, but what do we want to do?"

"Maybe we can go to the ocean together."

I shook my head. "Uh, no thanks. I'd like to have some variety. Oh, maybe we can go to the mall and pick out some things to help redecorate my room. That's what we need to do." I nodded, laying my head sideways.

He snapped his fingers. "That's right. We do need to decorate your little girl's room," he joked.

I scoffed. "Shut up. I didn't live in it for seven years. I grew up, okay?"

He smiled, watching me. "I know. We all grew up."

"We all did grow up. We've become different people. We're not kids. We are now adults who will be graduating this year and we have to decide on our future. Too many things have changed." So much had changed in just seven years that I feared Dylan and I couldn't be friends forever—and someday, we'd part ways.

Six

"DYLAN!" I GASPED.

He laughed. "It's only paint."

"Paint is hard to get off of clothes!" I looked at my shirt and sighed. "You are so cruel." I shook my head with a big frown on my face.

"I'm also your best friend. Best friends and cruelty come as a package deal." He shrugged his shoulders and looked at my walls. "I think this light mint color is fitting. It screams Mia."

Changing the subject. How clever.

I glanced around my room. "It does." I grabbed a shirt and went to the bathroom and changed into a clean one. I brought a garbage bag and a box from downstairs.

Setting it on my bed, I took all my old belongings, including my old clothes, and put them in a box to give away. I threw away all the painter's tape and plastic around the baseboards, ceiling, and floor to clean it up.

"Help me finish decorating, you dope." I gently hit Dylan on the back.

He looked inside my shopping bags.

Olivia decided not to join us today. She said something about letting two old friends catch up, whatever that meant. We'd already caught up the first time.

I opened my new bed set and removed the old sheets before replacing them with the new ones. "I'll forever be stuck in this bed until I move out." I sighed. It was a twin-size bed, the same size it was when I was still small enough to sleep in it. My parents found no use in buying me a bigger size for one year. I'd be moving out for college if I decided to go, and I would have to learn to use a twin size anyway.

Dylan shrugged. "It's not so bad."

"It is when you want space to spread out with your animals." I pulled a stuffed animal from the bag. "Isn't that right, Cocoa?" I showed him to Dylan. "Meet Cocoa. He's named that because he's a brown bunny that smells like chocolate."

"Why do you have a chocolate-scented bunny?" Dylan lifted an eyebrow.

"Why wouldn't I? I'm a girl. I like chocolate and he smells like chocolate. If my future husband can smell like this, I will be complete." I smelled Cocoa.

Dylan shook his head. "Girls are so weird."

"And boys aren't? You pee next to other guys. That is weird."

He helped me shove my old bedding into another black garbage bag. "We have the same parts. Why do we need stalls if we can just unzip and do our business quickly? We don't stare at each other. We all keep our eyes to ourselves."

"Still. I would feel awkward peeing next to strangers even if they didn't look at me."

He stopped to look at me. "Okay, but didn't you change

into gym clothes when you were at your private school? Other girls saw your bra."

I shook my head. "Of course we had a gym, but we also had a bathroom attached to the locker room. I changed in the stalls. I personally feel weird about it. I guess it's just a privacy thing." I pulled the fitted sheet over my mattress.

"I guess," he mumbled.

I stood back and smiled, admiring the bedspread.

"Okay, so now we just need to decorate the vanity and put my new clothes away." I started digging through bags.

"Wait, did you only wear uniforms? I wonder what that was like. Mia Dawson wears a tie." He laughed.

I looked at him. "Of course we had uniforms. They wanted us all to feel included despite being so different. It didn't work well. I was still very excluded." I realized I had said too much. I couldn't even take back my words.

"Why were you all different? Weren't you all girls? And who excluded you?" He got down on his knees and helped me take my clothes from the bags and hang them up in my closet.

I knew I could get away with an excuse. "Everyone is very different in their own way. It may have been a private school, but the judgment wasn't nonexistent. Girls can be very judgmental. They judge you for such petty reasons. That's what they did to me. I'm not like them. I just do my own thing." It was mostly true, so at least I had that lie to cling to.

It wasn't that I wasn't like other girls. I was, in many ways. And I badly wanted to be like them, but they said I was too different. In reality, I was like some girls but not the other girls. I despised that I couldn't fit in with the girls I wanted to.

The mermaids thought they were better than me. They practically owned the school. They were so perfect with their tails and voices. They could easily find love, and yet they were the meanest of them all.

Then I was there. I couldn't do that. I was not part of the group. The mermaids were always beautiful, but I wasn't. I didn't even have my tail yet. Of course, a lot of them didn't have theirs either, but that never mattered. I wasn't like them so they wouldn't accept me at all.

Dylan changed the subject. "What did your uniforms look like?"

"Our uniforms were a navy-blue color. Ties were optional. We wore blue skirts that fell to our knees, and we had short sleeves, white button-up shirts. Sometimes, I wore them for fun. I think ties are very cute to wear. It's like tucking in a shirt. During winter, we wore blue cardigans. The ties were usually a lighter blue to follow the color scheme." I nodded.

Dylan laughed. "I can barely imagine you in such an outfit."

"Hey, I wore it for seven years."

We finished putting my clothes in my closet. We got the rest of the décor out. I'd chosen five colors. Teal, light pink, purple, black, and white. I even got ocean décor to show my personality. "This is the best part." I finished putting my perfumes on the vanity. I smiled, looking back at Dylan. "It's perfect."

"It speaks from your soul that I doubt is real," he joked.

I glared. "Dylan, my soul is very real." I believed I had a soul. Didn't I? Animals had souls. Being an animal, I had to have a soul. Although, fish were more on the aquatic side of animals. Were fish filled with souls? They had to be.

He smiled and nudged me. "Shall we take a visit to our old hideout?"

"It's still there?" I was surprised that our hideout existed after all these years.

"It sure is. Come on." We left my newly decorated room to go visit our hideout. We walked to the end of our street and followed a path behind the neighborhood. It was lined with trees and a river. When the structure came into my sight, I stopped.

"That's..." I grabbed onto his arm, staring at the treehouse in disbelief.

"It sure is." He grabbed my wrist and pulled me to our treehouse. This old thing was built here long before we ever found it, but we made it ours as kids. The treehouse was up in a tree that barely hung over the edge of a wide river.

The tree was at an angle, making the ladder steps more like stairs as we climbed up.

I sat down inside and looked around, smiling like a child who just got a toy they begged for. "This old thing is still standing."

Dylan sat against the opposite wall from where I was sitting. He stretched his legs and looked at me. "I still have a hard time believing you're really back."

"I have a hard time believing we still love being around each other. I mean, we changed a lot growing up, but we are still best friends, and I'm thankful. We reconnected like old times." I smiled.

He gestured to me. "Well, to be fair, you haven't changed. You're still the same girl who lets me pick on her." He chuckled.

"Excuse me, no. No, I don't. I defend myself. I'm good at

defending myself and with Olivia around, you're definitely going to see me defending myself. That girl is teaching me everything she knows." I pointed my finger at him.

"You're getting along with her better than I thought. Should I be scared?" He leaned back some more.

I nodded, smirking. "Yes, very scared. I also wanted to ask a weird question if you're willing to answer."

"Yes, madam?" he joked.

I pulled my knees to my chest. "How long ago did you befriend Olivia?"

He repositioned himself. "Well, about a year after you left for private school, Olivia showed up. She had no friends, and I had no friends, so I decided why not try to make a new one? We instantly became friends over my shared cookie." He smiled.

I nodded. "And for these past six years, have you started to wonder what it might be like to...date or kiss Olivia?" I gestured.

He choked on a laugh. "I already told you Olivia is into girls."

"Yeah, but I was just curious if you ever liked her before she told you her sexuality." I shrugged. "It's a simple question but if you're not willing to answer..."

"No. Olivia and I honestly see each other as siblings. There was never a point where I thought I wanted to kiss her. I know for a fact that I see her as my sister. Olivia and I have always been a good pair when it comes to siblings, since I don't have any of my own. I guess my parents decided they were done."

I nodded again, thinking to myself. "Okay." I clicked my tongue. "Your parents stopped because you met me. They figured they could get away with not having more kids because you had me to keep you company and we lived next door, so we were...friends." I didn't want to say we were siblings because I didn't see Dylan as my brother. I never had seen him that way.

Dylan stood and grabbed me, pulling me up. He glanced at the window that hung over the river. I swallowed, hoping he wasn't about to do what I assumed he was.

He pulled me towards the window and I began to struggle. "No, Dylan! Don't!" I leaned back, hovering over the window with my legs still inside the treehouse. I squeezed his wrists, holding on for dear life.

Dylan's lighthearted demeanor changed into a more serious one. "You're really scared."

"Dylan, please, just don't throw me in!" The last thing I needed was to grow a tail against my will, in front of my best friend.

He gently pulled me up, studying my face. "I-I was only joking. I wasn't actually going to throw you in, Mia."

I looked at my hands, refusing to let go of his wrists. Until I knew I was safe, I wouldn't let go. "I wouldn't know that after all this time." I looked at him, realizing just how close we were. I'd never noticed how brown his eyes were. They resembled the color of *chocolate*.

He pulled us away from the window, letting go of me. "I understand." He nodded and put his hands into his pockets. We both stood in silence for a few more minutes. "I'm sorry, Mia. I shouldn't have scared you."

Tell him. Now. Tell him or your friendship might never recover from this.

"I need to tell you something, the real reason why I was terrified to be thrown into the river. It's not what you think,"

I said in a quiet voice.

Dylan nodded. "I'm listening."

My stomach knotted. My mouth went dry. "I didn't leave for seven years to go to an all-girls private school. I mean I did go to a private school, but it wasn't for what you'd think." I looked into the water below. "The Academy of Naiad is a school for sea creatures."

Dylan laughed at that one, assuming it was all one big joke. But I wasn't laughing.

"I'm not the person you think I am. When my mom sent me away, she told me about what I was. I went to go learn about myself, Dylan, and I learned that I'm not human. I'm a monster. I can eat men, and I swim in the ocean. I breathe underwater. I can sing and put men into a trance if I want to," I said.

His smile faded. "Like...a siren?"

I nodded.

"Mia, you have to be pulling my leg."

"But I'm not. You can ask my mom. You can ask my brother. But you can't tell Olivia. I know you'd never hurt me or put me in danger. That's why I can trust you."

He crossed his arms and tilted his head. "Prove it."

"What?"

"Prove it. I want to see proof, so I know this isn't a joke that you're trying to make me fall for." He pointed to the river. "Let's go there." He grabbed my wrist before I could decline, and we climbed down. We stopped in front of the water.

I clenched my jaw and took off my shoes. "Fine. I'll Prove it." I threw them to the side and sat down on the little bank while I dipped my feet in. In an instant, they turned to a tailfin, rippling through the waves.

Dylan immediately dropped to his knees. "Mia!" He grabbed my shoulders, shaking me. "Do you realize how amazing this is? You can grow a tail!"

I furrowed my brows as I stared at what used to be my feet. I'd never expected such a reaction, yet here we were. If Dylan could accept it, why couldn't I?

"You really like this?" I asked.

"I love it!" He laughed as he stood. "I mean you have power that others dream of. People write stories about these creatures all the time as if they're cool, but they know if they met one in real life, they'd be terrified. I'm not. I know you have a kind heart and I'm amazed by what you can do."

My muscles relaxed as I dried my fin, putting my shoes back on my feet. Maybe he was right. I'd been so worried for no good reason. My best friend loved what I was. Maybe humans really were the most accepting of all the species.

We left the treehouse eventually and walked back to our homes, not saying a word.

Taking a deep breath, I pushed my hair behind my ear. We stopped in front of my house. Dylan turned to me. "I'll see you tomorrow."

I nodded and went inside my house, putting my hand over my heart.

"What's wrong?" Dad came over, looking at my posture. "You look like you just saw a ghost."

"We went to that treehouse of ours above the river and Dylan was going to throw me in. Not really, but I thought he was." I sunk down, but my father's arms wrapped around me.

He planted a kiss on my head. "Hey, don't you worry. Dylan has always been a good friend."

I groaned. "I told him, Dad. I told Dylan what I am, and he actually thought it was the coolest thing ever." I shook my head.

Dad shrugged. "That's what I thought about your mother, too."

Was that his way of saying he expected Dylan and I to end up together? He was cute, but I wasn't romantically interested in him.

I let out a sigh and walked up to my room, falling back onto my bed. I took a moment to look around again, studying the new look. Dylan helped me with it, but it was ultimately my room. It expressed the deepest parts of me.

I, more than anything, just wanted to calm down and be reassured that I wasn't going to have to give up Dylan in order to keep my secret anymore. I could not lose him, and now that he knew, I never would. Unfortunately, I just couldn't see a victory in this battle. I was bound to lose by whichever path I'd taken.

Seven

I KICKED OFF MY flip flops as I walked down the beach. While in the middle of removing my shirt, someone walked by.

"What are you doing out here at night?" a familiar voice asked.

Pulling my shirt down, I faced Dylan. "I could ask you the same thing." I cleared my throat. "I like to swim at night. It's calming and very private."

He nodded. "I just like the sound of the waves. Although sometimes I hear singing and it's mesmerizing. I assume those are the other sirens?"

I swallowed as he mentioned singing. Who else came here, and why would they want to hurt Dylan? I refused to let that happen. I'd be his protector if I needed to be.

When I didn't respond, he asked, "Can I sit?"

"No." I shook my head. "Sorry, I just like to swim alone. I'm very private about being half-naked around my best friend. Insecurity issues." I scratched my head.

He said something that threw me off guard. "Insecure? Mia Dawson was never insecure, but I guess puberty changes people. You also mentioned not being able to change in front of other girls. I get not wanting to be seen naked but when I pretended to throw you in the river, you freaked out. Are you also pregnant? You know, aside from growing a tail."

I choked on my laughter. "Dylan, shit, no. I am not pregnant. If I were, who would be the baby daddy? I'm not exactly a virgin by choice. Men are not running to me to sleep with me."

His cheeks reddened as he lowered his head. "Ah, so Mia Dawson wants to have sex but can't."

This was treading dangerously close to territory I didn't want to visit. "Can we please drop this? I'm not pregnant and I'm not trying to have sex right now. I just...want to be alone." I buried my toes in the sand. "That's not the point I'm trying to make. I'm just insecure about my body and I don't want to be seen in this form. Is that a crime?"

"No, of course not." He rubbed his neck, backing away. "I won't look."

"It's not about that."

"You just said it was."

"But I want to be alone!"

"The beach is not just for you, Mia. I've been coming here for the past seven years while you were away at a boarding school." He pointed off in some direction, his arm extended all the way. "You can't *will* me away. I used this beach to accept that you were never coming home."

I swallowed my anger as a tear welled up in my eye. I would not do this tonight. "I didn't have a choice, Dylan. I didn't get a say in where I went to school. I was eleven, so you don't get to pin this on me, but I'm trying to cope with moving my life back here." I glanced at the waves crashing against the sand.

"Go home," I said. I didn't hear a word come from him after I said that, so I assumed he was crossing his arms and defying me. However, as I faced him, he was backing away. "What are you doing?"

He furrowed his brows, but the frustration and pain still lingered in his eyes. "I don't know, Mia."

"What do you mean you don't know?"

"I don't know! I have no control over my body!" He continued to back away, and as soon as he disappeared down the street, I looked down at myself.

My hands glowed but I couldn't wrap my mind around what just happened. Had I willed Dylan to leave all on my own? It couldn't be possible, and I doubted myself either way. We didn't get magic, did we? No, we weren't superheroes.

However, a part of me still feared that I might have been the reason Dylan had no control over his body.

ALL WEEKEND, I STRESSED over what had really happened. I couldn't keep my thoughts straight no matter how hard I tried to distract myself.

When I walked into school Monday, I attempted to avoid Dylan. That didn't go according to plan when Olivia caught me, and Dylan followed behind.

"Mia! How was your weekend?" she asked with a big smile. Olivia always had such a pretty face. If only I could have looked like that...

I shrugged. "It was okay." My eyes darted to Dylan, but he wasn't looking at me. He must have been pissed about the other night. I got to stay when he didn't.

Olivia looked at Dylan. "Did something happen between you two?"

"We got into a fight," I said before Dylan could answer.

She nodded a bit. "Oh." She didn't pry any further.

When I glanced at Dylan again, chills ran up my spine. We both had wanted to swim at the beach at night, but I didn't feel comfortable with him seeing me half-naked. Somehow, I had made him leave against his wishes. I couldn't explain that to him.

Olivia leaned against the locker, moving her black hair over her shoulder. "Whatever it is, I'm sure there's a way past it."

Dylan and I were fighting over a spot. How did we move past that?

With a sigh, I said, "Finding a solution isn't as easy as you think it is." I'd been partying it up according to his logic.

She laughed. "I think maybe you should come to a compromise. Compromise is a good solution."

I couldn't wait every other night to see my true form. That wasn't fair.

If we both wanted the spot, we'd have to come up with an agreement though, right? He technically owned the spot because he had dibs for seven years and if I couldn't compromise, he would get it permanently.

She was right. If I didn't share, Dylan would claim the spot himself and I'd never get to see my tail unless I was in the bath. I wasn't willing to give it all up. "Fine. I'll compromise with him." I nodded as I looked over to Dylan. "We need to come to an agreement about that spot."

"We need to?"

I released a sigh. Wrong choice of words. "I'm sorry. Can we come to an agreement?"

He smiled a bit. "I think I can make that work. What were you thinking?"

"Every other night. I get it one night, you get it the next, or something like that."

He nodded. "I can agree to that."

My muscles relaxed. "I just want to ask one thing. Can I get it tonight at least? Tomorrow could be your turn."

Dylan pondered that thought for a moment, but to my luck he was still the sweet boy he'd always been. "Sure." He nudged me. I was thankful he wasn't bombarding me with questions about what happened. I wasn't sure myself but tonight I needed to find out.

The school day dragged on, and I was itching to go to the beach again. When the bell rang, I rushed out of the building and ran to the spot.

I faced a stranger who was passing by, and said, "Walk the other direction."

They gave me the strangest look, but they kept walking forward. Eventually they disappeared down the road. I dropped my hands and frowned. They seemed so lifeless. Why had they glowed last night? It didn't make any sense.

I kicked the sand and dropped into it, folding my legs. The waves continued to roll across the beach in one motion, capturing my attention for quite some time. Something about the rhythm was mesmerizing to watch. The way the ocean breathed was a miracle that nobody could replicate elsewhere.

It wasn't difficult for me to watch the movement for hours until the sun had set. When it had, I stood and grabbed my backpack, ready to head back home. Maybe I could ask Mom about it. Would she know anything about it? She had to. She was just like me since I was her daughter. Why didn't the academy teach this, though? Maybe it was all in my head and I'd been imagining it.

I put in my earbuds and turned on some music as I began my journey home. Some creep was walking a little too close for my liking and I glanced at him just a bit. "Don't get close to me," I whispered. I feared what could have happened if he did.

His steps sped up and I swallowed a bit. No, this was not going to happen tonight. He was getting closer, so I started walking faster.

I could see his figure right there behind me and I immediately turned to face him without thinking. I shouted, "Don't touch me!"

His eyes were black without a soul in sight, and they screamed *monster*. Despite his hunger for horrid things, he backed away from me. "What the hell did you do to me?" He growled. What had I done? Why was he listening to me and not his own demons?

Gulping, I backed away from him. "Don't come any closer."

And he *didn't* come closer. He stayed glued to his spot, unable to move as if I had control of him.

I turned and ran home, closing the door behind me and grabbing my chest.

"Mia?" Mom asked. "What happened?"

Dad looked over at me from the couch.

I shook my head. "Nothing." But it wasn't nothing. Whatever happened, nothing good came of it. I ran up to my room, locked my door, and dropped my backpack.

As much as I wanted to cry, I didn't. I had never had a scary encounter like that since I left the academy. I popped in a CD to my radio. The music didn't help me much, but it kept me from overreacting.

I grabbed my phone and pressed the call button. I put it to my ear as I nearly pulled my hair from my head. "Please pick up. Please, please." I paced back and forth but the phone went straight to voicemail. "Shit." I rubbed my face. I had nobody to talk to. Who did I tell? If I told my mom, she'd never let me leave the house again.

My heart pounded in my chest as I sat on my bed. Maybe I was just throwing this out of proportion but what did I do? If I didn't have whatever power I did, that man would have raped and killed me.

I must not have heard the knock on my door because when I looked up, Christian stood in my room. "What happened?" Would he tell our parents if I said something? No. Would he?

"I... I can't even begin to process it." I ran my fingers through my head. "He was right there. He was so close, and I could see the way he looked at me. He wanted to tear me apart, and he was about to." I rubbed my eyes. "I don't know how I did it, but I told him to not come any closer and he didn't. He just...stayed there. I think I could control him in a way."

He furrowed his brows. "What are you talking about?"

I closed my eyes as a tear escaped. "When I was walking home tonight, a man was following me. He was going to hurt me but somehow I could control him. He knew I could control him, too."

"Shit, Mia, why haven't you told Mom and Dad?" He sat beside me and wrapped an arm around my shoulders.

"Because they'll worry! I'll never be allowed to go out again.

She'll know I've been going to the ocean. I can't take that risk." I shook my head. "I don't want anyone to look at me and see me as a weak little girl. Yeah, he was going to hurt me, but he couldn't. I told him not to and he *didn't*. He couldn't because whatever I did, I put him under my spell. I have some kind of power, Christian. If anyone tries to hurt me, I can—" I looked at my hands. "I can tell them what to do. I think I have magic."

Eight

I SHIVERED ON THE way to the beach. The past few nights have given me time to think, and I had a theory on how this all worked so I was going to test it tonight.

Stopping in the sand, Christian stood just feet away. I turned to look at him as I held my palms out, facing them to the sky. "Walk towards me."

He walked towards me, then stopped.

My eyes flickered to the cliff and an idea popped into my head. "Jump off the cliff."

His eyes widened, but as hard as he tried, he couldn't fight it. He backed up and headed to the rocks, walking up the cliff. He got closer and closer to the edge where the waves crashed against the rocks below. "Mia," he said.

After he got just inches from the edge, I said, "Stop."

He stopped.

I looked at the moon, confirming what I had thought. I couldn't use my magic during the day when the sun was shining, but I could when the moon was.

My hands glowed the same color as the source of my

magic—the *moon*.

A couple walked past the beach, and I didn't think for a moment to hide my magic. Maybe the adrenaline had me going, but I wanted to keep trying it out. Deciding to test my limits, I took a deep breath as I looked at Christian, then the couple. "Everyone come here."

Christian followed the instructions and soon all three of them stood before me. The look on my brother's face told me I was crazy.

"Strip down."

Everyone got crazy eyes, but they complied.

"Mia, what are you doing?" Christian asked me as he removed his pants.

I closed my eyes. What was I doing? This wasn't like me to make such stupid and reckless decisions. Yes, I had magic, but I couldn't just control everyone for fun.

Facing the couple, I said, "Go home and never talk about this again." They did exactly as I said.

I squeezed my fists shut, letting Christian go from my hold. "What did I do?" I asked in a whisper.

He pulled his clothes back on and shook his head. "I don't think we should be out here anymore. Let's go home."

I nodded but all feeling left my body, and I couldn't seem to make myself do anything.

"Mia?" Before he could ask more questions, I lost consciousness.

I OPENED MY EYES and groaned from the strange feeling in my head. It was almost as if my brain was nauseous. It wasn't an ache or exhaustion. I just wanted to throw up whatever was *in* my head.

As I sat up, I screamed at the figure sitting at the end of my bed. He shushed me and leaned forward, and I calmed down. "What are you doing here?" I asked.

My brother frowned. "Mia, you passed out. I had to keep an eye on you."

I glanced at the time, and it read 2:48 a.m. "You've been staying up for me? We have school in five hours."

He shrugged. "Yeah, well, I also want to make sure you didn't kill yourself. Whatever happened tonight is serious. You passed out. I think we should tell Mom."

"What? No way."

"I had to lie to her and say you fell asleep. I can't keep doing that. She will be able to help you more than I can. You two are the—"

"Don't say it."

Christian swallowed. "You know what you both are. She knows way more than I do, and she can answer your questions. You can't just do this alone anymore, all right?"

I wanted to tell him to shove off, but I knew he made a good point. "Fine, but I decide when I want to tell her."

"Then promise me you won't use your magic until you do."

That was far too much to ask of me. "I can't."

"I can't let you hurt yourself or anyone else. We don't know what kind of power this is. You can control people, Mia, and that's a dangerous kind of magic."

"Fine, I won't use it."

After I made my promise, Christian left and tried to get some bit of sleep before we got up for school.

When the sun did start to rise, we both got ready and

ate breakfast. Mom and Dad didn't bother to ask us what happened which means Christian must have given them a pretty good lie.

We both left for school, and Christian told Olivia and Dylan to keep an eye on me today. Well, they could only do so much when we had different classes.

I spent my time in classes looking up magic and what kind of magic came from the moon. They didn't talk about the moon and its magic much, but they did mention types of magic. When I read through those, I concluded that my magic was mana magic. It needed an energy source, and mine came from the moon. However, what happened to me last night wasn't abnormal. I'd used too much at once. I was limited with how much I could use, and I'd need to keep practicing with it so I could recharge my magic the proper way.

Lunch came quickly, and while Olivia and Dylan talked to each other, Christian was looking over my shoulder at what I was researching. "Mana magic. What's that?"

"It's what I have," I said in a quiet voice. "That's what I've realized. I need the moon to recharge my magic, and I'm only able to use it during the night."

"So you can't use it on a new moon."

"Nope."

He nodded. "Interesting. And you passed out because..."

"Because I used too much of my energy at once. I have to learn how to control it and build it up. If I can just figure that out, I'll be able to use more of it without burning it all."

Christian laughed. "Well, it makes sense. At least you'll figure it out." His smile dropped. "But why would you need to use more of it? You don't have a purpose for controlling people."

"Because I have a power that I want to learn. If I never do, it could be used against me, just like my ancestry is." I closed the tab.

I wanted to ask him if this meant I could use my magic without telling Mom, but I knew Christian would tell me to let her know. He worried about me, and I got that, but if Mom never told me that we had magic to begin with, there had to be a reason she didn't want me to know or use it. I couldn't promise her I wouldn't use my magic. I couldn't make such a promise to anyone.

"What are you two talking about?" Olivia asked.

"Nothing," Christian and I said at the same time.

Dylan gave her a look. "It was definitely not nothing."

Clearing my throat, I furrowed my brows. "I'm sorry but don't we have like a minute until our next class? I don't want to be late." I hurried to my next class before the bell rang, avoiding the questions swirling around in their heads.

Dylan had already experienced a bit of my power, and if he questioned that at all, I'd be in deep trouble. He'd see me for the monster I really was, and I couldn't lose my best friend.

As soon as I got home after school ended, I feared Mom would be waiting for me and Christian would have said something. I was wrong. He kept his word, and he was expecting me to keep mine.

How could I do that? She had already forbidden me from going to the ocean. She would never let me go there and practice my magic. She'd rip it all away from me. It never made sense either, considering what she ate. She refused parts of herself and tried to shelter me, yet at the same time tried to make me embrace it. She was two sides of the same coin.

I couldn't take advice from her. She had no idea which side

she was on. No, the only choice I had right now was to find another like me to ask her if she had magic, too. I needed help with mastering this power without being told I could never use it.

Where did I go? I'd hardly ever come across them. Even at the Academy of Naiad, they didn't like me for the sole reason that I was ashamed of being like them. Everyone hated me except for Natalia.

I gasped when someone said, "Mia." I turned around, facing Christian. "What's wrong?" he asked.

What did I say? Did I tell him I lied and I was going to learn on my own? No, of course not. I was older and I was an adult. I had the final say in my own magic.

"Nothing. I'm just... I have a lot of homework and it's overwhelming. Senior year is too much, right? Wait, you're not a senior." No, he was a junior.

He saw through all the lies. Was the proof in my face—my eyes? Maybe.

Christian gestured to the couch and sat down with me. "I can tell you're having second thoughts about telling Mom."

"What if she says I can't use my magic? She's going to rip it away from me."

"Is that so bad?"

"Yes! It's my magic! I want to use it!"

"What if your magic is bad?"

I clenched my jaw. "Are you saying I'm a bad person? Are you saying I'm a monster like the rest of them accuse me of? Tell me how you really feel."

He groaned. "That is not what I'm saying." He rubbed his face. "I'm just telling you that maybe Mom will come to her senses and realize that you'll do it no matter what. Maybe she will help you master it."

"Doubt that." I crossed my arms. I doubted everything at this moment. I doubted the good parts of my mom the second she told me I couldn't go to the ocean. She was keeping me from my true potential. How could any good intentions be behind that? Did she not realize I would live on my own someday and I needed to be prepared for everything?

"Mia, we're only trying to help."

"How?" I yelled, standing up. "You don't know what it was like there—what they did to me. They despise me. If they find out that I have magic I can't *control*, what then? They'll use it against me. I'll be vulnerable. This is not the human world we're talking about, Christian. This is the world of sea creatures. There are mermaids, sea nymphs, sirens, water sprites, selkies, and so many other creatures from different backgrounds. I hate myself, but this is the one thing about me that I don't despise. If I can embrace pieces of my identity, why can't you support that?"

He nodded. "I'm sorry. I didn't realize."

"No, you didn't. I'm already in a battle with society not being able to accept me. They've taught me not to accept myself, so when I do like parts of me, let me have that. It's easy for Mom to ignore this. She's had years of experience. She has people who accept her for who she is. What do I have? I have nobody. You are forced to accept me because you're my brother. Dad accepted Mom, and I fear Dylan will never be the same way. That is a huge risk that could make or break my future. I have nobody, but I have at least something to help me. I have magic, Christian, and I want to use it."

Christian didn't say another word as a figure stepped into the living room from the front door. *Mom.*

We faced her, hoping she didn't hear what was just being said. Wishful thinking, I guess.

"H-Hi, Mom," I stuttered.

She folded her arms, narrowing her eyes at me. "You want to use what exactly?"

Nine

I THREW MY ARMS up, ignoring all the rules I gave myself the past few days. "I have magic!" I faced my mother. "I have magic, Mom. I can...control people."

Christian had left to go to his room when Mom told him to, leaving the two of us alone. I wasn't happy about it, but I couldn't make up a lie this time.

She stepped forward, holding my hands up. "Magic from our kind is evil, Mia. We must never use it."

"How can you say that? Why wouldn't we use what we are given?" I ripped my hands away. "I haven't hurt anyone! I've been trying to practice so I can control it. If I can't control it, the mermaids can use it against me. They'll find out the truth. They always do."

"Damnit, Mia! They already know the truth!" She used her forefinger and thumb to rub right above her eyes.

I dropped my shoulders. "What truth?"

Releasing a sigh, she met my eyes. "Mermaids have magic, too. We all have magic, Mia. It's not just you."

The skin around my nose twitched. "What? Why haven't

you told me?" More importantly, why didn't the academy tell me? Were they so afraid of us having magic? Did they believe we'd use it for evil? Mermaids knew before we did. That had to be the explanation.

She stepped forward, grabbing my shoulders. "I was afraid of this day. I knew you'd want to use your magic, but you can't. If you use it, it'll control you. Our magic is evil, Mia. Our magic comes from the moon, and theirs comes from the sun. Only we get this magic. If we use our magic, it will take hold of you. There is nothing good that comes from controlling people and you know this. You can't use your magic."

"You expect me to just sit here? If they know I have magic, then why wouldn't I want to master it? What good is having magic if I can never use it?"

Mom shook her head, moving her hands up to my cheeks. "Your magic will never be what you want it to be. The power is too great. It will eat you alive and turn you into someone you're not."

I scoffed, backing away from her touch. "You're ignoring the fact that our entire race is evil. The meat that you eat makes you evil. You want to pin it all on the magic, but the truth is—it's us. *We* are the ones who are evil. We are the bad guys. You can't keep denying this."

"But you think you can deny who you are."

"You're telling me to! You won't let me use magic, but you still eat that meat! You make no sense. None of this makes any sense." I pushed hair out of my face.

Silence fell between us both. Mom was unsure of what else to say to convince me not to use magic, and I didn't want to admit the truth.

If I didn't master my ability, I could never protect myself from the bad guys who aimed to lump me in with the rest of my kind. I could never stop the mermaids from harming me, just like when I couldn't stop Jason from forcing me to eat something so vile.

I needed to stop them. No matter what my mom said, nothing could keep me from learning the art of magic.

"Mia?" Mom whispered.

I didn't look at her. Instead, I turned the other way, ignoring her stare. "I hate who I am. You made me this way. You turned me into a monster, and now you're trying to ask me not to use my own magical gift. If you didn't want me to use it, why did you have me? Why didn't you abort me the moment you found out I was a girl?"

Arms wrapped around my torso and a chin rested against my head. "I could never do that to you. I wanted you. I always wanted a daughter even though you'd be like me." She pressed her lips against my hair. "I don't regret any of my decisions."

I didn't respond to her. A few tears rolled down my cheeks, and eventually the silence ate us whole. Mom let go of me, and I sauntered up to my room. I locked it behind me and pressed my shoulder against it with one palm flat on the door.

More tears left my eyes, eventually turning into sobs. I slid down to the floor and let the sorrow sweep me into its arms.

PLANTING MY FEET IN the sand, I glanced at the moon. "If our magic is meant for evil, then mermaids must not be able to use their magic for anything but good." Those words tasted bitter on my tongue. "No, that's false. I refuse to believe I can't use my magic for good."

As I closed my eyes, the moon's light radiated off me, fueling the energy inside. My fingertips tingled and goosebumps covered every inch of my skin. All my worries were washed away with the waves. Every ounce of my being was at peace. This was the one time when I could feel complete serenity take over and I didn't want to lose that feeling.

I walked towards the water, losing my shirt and shorts along the way. I removed my underwear, then my bra. The ocean rushed over my toes, filling every nook and cranny.

Within a minute, my legs had fused as one and my fins emerged. I swam away from the shore, spinning in every direction possible.

The saltwater coated my skin, welcoming me home.

I smiled as I swam further into the depths of the ocean. Fish swam around me for a while until they disappeared for good. I stopped, floating in one spot. I searched every corner for the fish, but they were gone. Were they scared of me?

An arm snaked around my waist, yanking me into the darkness. I reached for the surface, trying to claw my way back but nobody knew I was down here.

After I was thrown onto a ledge, I glanced back at my kidnapper. No...

A woman folded her arms across the edge of the ledge, leaving only her head exposed. "Hello."

I scooted away from this man-eating monster. "I'm nothing like you," I said. Another one appeared from my right.

Sirens.

The first woman sighed. "You can't just run from the

truth." She climbed up onto the ledge. "My name is Calliopé. Her name is Kysana."

Kysana leaned forward. "You must be a different breed. Most of us don't have..." She pointed to the gills under my breasts. "Well, those of us who kill."

"I don't kill." I covered my boobs with my arms. "I want to go home."

Calliopé laughed. "This is home! The human world is chaotic, and you shouldn't be living there. That's why we eat them." She leaned forward.

"I would never eat them. I could never." I swallowed.

Calliopé grabbed the fin on the right side of my tail. "Don't lie to us. You're lying." She placed her hand on the rock, closing the gap between us. "I can smell the lies."

Kysana giggled. "Lies! She smells those from a mile away. Part of you is curious about human meat, is it not?" She leaned in closer, laying her head on my shoulder.

They couldn't be serious. I would never be curious. I was not telling any lies.

Calliopé pulled away, giving me room to breathe. "She's friends with them." Her eyes narrowed. "She trusts them."

Kysana gasped. "What? You trust humans?" She lifted her head.

I scooted forward, refusing to show fear. I couldn't show that I was afraid of them. They'd use it against me. "I have no reason not to. They didn't kidnap me."

"Not yet. They don't know your dirty little secret." Calliopé smirked. "But they will, child. They will know everything about you."

"How do you know?" I asked.

She shrugged, twirling her hair. "I know things. You can't

hide your secrets from those you care about, and they will never accept you, either. Humans see us as monsters. They don't love us the way we may love them. Cut your losses now and embrace yourself."

I leaned forward on my hands. "You loved someone, didn't you?"

"That's none of your business," she snapped.

Kysana grabbed my hand, holding it against her chest. "Humans hurt us. They see us as beautiful women they can control. They would never see us as people with feelings. It's foolish to believe they'd love us."

I pulled my hand from her grasp. "I'm sorry you got hurt but this is my life. Not all humans are bad." My brother was human, but I'd never tell them that. It would put him in danger.

I slipped from the ledge, into the water. "Don't come back for me." I swam out of the cave.

The swim back was long as I tried to navigate my way through the abyss that held on tight. I popped up above the water a few times to see if I could spot the shore, and I couldn't.

"I can take you back," a girl said.

Facing her, I glared. "No."

Kysana swam closer. "I know the way." She swam off, leading the way.

I groaned, not having any other choice. I followed her.

When we approached the beach I'd left my clothes on, I turned to thank her, but she was gone. I wasn't going to tell my mom about this. She'd never let me out of her sight again.

When I dried off and got dressed, I walked back to the house and snuck up to my room before anyone caught me.

The window across from mine was dark. Dylan was fast asleep. He needed the sleep for his soccer games, and I needed it to process that I had met other sirens.

Sure, sirens went to the Academy of Naiad, but there was a difference between those raised on land and those raised in water. Calliopé and Kysana were not like any of the others. They scared me, yet I wanted to learn from them. Who else was supposed to teach me to master my magic?

Kysana had mentioned that I had gills. What did that mean? I thought all sirens had them, and yet, they seemed so intrigued by them.

I couldn't ask Mom, or she'd question how I even got such information. I had nobody to teach me about this world but the two of them. Did I want to take such a risk?

Maybe. Maybe I didn't. They could teach me, and I could teach them. Together we could balance each other. If I could show my mom that they weren't all evil, maybe she'd let loose on the reins. I'd be allowed to be who I was and not what others wanted me to be.

I changed into pajamas and laid in my bed. There had been a day when I never had any idea about what I was. Mom came and told me the truth and since then, I'd denied the truth. I wasn't going to be like them—the monsters they thought we were. I would have to prove that I could use my magic for good and I'd make my own path.

Mermaids were quick to believe this world was so black and white, but they forgot that even black and white movies had shades of gray all over. Good and evil weren't so crystal clear anymore, and they never had been.

What if I was a shade of gray? What if I was neither black nor white?

The world refused to accept the morally gray areas that surrounded us every day. They were quick to want to say whether something was good or bad, and it was solely to validate their decisions.

I *was* a shade of gray, and I'd have to show everyone that we existed in black and white movies, too. We'd been left out in the dust, but we were just as valid. We were real colors.

Ten

I WALKED DOWNSTAIRS, RUBBING my eyes as I listened to the obnoxious voices. They woke me up, and I was not happy to be woken up early on a Saturday.

My feet hit the first floor and I looked at the culprits of my nightmare. "What is the meaning of this? I was trying to sleep."

Christian looked at me and chuckled, shaking his head. "Dylan came over and I'm telling him embarrassing stories."

About me? Hell no.

"No, Christian!" I whined, stomping my feet. "You can't ruin the way he sees me. I'm supposed to have power over him."

Dylan turned to look at me while the stool he sat on squeaked. "Too late. I know your secret. I know all about you."

I swallowed, looking at my brother. He told Dylan about my magic. We had a deal, right? Wrong. But it still should have been my decision.

"I know that you would wet the bed as a kid." He crossed

his arms. "I'm surprised I never noticed."

Relief washed over me as my shoulders relaxed, realizing Christian didn't tell him anything. "Yes, I did wet the bed. What are you going to do about it? A lot of kids do that." I walked over to the counter, putting bread in the toaster. "I don't do it anymore."

Dylan looked at my brother and shrugged. "If you say so."

"Oh my gosh, you think I still do it. No. That's disgusting."

"Isn't that why girls made fun of you?" Christian lifted his eyebrow.

"No, they made fun of me because I was different." My toast popped up and I spread butter and jam on it. I took a bite.

"And why was that? Why were you different?" Dylan questioned.

I looked between them. "Why wasn't I different? I'm not exactly cool. I'm not popular. I'm just me. I always have been and always will be." I sighed and sat. "Look, I had my troubles at that school and it's true but... I still enjoyed it. Natalia made it all better."

Christian squinted at me. "So you say. But what troubles did you have?"

Taking a deep breath, I said, "I developed late. I was a late bloomer. All the girls got their boobs and curves and I still looked like a child. When I tried to join them, they wouldn't let me. I wasn't good enough because I couldn't attract boys. They knew what I was. They knew. I was a complete joke. I tried to stuff my bra and it didn't work. One boy found out and he embarrassed me in front of the entire school. I hated being a late bloomer. I just wanted to look like the other girls. I was always left out. A private school still has its bullies.

They're no different from the rest of the schools." I slowly ate my toast.

Dylan scrunched his face, confusion setting in. "I thought you went to an all-girls school?"

I was a horrible liar. I knew my lies would catch up to me eventually. Swallowing, I averted my gaze downwards. "Well, I lied. It was boys and girls. Natalia was always there for me. She helped me feel better about myself. When I finally bloomed, everyone noticed." I looked at my chest. "So, Natalia helped me get revenge on the boy. We poured paint on his hair in front of everyone. It was perfect."

Christian nodded. "I'm glad she helped you. I'd punch any boy who makes you cry."

"It went on like this for years. We constantly pranked each other, back and forth until we left school. He was just so cruel to me. I can't control my body. I can't control when I grow. Well, he learned. Everyone learned. I wasn't a late bloomer for the sake of it. I was a late bloomer because I had a lot of good stuff that needed more time to grow." I finished my toast.

Christian's face was red as he looked at the counter, avoiding all eye contact.

Dylan's eyes wandered down to my boobs and I slapped the table. "Excuse me, control your eyes. You're my best friend, so act like it."

"I'm a man, Mia. We were kids when I last saw you. Seeing you like this is a whole other ballgame." He gestured to me.

I gasped. "What does that mean? I'm still myself. I just have boobs! Getting boobs is part of growing up for a girl. It's not abnormal."

He shrugged. "It is as if I saw you differently when we were kids."

"Differently. What does that mean?" I eyed him.

"It means I saw you as a girl who played in the dirt and got scrapes. Now you really are a girl."

I wasn't sure if that was an insult or not. Did Dylan want the tomboy back? He'd be out of luck if that was the case. "I was always a girl, Dylan. I'm just girlie now because I like more feminine things and I have boobs. There's nothing wrong with who I am now. I'm not ashamed of being a girl." Unfortunately, I was ashamed of something else. Being from the sea had amazing perks, but having human friends and family made it that much worse. Even other sea creatures hated me, and I never understood why. I wasn't an evil person. I was never wicked.

He rubbed the bridge of his nose. "I know and I'm not saying there's anything wrong with it. It's just different and I'm getting used to it. There's nothing wrong with you liking girl things."

I smiled. "Good. Because I like painting my nails and wearing jewelry and being a girl. I find nothing wrong with embracing my femininity."

Dylan sat back in his chair. "That's fine. Plenty of people like girls like that. In fact, Olivia likes girls like that. Not that I'm saying she likes you, because I'm sure she knows you don't like her. Unless you secretly do, and I just have no idea. I'm just saying that there are people attracted to feminine...people."

"Not romantically sure, but platonically, yeah." I scoffed. "Are you telling Olivia that I don't like her? Was I a bit jealous when I found out you made a new friend while I was gone? Maybe."

Christian coughed. "A lot jealous."

With a glare, I straightened my posture. "My point is that I understand you had to make friends. I was jealous that she replaced me, but I've gotten over it."

"Nobody replaced you. I simply made a new friend." He shook his head and looked at my brother.

I folded my arms on the table, but I began rubbing my forehead. "My head is starting to hurt." Facing my brother, I asked, "why are you both up so early? Do you not sleep in like normal people?"

"Dylan came over and decided to talk to me. He needs guy friends, too, you know." He tapped his fingers on the counter. "I'm not against making more friends."

"He's my friend. You have your own."

"Why are you jealous? You just said you got over it."

"You're my brother and he's my best friend."

Dylan patted my hand. "Don't worry. I'm still here. I have plenty to go around. He won't steal me away."

I grumbled and pulled my hand away from him. "Don't touch me."

Dylan chuckled and looked at my brother. "Do you want to go play video games?"

"Hell yeah!" Christian got off the stool and took Dylan to his room.

As I stared at the empty stool, I frowned. Dad came out of his room and started a pot of coffee. "Is something wrong?"

"Christian is taking my best friend. If he's going to take my friend, then I won't have time to spend with him myself. It's rude. I can't even have my own friends." My shoulders slumped.

"Maybe Olivia is available." He patted my shoulder.

"No, I don't have her number yet. I keep forgetting. I only

see her at school for the most part and when we hang out with Dylan. I just wanted to have my cake and eat it, too. My brother is stealing my cake." I laid my cheek flat against the cold surface of the countertop.

Dad sat next to me and shook his head. "I know it's hard, but you have to realize that Dylan is allowed to have however many friends he chooses, and he can choose those friends himself. There is no limit to the number of friends someone makes. You just have to make friends to hang out with when Dylan isn't available. Be sufficient without him."

"I have a hard time making friends. I try but I'm just not like everyone else. I'm not like the humans or the mermaids. I'm different and people don't like different. How am I supposed to do that?" I checked my phone, my eyes lingering on the contact I hadn't spoken to in a while. "Even the sirens hate me, Dad, and I'm apparently the most like them if you ask the mermaids."

"It takes time, but the effort is worth it. When you have real friends, you will be much happier." He smiled and took his coffee back to his room.

I set my phone down and looked at the fridge. Dylan was with Christian. I only had one other option. I was going to go swim in the ocean today. Who needed friends?

After walking back to my room, I changed into other clothes and I made my way to the ocean. I stripped down on the beach to nothing but my bikini top, and I walked into the water. I fell over as my legs transformed, leaving me with nothing but a fishtail. I swam deeper, away from the shore. I took this time to really enjoy the aura of the water. I was home now, and I was free to be me.

I swam up, poking my head out of the water. The air was

pure here. The ocean was exactly what I needed to wear off the stress and worry of my loneliness. Without Dylan, I barely had real friends. I needed to accept that and use this time to get to know *myself*. I would have to spend my time swimming around in the one place where I felt okay.

As I swam back to the shore, I noticed someone sitting on the beach. I couldn't return. Nobody could know about my secret. I swam to the rocks further down, keeping myself hidden from view. Who were they and when would they leave? I was in a dilemma. I couldn't go home until they did first.

There wasn't any way I was going to use my magic on him. Not after what happened to me the last time I did.

I hung onto the rock, keeping an eye on them. They weren't leaving anytime soon.

I watched the grown man relax on the beach and go for a swim here and there. At some point, he noticed my clothes and didn't see me anywhere in sight. I knew I screwed up when police sirens wailed and officers arrived.

The police weren't sure what to do because my clothes were not bloody or torn but their best guess was I drowned somewhere. With this information at hand, they started to let the station know, sending out requests for who the clothes belonged to.

When they finally left the beach, I got out, drying off. With my clothes being taken to the station for evidence, I was left completely naked. I could not walk down the street without any bottoms.

How was I going to go home? When my parents would find out, they'd kill me for coming to the ocean. The only solution was to go home as if I wasn't at the beach at all. The only issue was I had nothing to cover my front or back.

All my ideas were useless. I wasn't going anywhere without clothes. I gave up on the whole plan, sitting on the beach all night. I didn't know what time it was, but the crickets were out and the waves were still rolling.

"Mia!" I heard Mom's voice yell behind me.

I looked back to see her running to me before embracing me in a big hug. "When they said a girl's clothes were found on the beach, I didn't think it could be you but then I realized you weren't home, and you hadn't come home all night." She was thankful I was alive now but tomorrow there would be hell to pay for going against her word.

Dad brought me a blanket, letting me wrap it around my naked body. Dylan and Christian both came over, making sure I was okay. I would need to hide my clothes for now on or else this was going to happen again. I was most likely already grounded for scaring my family half to death. This never would have happened if Christian hadn't stolen my best friend, and I had him to blame for getting me caught at the one place I was forbidden from going.

Eleven

My body was growing restless. I sat in my room, fiddling with my cold fingers as my hands shook. It was hard to sit here and do nothing, but I had no choice. Mom and Dad grounded me for such a thing I pulled, and I was not going to come out of this for a long time.

A light clunking sound bounced off my window, getting my attention. I walked over to see the very criminal himself. I opened my window and narrowed my eyes. "What, are you trying to break my window and get me into more trouble?"

Dylan shrugged, his arms laying across the pane. "It was barely harmful to the glass. It wouldn't make a crack."

I rolled my eyes and sat on my floor. "What is it that you want, Dill Pickle?"

He gasped. "Excuse me?"

"You heard me." I smirked. "Did you think I forgot your nickname?" I leaned my elbow onto the pane and rested my jaw in my hand.

He grumbled and looked anywhere but at me. "Yeah, because it's weird."

"Oh come in. Your name is Dylan. Dill. You have a pickle between your legs. It makes sense." I laughed, putting one arm against my stomach.

"Damn, Mia. Where is your brain at?" His cheeks turned a light shade of pink as he cleared his throat.

"Everyone knows it. You either have a pickle or a banana. Your pick." I gestured.

"And what do you have?"

"Coconuts and a donut." I smiled. "Like every other woman out there."

His facial expression changed. "Not every woman has boobs."

I stopped laughing, nodding my head. "That's true. It was insensitive of me to imply that you must have them to be a woman. You don't. Breasts don't make a woman. It's so much more than that." I rubbed at my red cheeks.

"Of course." Dylan nodded.

"What would you say if I made a crazy offer?"

"Depends on the offer."

"I want to buy an apartment. And I want you to be my roommate." I chewed my lip.

A smile formed on his lips. "You want me to be *your* roommate? You sure about that?"

I smiled in return. "Beats getting grounded for going to the ocean when I'm eighteen."

Dylan leaned against his windowsill and chuckled. "Let's do it. Let's find an apartment together. You and me. Then you won't be restricted by their rules anymore."

Their rules. Right.

I let out a little sigh. "Life sucks, doesn't it? There is so much in this world that sucks, and I've been looking for the light, but it's so hard to find. When you do find it, it's barely in your grasp for a short time before it vanishes again. There is so much hatred, misery, and disease. I wish I could change the world."

Dylan nodded. "You can, in your own ways. Small steps help lead you to the big goal. It all starts somewhere."

"Right. It does start somewhere." I sat back, looked up at the stars in the sky. "Do you think anyone will ever like me?"

"What are you talking about? Why wouldn't they?" he asked.

I shrugged, looking at him. "Because there are things about me that people don't know. I'm not exactly desirable if people know where I come from, and I want to know if anyone would accept that."

"This is a new day and age. I'm sure most people will accept anything."

I shook my head. "No, not most people." The mermaids wouldn't accept me as I was. The sirens wouldn't accept me as I was. I didn't belong anywhere, and I was beginning to think maybe something was wrong. I wanted to choose the right side, but they didn't want me around, and the other side wanted me to be exactly like them.

"Why?"

"Because even if the world changes, people don't always change. Some stay the same and they want to judge people rather than getting to know them as a person." I grabbed my pillow from the bed and put it against the windowpane, cushioning my head.

"I guess that's true." He nodded.

I stared at him, wondering if he would judge me for who I really was. He would, wouldn't he? Dylan would never understand my side of things. He would never be able to accept this.

"They were mean to you, weren't they?" he asked me.

"When are they not? This is part of who I am, and I can't make it go away. It's who I am. People don't seem to understand that it won't go away, but it doesn't define me as a person. I still control my actions. It might be part of my identity, but it doesn't define my character. They judge me for it and assume these other actions of me, but they are not me. I control myself." They'd never understand that because DNA always stood out above actions. People believed that if it was ingrained in my system, it would eventually come out.

"What did they do?"

"I can't say. It's too personal. It's too risky. I can't trust a single soul." The only people who knew were those who were meant to know, like Natalia. "I struggle with it every day. Nightmares haunt me. Both sides treat me like the villain, leaving me nowhere to turn to. People like me are left out in the dust to fend for themselves. They tell me to follow my ancestors, but if I did, they'd hate me more than they do when I resist it. I'm in a losing battle."

Dylan didn't say another word. I looked at the stars again, admiring how they could all shine so brightly. I wanted to shine, too.

Breaking the silence, I said, "I should probably go to sleep. I know that my parents will never unground me and I may as well sleep during the night like a normal person."

"All right, I'll sleep, too, I guess." He said goodnight.

We both closed our windows and went to bed for the night. I wasn't all that surprised that I had told Dylan about how I felt even if I didn't tell him what Jason did. He was my best friend, and I couldn't keep my feelings from him. If he were the real Dylan, he wouldn't pester me for more.

THE SUN BLINDED ME while birds chirped as if they'd been up for hours. I rolled over and got out of my bed. I went downstairs to eat breakfast.

Mom watched me eat, dropping a package of bloody meat on the counter. "When will you try it?"

"Never."

"Why?"

"Because *they* didn't deserve to die."

"Nobody killed them for us. They were already dying, and we just so happened to get their meat. It's not wrong."

I put my toast down. "It feels wrong."

"If something feels right, does that make it right? No. I didn't send you to the academy to hide away in a cave. Someday you must accept the truth."

The laugh that escaped me didn't hold an ounce of humor. "The same way others accept me? Sure, Mom." I rolled my eyes, eating my toast again.

"You can't survive on toast forever." She sighed and put it back in the fridge. I swallowed, barely managing to finish my breakfast before my appetite completely dissipated.

I wasn't sure what I wanted to do today. There wasn't much I was allowed to do.

Christian came over to me and sat down. "You look miserable."

"I want my Dill Pickle."

He jabbed his thumb at the fridge. "There are pickles in the fridge. Get one yourself."

"I mean Dylan. I want Dylan, my best friend. He always knows how to comfort me. I'm sure he's spending his day with Olivia, right?"

"Are we still going on about this? Olivia is his friend. Get used to it."

"I am! I've become her friend." I crossed my arms.

Christian sat back, leaning his arm against the counter. "That's not how it works. The jealousy is obvious."

I dropped my jaw, completely taken back by my brother's bluntness. "I am not jealous!"

"You are. You really are." He chuckled.

I got off the stool. "I am not jealous." I walked up to my room. Why would I be jealous? He was allowed to have his own friends.

Dylan was also my best friend, and he always would be. If he wanted to be her best friend, I'd be fine with that. I was even learning to like Olivia.

I had *no* reason to be jealous.

I checked out my window and noticed the empty room across from mine. He was out doing something, and I didn't blame him. I closed my curtains and looked around my room, not sure of what to do. I didn't have a TV like most kids my age.

An idea popped into my head, and I looked out of my window. I wanted to prove I wasn't jealous. I was going to go hang out with them whether I was grounded or not—and I still was.

I locked my door as I left my room and walked downstairs. Dad was watching TV and Mom was doing the laundry. My brother was probably somewhere with his friends.

I quietly walked into the kitchen and hid behind the counter. I peeked up and checked on my father who was completely distracted by the football game. I crawled towards the back door and slid it open, crawling out. I closed it behind me and ran through the gate. I finally stopped running once I was a few houses down the street. I texted Dylan to ask him where and Olivia were. When he responded with the mall, I headed in that direction.

The mall was close to our house. When I arrived, I asked them which store they were at. I found them in the food court which was to be expected. They were munching on some fast Chinese food as I sat down between them. "Hello, fellow friends."

"Aren't you grounded?" Dylan asked.

I shrugged. "I am."

Olivia laughed and nudged my arm. "I like you."

Along with their Chinese food, Olivia had an orange in her hand. It was an interesting snack to go along with Chinese food.

They both finished eating and Olivia smiled at me. "Hey, now that you're here, I want to go get some bras and panties."

"I can do that." I stood up with her.

Dylan groaned. "Really? Do we have to?"

Olivia looked at Dylan, replying, "Hey, you don't have to come. You can meet us somewhere else."

"Then what's the point of going to the mall together? Only children and their parents who go together will meet up later." Dylan got up from his seat and sighed. "Let's just go."

We headed to the store and walked inside. I looked at everything and frowned. "It's all so adorable. I want this." I touched a bralette hanging on a display. "This is so cute, and it has no wires! Perfect for wearing under tank tops. They have that band around the bottom, and it makes it so much cuter. I love this one, too." The realization dawned on me, and I stopped looking through the different styles. "I have no money right now." I'd put all my money into savings with no plans of using it for anything but the apartment now. And a car.

Olivia looked at me. "How about this? You can pick out one bra and I'll pay for it. I have a credit card here."

"Really? Your parents allow that?"

"I pay all my bills off. I'm not an irresponsible teenager." She shrugged. "As long as I pay off my bills, I get to continue to have it."

"That's a good idea. Your parents sound great. But you don't have to pay for my stuff. I need to learn to get a job anyway." I sighed.

"Are you sure? It's not a big deal. You can just pay me back." She picked out some bras in her size.

I thought about it for a moment and looked at the price. The bra was a washed-out version of bright red with a floral pattern, and it was just so cute. "Okay. I'll pay you back."

Olivia smiled and grabbed the bras, taking them to the counter. She paid for them and gave me my bag.

Dylan's posture was stiff the entire time—including a certain part I wasn't supposed to see—at least until we left the store full of women's undergarments. We walked around to multiple stores and looked at the different items but didn't buy anything else. I never understood the purpose of walking around stores if you knew you couldn't buy anything. What about that was so fun for teenagers?

I looked over at Olivia and Dylan as they nudged each

other. I was not jealous of their friendship. Why couldn't anyone else see that? They were great friends, but Dylan was still my friend and I had to remind myself I was thankful he still welcomed me back after being gone for so many years.

Olivia came over to me. "We're gonna go now. We should hang out again. I may need to give you my number for that." She grabbed my phone and put in her number and handed it back. "Text me anytime." She smiled.

I nodded in return. She was nice and I knew there was no way I was envious of her. Christian was a liar. Maybe Olivia and Dylan could both talk about cute girls together, but Dylan and I had history together. We had memories that went far back, and I had to hold onto that if I didn't want to mess up this friendship.

Twelve

"WHAT THE HELL ARE you wearing?" Olivia asked as she looked at me. "It's Halloween. It's the time to dress up as whatever you want."

I looked at the giant T-shirt with an orange design. Olivia liked oranges, right? "I'm an orange. I am dressed up."

"Sure." She shrugged. Olivia was dressed up as a bee. She pulled it off well. "We need to find Dylan."

"Why?"

"Believe it or not, the moron is our friend."

Right. He's our friend.

Christian thought I should have dressed up as a mermaid or something ironic. Well, it was a good thing he wasn't making the decision.

Dylan showed up, and both Olivia and I groaned. "No, Dylan. What the actual fuck is that?" She asked, gesturing to the giant soccer ball on his body.

He frowned. "What? I like soccer."

"And Olivia likes oranges," I said.

Olivia looked at us both, giving us a look of

disappointment. "You both are a disgrace to Halloween." She headed to the kitchen to get what I assumed was some alcohol to properly deal with the us.

Dylan tried to get closer, but his ball kept us apart. "Sorry."

I cleared my throat. "So it seems we both suck at Halloween. What happened? Weren't we the best when we were kids?" I laughed, basking in the memories. Dylan dressed up as the superheroes and I would always dress up as the monster from a horror movie. How ironic it was back then.

He chuckled. "I suppose we were. Now we can't seem to keep Olivia happy."

"Maybe I could spice it up just a bit." I grabbed some red punch, splattering it onto my shirt. Using a stick of red lipstick, I drew all over my lips. "There, now I'm a bloody orange. Blood orange. Get it?" I laughed.

Dylan laughed, too, before trying to sit down. That plan failed. "Maybe I should have gone with just a soccer player."

"Yes, very original."

"Hey!"

Laughter erupted some more before my smile faded. Olivia returned with a drink in hand. "Any of you want some?"

With an ounce of freedom, I decided what my parents didn't know couldn't hurt them. I was legally an adult, and in other countries, I was allowed to drink alcohol.

In a matter of thirty minutes, the tingling kicked in and I lost most control of my mind.

"Did you guys want to see my real costume?" I asked. I could get away with it, couldn't I?

Olivia nodded. "Hell yes! That costume you have on is ugly. Show us."

I waved the two of them to follow me and we all headed

to the beach. The beach was filled with dressed up people drinking, and surprisingly a lot weren't dressed up as sea creatures.

As I climbed behind some rocks, Olivia and Dylan followed. Dylan struggled the most and Olivia had to pull him up herself.

The shirt I wore was big enough for me to remove all my bottoms without having my butt exposed. I took a deep breath, stepping into the water, but sirens echoed into the sky as people ran from the beach. The police were here to catch underage drinkers.

Olivia cursed and pulled her costume off until she was naked. She ran into the water, trying to form a cover-up. "Dylan, get in here! Now!"

"No! That water is freezing!" Hardly. It was nothing compared to the west coast.

I hurried into the water before my legs disappeared, pulling my shirt off in the process. I threw it back up on the shore. I would have to be Olivia's back up story.

It was dark enough that nobody could see the large tail under the water.

The police arrived, shining their flashlights on us. "What are you kids doing?"

"Sorry, officer. We thought we'd skinny dip on Halloween." Olivia smiled.

He shook his head. "Are you old enough to be out here?"

Olivia nodded. "We all are." She laughed. "But Mia and I were...having fun. What else do two girls do in the water at night?"

The officer grumbled. "Get home safely, all right? There was underage drinking and I had to shut it down. I don't want to hear about another kid going missing around these parts."

He turned on his way, but I called out, "Another?"

He faced me. "Yes. Another. One of the kids here went missing tonight, and we came to shut down the underage drinking before more followed suit. Halloween is the worst night for all first responders and those on the force. Get home, please." He disappeared behind the rocks.

Olivia swam towards the shore. "Mia, are you coming?" She glanced back at me.

I nodded. "Yeah, give me a moment."

Dylan helped Olivia out and she wrung out her hair before putting her costume back on. She and Dylan walked back up the beach, behind the rocks again.

"I'm sorry, but I must find that kid. I'm not the bad guy and I'm going to prove it." I backed up some more before turning and swimming below the surface. He couldn't end up like the first boy.

I'd memorized the path taken towards the cave where Calliopé and Kysana lived, and this time I arrived before anything could happen. "You..." I choked, watching the boy writhe in pain.

Calliopé looked at me. "What are you doing here?"

"Stopping you from killing an innocent kid!" I swam over and pulled her away. "Don't do this."

She pushed me back into the rocks. "Don't tell me what to do! You have no authority over me, and I am hungry."

I swallowed. "I can get you meat. I can get you the meat from my house. My mom eats humans, too, but I don't want you to kill someone over it."

Kysana frowned. "Why do you care about what we do? You don't like us."

Taking a deep breath, I shook my head. "That's not true. I never said I didn't like you. I... Look, I know nothing about sirens. I've only learned what they taught me at the academy and my mother doesn't want me to know much about them."

"Us, child, us. You're one of us, too," Calliopé said.

Closing my eyes and nodding, I continued, "I want to learn more. I want you to teach me things nobody else will."

When I opened my eyes, Calliopé gave Kysana a look. "All right. We can do that, but you must understand that this is who we are. We eat fresh, live humans."

Without a second thought, I rushed over and grabbed the boy, dragging him off the ledge. I swam under the water, through the cave, and up to the surface. I swam as fast as my tail would take me with Calliopé and Kysana on my back. Just when I made it to the shore, Calliopé grabbed my fin, ripping it. I yelled out, letting go of the boy. I scooted up towards the sand, shaking from the pain. It was like having an ear torn.

I looked towards the boy struggling, and as I glanced up at the moon, I lifted both hands as they began to glow. Turning to see the boy, I yelled, "Go home and never return to this beach again!"

Just like that he stopped struggling from my power. He walked up the beach and disappeared beyond the road.

Kysana approached me with caution, but it was Calliopé that I feared. "What did you do to him?"

"I saved him." I hugged myself. I *saved* him. That was what mattered.

Calliopé smirked as she came closer. "That is quite the gift you've been given."

"Don't you dare touch me." I scooted further up into the sand. "You're evil."

Calliopé stopped, rolling her eyes. "You took my food away from me. You're controlling what I eat when I barely know you, and this particular diet has been in our ancestry for centuries. Excuse me if I seem a little pissed off about it. I haven't eaten in days."

"Days? Why?" I narrowed my eyes.

She shrugged. "It's not easy to steal a man when the beach is filled with them. I only got this one because most of them were drunk out of their minds." She leaned forward, resting her cheek on her hand. "Tell me more about this gift."

"Tell me about yours, first."

Calliopé gave Kysana a look. "Do you want to tell her or should I?"

Kysana nodded. "Go ahead."

Clearing her throat, Calliopé planted herself beside me. "Not every siren gets a magical gift."

"But my mother said..."

"You said she won't tell you much about sirens, so why are you taking any advice from her?"

I didn't respond. Maybe she was right, and my mom had been lying to me. Why, though?

Calliopé pointed towards the moon. "The moon is our energy source. That is what we call mana magic. Sirens and mermaids use mana magic, but mermaids get their magic energy from the sun. Sirens feed best at night which is why our source is the moon. Mermaids don't eat humans but instead seduce them, hence why they need the sun. See the difference?"

"If every siren doesn't have magic, how do you know this?" I gestured to the ocean.

She gave me an insulting look. "I'm not stupid, child. We

might live in the water, but we know about the human world and what goes on. We also know about sirens, more than your mother wants you to know. We are not bad people. We just have to survive off of humans and that's not our fault. We were born this way."

I reached down and touched the rip in my fin. The salt had stung at first in the fresh wound, but it was gone by now.

"Kysana and I don't have gifts. Not like you. We can sing to attract men, but..." She shook her head. "It explains the gills. Not all sirens have gills, either, and I believe those who do, have magic."

"But why? Why me?"

Kysana pointed to the moon. "See that? Your magic comes from the moon. They say the moon chooses which sirens have magic, and which don't. The moon seems to think you're worthy of this magic."

It explained why I didn't get my tail and gills until I was eighteen, but it didn't explain why I was chosen to have magic. Was the moon trying to prove to me I was just a monster?

"My mom said that all siren magic is evil, and can't be used for good," I said in a quiet voice.

Calliopé nodded. "That part she got right. We eat humans, and our magic should only be used to help us with that. If you try to use it for anything else, there could be consequences."

Could be. That didn't mean there would be.

"So mermaid magic is used for good to help them seduce men. Then why are we deemed the bad guys? You said we aren't bad people, but our magic is only meant to help us kill."

She released a sigh, leaning back on her hands. Her hair slipped back behind her shoulders and her breasts saw the moonlight. She'd been right. She didn't have any gills, but *I* did. "Because in the eyes of the sun, mermaids being able to reproduce is a good thing. That's why they are the good guys for reproducing to keep their race alive. We are the ones who eat and kill men, the men mermaids use to reproduce and the men that sirens need to stay alive." She glanced at her stomach. "But I will never get pregnant."

"Why is that?"

"I don't want to," she snapped. "I don't want to destroy my body for a baby. I want to live my life as I please."

Shivers ran up my spine as I leaned forward again. "I'm not judging you."

Kysana grabbed my hand. "We don't have to get pregnant, Mia. Sirens...reproduce in another way."

Calliopé leaned in. "Ah, yes, we do." She whispered, "We're like vampires, child."

Nausea swirled in my stomach at the thought. "What?"

Kysana ran her finger down my hairline, moving my hair behind my ear. "We're the one species that is given the choice to get pregnant or not. Most of us have no interest in having sex with our prey. The moon gave us options. What did we choose, you ask?" A cunning smile formed on her lips. "We chose to bite the hand that fed us. That is how a siren is born."

Thirteen

As hard as I tried to forget those words, I couldn't. It was beginning to fall into place now. Purebred sirens were those given magical gifts, like me. I was born of another siren. However, sirens who were created through the bite of another were not purebred, and therefore they did not get the magic that the moon offered to the rest.

I was a purebred. Kysana and Calliopé were not.

Kysana had said they bit the hand that fed them, but men couldn't be sirens and sirens didn't eat women. That meant there were human women who were feeding human men to the sirens. That's how Calliopé and Kysana got their food.

When we exited the cave, I flexed my fingers, looking up towards the moon. It was worth a try.

"I forbid you from ever eating another live human again," I said with power raging through me.

Calliopé and Kysana both looked at each other and laughed. What had been so funny? "Mia, your power doesn't work on us. We are sirens, too. We are immune to the magic our kind possesses."

Part of me felt sick to my stomach to hear those words, but there was nothing I could do about it. The other part of me was relieved to have more limits. To have this much power was terrifying yet exhilarating. I needed to have limits if I was going to trust myself with such magic.

Calliopé cleared her throat, scooting out of the water. "Let's go for a walk."

"What?" I looked at her as Kysana did the same.

Calliope gestured to the empty beach littered with bottles of beer and alcohol. "I said let's go for a walk. You seem to think your magic saved that boy, but you have no idea what you've done."

"He's safe and alive. I think I did great."

Calliopé's tail turned into legs. "No, he's not. Let's go."

As soon as I dried off and put my stupid costume back on, the three of us walked up the beach. I stopped almost immediately. "Wait. You both need clothes."

"Who says we do?" Kysana asked.

"How old are you, really?" I turned to face her.

She shrugged. "I think I'm eighteen."

"People will stare and ask questions and we need to not draw attention to ourselves. Trust me when I say there are perverts all over this place."

Calliopé scoffed. "We aren't going to magically get clothes."

I saw a few people walking down the street, and a smile slowly formed on my face. "Leave that up to me."

With my palms facing up, I watched the couple. My palms began to glow the same color as the moon. "Walk over to us and give my friends your clothes."

Within seconds, they approached and stripped down, handing Calliopé and Kysana their clothes. Kysana wore the girl's clothes and Calliopé put on the boy's.

"Leave," I said. And they obeyed.

Once out of sight, I dropped my hands to my sides, but exhaustion washed over me. Kysana caught me before I fell to the ground.

Calliopé shook her head. "You've used too much magic tonight. You have to stop."

I knew she was right, but I didn't want to stop. It was the one thing that separated me from them—the ones who ate humans alive.

Despite being a smaller girl, Kysana carried me as the two of them looked for that boy I saved. Sirens had a bit more strength than humans, and that was fair considering they were supposed to eat them for dinner. They had to be stronger than the prey.

Calliopé spotted the boy from afar, showing me what had happened. "Your magic isn't as innocent as you seem to think."

I turned to see the boy who was now sitting on the lawn in front of what we thought was his house. His lips were moving, but he was quiet as he spoke to himself. His eyes darted around the area, and he shook his head quickly before smacking his hand against his head.

What was wrong with him?

Kysana set me down. "You did this. You used your magic on him, and now he's seen too much. His small human mind is having a hard time processing what happened, and he can't even come back to ask whatever questions he has, because you forbid him from doing so. He's going insane."

"No, that's impossible. I saved his life."

"You saved his life, Mia, but you also stole his sanity just to be a hero," Calliopé said.

"So I'll just go over and explain to him so he's back to normal." I nodded.

Calliopé laughed. "You think that's going to help? Face it. You're a siren and your magic is meant to be used for selfish reasons. Using it to save people is only going to backfire on you. Stop trying to defy nature. Stop denying who you really are."

I pulled my knees to my chest. "I'm not a monster. I'm not. I won't be."

Calliopé's entire demeanor switched. "Is that what you think of us? We are not monsters. We did not choose this life. It chose us. We don't deserve to starve just because of our diet." She narrowed her eyes. "Your precious humans seem to believe they're all overpopulated anyway. We're only solving a world issue for them."

"You don't get to murder people because of overpopulation. That isn't how this works!"

"Why, because murder is wrong?" Calliopé squatted down to my level. "It's the circle of life, Mia. You don't get to come and tell us how to live our lives just because you think you're above us. You're not better than us. You're a siren. Admit it. You're just like us."

I gritted my teeth. "I am nothing like you."

Calliopé leaned in closer, glancing at the kid. "Tell me. Is it better that he spends the rest of his life questioning his sanity than being used to keep another species alive?"

Gaining some energy, I stood from the ground. "I refuse to believe the lies. I'm not going to tolerate this any longer. He did nothing to deserve to be your meal."

I turned and started walking in the direction of my house.

Calliopé called out my name, stopping me in my tracks. "Sirens don't deserve to starve because of what the moon chose as our food. You're on the wrong side. Please don't let the mermaids cause you to hate yourself."

After leaving the two of them there, I arrived back at my house, but I didn't step inside yet. Her words kept echoing inside my head. As much as I wanted to say I knew it all and I was morally right, I had to admit that I wasn't.

Calliopé had mentioned it again and again, reminding me that sirens didn't have a choice in what they ate. They didn't have any choice in being a siren. So, why did I continue to let the mermaids feed me with self-hatred? None of this was the sirens' fault. They were only trying to survive like any other living creature.

"Mia!" someone yelled.

I spun around to see Dylan. He no longer wore his soccer costume. "Hi."

He wrapped his arms around me, refusing to give me room to breathe. "We got worried. When that kid went missing, we thought maybe something happened to you, too. Olivia has been out searching for you. I was here, trying to tell your parents what happened so we could call the police." He released a sigh of relief. "But you're okay now. All that matters is you're okay," he whispered.

My entire body relaxed in his arms. Somehow, he made it better. With my best friend by my side, it was easy for me to realize my problems were solvable. No problem in this world couldn't be solved, and I had no reason to bring about wrinkles before I got old.

I reached up, wrapping my arms around his back. "I'm okay, Dylan. I promise that nothing can hurt me." No, because I was the threat to everyone here. I was the one with all the control.

He pulled away a bit, looking at me. "Can I ask what happened?"

With a small smile, I said, "I just went for a longer swim than I had planned. I wasn't in any danger." He knew what I was, but I didn't want to tell him about my friends from the ocean just yet. There was no need to worry him.

Nodding, he planted a kiss on my forehead and rested his chin on top. It filled every part of me with warmth. Dylan made me feel safe and loved. Even if I was a monster in the eyes of the mermaids, he cared too much about me. Every time I went missing, he was left worrying about me.

What scared me was how he might react if I told him the full truth. Would he change? Would I become the monster?

"You two seem close," Olivia said from behind Dylan.

Dylan pulled away from our hug and faced her. "I'm just happy she's home now."

Olivia smiled. "You and me both." She came over and pulled me in for a hug. "We were worried sick."

"Thank you." I returned the hug. After a few loving seconds, we both pulled away.

Dylan gasped. "Mia, what happened?" He closed the distance between us before bending down to look at the deep wound on my leg. My fin had been ripped thanks to Calliopé.

"I suppose I got hurt. I didn't notice." I cleared my throat.

Before my parents could come out and scold me for scaring them again, Dylan and Olivia led me to his house next door. Dylan took me to the bathroom and got out the first aid kit. "You need stitches. We have to get you to a hospital."

I shook my head. "No. We can't." I sat down on the toilet

seat with the lid down. "I mean, I'll do it."

"What? You want to stitch up your own leg? Mia, just go to a doctor and get proper drugs. Then you don't have to feel it."

I grabbed his kit. "I can do it. I can handle it." I grabbed a curved needle. "Why do you have a needle if you want me to use a doctor?" I needed to stitch both my leg and fin. And the doctors couldn't see that.

Olivia stood in the doorway, arms crossed. "He doesn't. I do. I mean, I gave that to him. I did the same thing." She laughed. "I hate going to doctors." She leaned against the frame. "We don't have health insurance so we have no choice but to save money where we can."

I frowned. "But you're young. Wouldn't you still be on the child healthcare plan?"

"I'm nineteen, Mia. I was held back a year, and my health insurance expired."

"Oh." I knew it was a lie because students were eligible, but I didn't want to push her to admit something she didn't want to.

I pulled out some string and looped it through the needle. I placed the tip against the edge of my wound, taking a deep breath.

Dylan gave me a look. "Are you sure you don't want a doctor?"

"I'm positive."

He groaned and grabbed the needle. "Let me do it." He grabbed a stool and rested my foot on it, keeping my wound steady. "You might want to think of other things."

"Wha—" I grabbed the towel bar and gripped it. I closed my eyes and leaned my head back. The pain came again as he poked another hole in my skin, bringing the needle up from the other side of the wound.

When he was finished, he wrapped gauze around the site. "All done."

I leaned back, still holding the towel bar. "I'll sleep here for the night."

Dylan laughed. What was so damn funny? "You are not sleeping on my toilet." He slipped one arm behind my back and the other under my knees. "Come on, let's take you home."

"No, Dylan." I shook my head, opening my eyes to show him how serious I was. "I can't. If my mom finds out I was by the beach and I got hurt, she will kill me. I can't go back."

"She's worried. She thinks you're missing."

"Tell her I'm okay and I'm sleeping here. Tell her that I was actually hiding in your house waiting to scare you as a prank." She'd believe that and I wouldn't get into trouble.

He gave Olivia a look, and she nodded. "On it." She left the house.

Dylan took me to his room and laid me down on his sheets. "Get some rest."

"I plan on it." I laughed a little, closing my eyes. I snuggled amongst his blankets but almost jumped when I felt the weight of the mattress sink. It'd just been Dylan laying down next to me.

"Sweet dreams, Mimi."

"Sleep tight and don't let the bedbugs bite, Dill Pickle."

Fourteen

My thumb hovered over the contact, making the decision to touch the call button. I put the phone to my ear until someone on the other line picked up. "Hello?"

My heart began to race but my emotions were begging me to have control. Nothing sounded better than crying at this moment. Her voice was still just as smooth as it had been when I left her. It brought back so many memories.

"Natalia, it's Mia," I replied before I sounded like an idiot.

"I know, I have your number saved in my phone." She chuckled.

That felt good to hear. Her chuckle warmed up the joy inside of me. I felt better knowing that she saved my number all this time. She never deleted my contact.

"Hey, long time, no chat," I whispered.

She let out a deep breath she had been holding. "I miss you."

"I miss you, too. It's so hard being different. It's hard having to hide who I am."

"Tell me about it. My girlfriend won't even accept me, and

do you know how hard that is? I think I may just dump her."

"You got a girlfriend? We've barely been back home for three months. What do you mean she won't accept you?"

"Oh I'm stunning. You think I can't get a girlfriend upon arriving back home? No, I can get any woman I want." She laughed. "And she is terrible. I try to tell her secrets and now she assumes I'm straight and just using her to make fun of her. Little does she know I'm half-fish." She scoffed.

"She won't let you tell her the truth? She just assumes something else?"

Natalia sighed. "I guess I can't care at this point. She clearly isn't trustworthy. Of course, we haven't done anything serious, but does she really have to be so rude about it? She needs to shut her damn trap and let me speak."

"Amen, Nat, amen. If that girl won't listen, dump her. She isn't worth your time. What is it with people? Do they think this is easy? Being from another species isn't easy. It sucks. We have to hide from everyone and contain who we are. What happens if we don't? Who knows? The government may kidnap us and experiment on us. It's better to be safe than sorry." I rolled my eyes.

"Have you finally got your tail?" She changed the subject.

I laughed, a small smile forming. "I did. It's beautiful, Nat. I need to send you a picture sometime. Unfortunately, Mom won't let me go out to the ocean. She's nuts. She won't let me go swimming in the freaking ocean! It's complete bullcrap." I spun on my stool so that I was now facing the counter. "Which makes no sense because she keeps asking me when I'm going to try meat. Does she want me to embrace my identity, or does she want me to hide it?"

Natalia gasped. "She won't let you swim in the ocean with

your new tail from the identity that you own when she sent you off to a school to embrace and learn about your true heritage? That's messed up."

"Yeah, tell me about it. I think maybe it's because she might assume that I'm going to do something bad. Can you believe her? It's crazy." I threw my arm up, slapping my hand against the countertop.

She laughed. "It is. She doesn't know what she wants."

"Apparently not. It's ridiculous." I shook my head. "Anyway, how has your life been other than that girlfriend being a butthole?"

"It's been fine. Dad is still so caught up in his work that he doesn't notice me. No wonder he sent me away for seven years. It was for himself. I could have sex with her while my dad's in the house and he wouldn't notice. I hate it. And don't even get me started on Jenna. She has been so cold since I returned, and I don't understand why. Sisters suck. Be glad you don't have one."

"Brothers suck just as much. The grass isn't any greener over here." I laughed a bit.

"What is your grass like, then?"

I thought for a moment. "It's okay. I snuck out to the ocean last week and how did that go? Well, the police sent out a missing person's report for my clothes that some guy found on the beach and now I'm grounded. I've made two friends, though."

Natalia laughed. "Good job on getting the police involved. And who are these friends?"

"Olivia and Dylan."

I heard a loud thump on her end of the call, and she yelled, "I'm okay! You mean... Dylan? As in... Dill Pickle?"

"The one and only, in the flesh." I smiled big. I could never keep Dill Pickle to myself. Natalia knew everything about me. She was the perfect best friend, aside from Dill Pickle himself.

"Oh gosh, how cute is he now?"

"Natalia!" I widened my eyes.

"It's a serious question. He can grow a beard and he got taller, and his voice got deeper. Things dropped in the southern region. I want to know what you'd rate him as." I could practically hear the smirk in her voice.

I started to chew on my lip. "Well, he's probably a nine or a ten. No, a nine. He would be a ten if he grew out that beard that doesn't exist."

"Ooh, I am so happy for you."

"Why? He's my best friend. We aren't dating. We don't see each other that way."

Natalia laughed again. "Good luck with that. I bet you'll be dating by Valentine's Day. I mean, sometimes these things happen, and you don't expect them to."

"Of course, but I don't see him that way. He's adorable but in a friendly way. He's my friend and I love that. I can trust him."

"Have you told him your secret?"

"I have."

"What did he say?" she shouted.

"I'm the coolest thing ever, but I have a hard time believing that. It's a work in progress," I defended.

Natalia let out a sigh. "You are so sad. You poor girl. Here you have a great Dill Pickle, and he even loves who you are, but you don't feel the same way."

I shrugged a bit. "It's not easy."

She paused. "Well, yes, but you deserve to be happy and love yourself. You are nothing like the stereotypes. Stereotypes are stereotypes for a reason. They don't apply to everyone, and they are not a mold you have to fit into or a guide you must follow. You have to ignore them and be yourself."

Why did she always have to be right?

I looked at the counter and tapped my fingers. "I love you, Nat. I wish you were here. I need someone who understands me, and you were always the best at that. I want you to come back."

"I will."

Swallowing, I asked, "What?"

"What is here for me? A dad who doesn't notice I exist? A girlfriend who won't listen to me? I want to be where you are because you make me feel like I matter. I want to be around you. I've been trying to save up. I'm sure all the hours my dad has put in got him enough money for me to steal. I can fly down to see you." Why could I hear the smile in her voice? She was taking a risk for me.

"Fly?"

"Yes, fly. In a plane? They're these big machines in the sky that take people from one place to another much faster than a car."

I mumbled, "I know what a plane is." I spoke up, "listen, Nat, I want you here, but I don't want to get you into trouble."

"You won't. This is my decision, and you can't stop me. I'm going to visit you. I will be there. You are amazing and I want to be there."

I chewed my lip. "Really? You're going to come for me?"

"Always. I would never miss a chance to see the only real sister I have."

I smiled, holding back the warm tears. "I can't wait. I want you to meet everyone and I want them to meet you."

"Now what's your address again?" She seemed distracted.

I texted her the address so I wouldn't have to repeat it. "Now don't let me down. I will be heartbroken if I don't see you soon."

"Break your heart?" She gasped. "Never."

"I'll see you down here. Anything else you want to tell me about?" I yawned.

She paused for a moment. "I mean, nothing that I can think of. I really can't think of anything important. Who's Olivia, though?"

"She's Dylan's friend. She replaced me when I left." I didn't mean for it to come out the way it did. "But she's sweet."

"She's sweet but she replaced you? I don't like her."

"Neither did I, at first, but she is really nice. She even bought me a bra."

"She bought you a bra? What kind of sicko does that?"

I couldn't help but laugh at her remark. "She does. I liked it and she got it for me. I've been earning my paycheck so I can pay her back. I've already got the money from my job, and even enough for me and Dylan to buy our apartment now. I'm so proud."

"How much was the bra?"

"It was, I think, thirty or twenty dollars? Something like that. I know it was worth it. The bra is so adorable."

Natalia scoffed. "Nothing is worth that much."

"Oh, stop. Quality bras are important for us women. Our boobs need the comfort and support, and these bras are worth the money. Cheap bras will not last me long. These bras will."

"Must be nice."

"What do you mean?"

"To have boobs you need to spend money on. I still wear sports bras."

"When I get elbowed, it's not fun. My boobs bounce when I run. They're not that great," I pointed out.

She cleared her throat. "Don't lie to make me feel better."

"I'm not. I swear." I put my hand up in defense before I realized she couldn't see me. "They hurt when I'm on my period. Besides, you can get more women than I can get men and I have bigger boobs. Boobs are not everything."

She was silent for a moment. "I guess that's true. I can get any woman I want. It's all in the ass."

"Right." I gave a small chuckle.

"Listen, I gotta go. But wait for me. I love you."

I smiled to myself. "I love you, too, Nat. I'll be waiting." I ended the call and took a deep breath. I needed that. Talking to the one person who made me feel normal, made me feel okay. I believed I would be okay in the end because I had her by my side to support me.

As I looked around the empty house, I went to the fridge. I couldn't wait until dinner. I tried to find something—anything really. I eyed the meat, and my mouth began to salivate at the thought of eating that. I closed the fridge and faced the counter. Toast. I would eat toast.

Mom was right. I really did live on toast.

I made myself some toast and scarfed it down to forget about the meat in the fridge. Once my toast was gone, I headed up to my room.

While staring out the window, I saw Dylan passed out in his bed. I smiled, watching him sleep so soundly. I couldn't wait to move in with him, but I didn't know when that would be or when an apartment would come up for us. We'd been searching endlessly. I needed to know for sure if it was safe enough to live with my best friend and not drag him down the rabbit hole with me.

~

"THAT'S THE LAST OF it," I told Dylan as I closed the front door. I shot him my biggest smile just as he came over and hugged me tight, spinning me around.

"We're officially roommates!" He kissed the side of my head. "I wouldn't move in with anyone else, Mia Dawson." He put me down.

I giggled, lightly hitting him. "Better not. I told you my secret and all. You're all mine now. I think it was a fair trade, eh? A secret for a roommate." Winking, I went to the kitchen for some snacks. "We do need to go grocery shopping though. Between school and work, we have hardly any time for anything."

"That's why we live on four hours of sleep," he said.

When I glanced back at him, his chocolate eyes scanned our new place, warming my soul. It felt amazing to know he knew things and now we could share an apartment. Life's puzzle pieces were finally falling into place.

Fifteen

Tears ran down my face, staining it along the way. They were hot yet wet, irritating my skin at once. My feet kicked the sand as I ran through it, peeling off pieces of clothing from my body as I went. I finally ran into the salty water, feeling the transformation begin. I fell in, swimming underneath, the ease of the ocean taking me in as if it were my mother. It comforted every aching bone in my body and soothed my broken heart.

This was the only place I could feel safe from the human world. They could never accept me. I was different and that meant I was not right. Nobody liked *different*.

I let the worries wash away in the water, being carried from my body. I felt free, and that was all that I could focus on. I turned over, facing my back towards the surface. I moved my fin up and down in a worm-like motion, swimming further below. This was where I belonged. The sea was the only home that I could truly be myself in.

After the much-needed escape to the ocean, I left before anyone could discover my secret.

My feet hit the grass that was dying in our front yard.

"Don't look so glum," a female's voice said.

My head shot up at the sound of her voice, my eyes as wide as they could get. "Natalia..."

She smiled and ran, hugging me as tight as she could squeeze. "I missed you!"

I didn't dare stray from her embrace because it was the only thing keeping me together right now. She was my rock.

She let go and I took her to my room before saying anything. I sat down and looked at her. "I can't believe you're here so quickly."

"It's only been a few days since I said I was coming, and I don't break my promises." She sat next to me and hugged me. "I missed you so much, Mia."

"I missed you, too, Nat." I laid my head on her shoulder, letting her comfort the loneliness inside me. I had someone here to understand me. That was all I wanted.

"Your eyes are puffy and red. Who hurt you?" Her tone became serious, and she pulled away from our hug.

I rubbed my eyes and shrugged. "It's a long story. These past few days have been crazy and I'm just having a hard time adjusting into a life where I have to hide what he did from half of the people I love."

"I'm here to listen." She sat back against the wall.

Nodding, I played with my fingers. "Yesterday, some idiot tried to mix some chemicals and it went wrong and caused a lot of smoke which set off the fire alarms. It set off the sprinklers on the ceiling."

"Oh no..."

"I ran so fast out of that building. People asked why I was running, and I had to make up a lie. Now everyone thinks I was in a serious fire back at the academy and I just get so sick of the constant lies." I sighed.

Natalia grabbed my hand. "It's hard, I know. I want to help you so much. I want to be everything for you, but I just don't know how."

"I don't know what to do anymore." I sniffled, wiping my runny nose and wet cheeks. "I just never realized how much water was involved in my life before this and now it's becoming too difficult to even pretend. I feel trapped. So much is going on and it continues to spiral downward. How do I continue to live this lie?"

"It's scary, telling people your secrets. This is part of your life, and you just want to make sure only the right people know or it could be the end of you." She began rubbing my back.

I looked at her. "How is Dylan going to react when he finds out I've been lying about what Jason did? He's my best friend and I'm supposed to trust him. He's always showing me that I can trust him and here I am, not doing that. He has never given me a single reason to doubt him and yet I do, and it makes me feel like the worst friend ever."

She nodded and looked at my white walls. "I wish I had the answers. You are one of the best girls I know, and you deserve to be yourself. I want you to be happy."

I wanted the same thing, but I didn't know how to achieve that without screwing everything up. I was a mess—an accident waiting to happen. I could end up exposing the entire species to the world with the wrong decision.

"Let's just forget about this whole mess and enjoy each other's company," I said. "Ironic that I'm spending Thanksgiving without my family but here we are."

The two of us laid back on my bed and continued to talk about other things. It was comforting to be able to completely be myself. I wanted to talk about my tail and the feeling of swimming in the ocean. I talked about these things, and Natalia listened to every word.

Before night fell, a knock was heard from the other side of my door. "Come in."

My brother came in and looked at Natalia. What was he doing here? "Who's this?"

Natalia sat up and cleared her throat. "Natalia. I'm Mia's best friend from the academy. You're Dill Pickle?"

Christian choked on his spit and looked at her. "Dill Pickle? Did you name me Dill Pickle?" He looked at me.

I laughed and shook my head. "No, I named Dylan Dill Pickle. What else would I name him?" I sat up and leaned against Natalia. "This is my brother, Christian."

"Ah, so wrong guy. He knows about us, right?"

Christian widened his eyes. "Us? You mean you're dating?"

Natalia burst out laughing, tears beginning to form. I chuckled and looked at him. "Christian, this is my best friend. She was referring to us being from the sea, not being together romantically."

He scratched his head, averting his gaze. "Oh."

Natalia calmed down and wiped her tears. "That was good. We need to do that more often."

I nodded, looking between them. "Yeah, he knows. He was there for my first ever swim in the ocean."

Neither of them said a word and I knew why. I changed the subject, "So I guess you two have finally met. Any reason why you're here?"

"Yeah, I came to tell you Mom was going to have a family

dinner tonight, if you wanted to come. It is Thanksgiving after all."

"Did Mom make enough for Natalia?"

"When does she not make enough even for just the four of us? She cooks for an entire feast." He shrugged and left.

I stood, leading Nat over to my house. The walk wasn't too far since Dylan and I had gotten an apartment close to our homes and the school.

I introduced her to everyone, and we sat down, eating the food. Natalia was practically moaning at every bite. "Mrs. Dawson, this is amazing."

Mom smiled at her. "Thank you, Natalia. Mia told us little about you and I want to know more. You two went to the academy together?"

Natalia gave me a look and I shrugged. "I barely told anyone about you. I don't like talking about my life from the academy very much."

She shook her head and smiled at my mom. "We did. We were roommates, actually. We became best friends. She was judged for wanting to be one of the mermaids and I was judged for being...as blunt as I am." She nodded and took another bite of the food.

"You're blunt? About what?"

Natalia shrugged. "I was always telling those girls off. They're so rude to Mia. I was her little bodyguard. She may be taller, but I can sure as hell pack a punch." She wore a proud smile.

Dad looked at me and lifted an eyebrow with a small smile on his face.

"It's true. Nat was always there to defend me. She taught me a lot and I'm grateful. She accepts me as one of the mermaids even if they don't. I'm okay with that. She's a sea nymph." I gestured to Natalia.

Mom looked at her. "Oh, I remember those. So, you attract a lot of humans?"

"I do. I can get any woman I want. I tell Mia this all the time. Although, I've been struggling to find a good one who will listen to me when I want to tell her something serious." She rolled her eyes.

Mom laughed a bit and chewed her food. "What is your kind like again? I mean, sea nymphs?"

"Well, you're correct that I can attract any human. But overall, we are still people and we control ourselves. I know that they teach sea nymphs are very sexual creatures but it's not always true. There are different kinds of nymphs if that helps. There are five. Sea nymphs kind of join two worlds and they can go wherever. We can go between sea creatures and nymphs." She took a few more bites.

Dad was focused on his food and Christian was barely listening. Mom and I were the ones most intrigued by what she had to say.

"The sea creatures are quite interesting because there are so many. You have mermaids, and selkies, and water sprites, sea nymphs, sirens, and even more. They're similar but different. It's kind of like being from America but not being from the same state. With nymphs, you have five different kinds of nymphs. Sea nymphs, celestial nymphs, underworld nymphs, land nymphs, and wood nymphs. We are creatures who attract other humans, but we come from parts of nature.

"Underworld nymphs are from the underworld, which is why it's in the name. Celestial nymphs come from the heavens and all that light stuff. Woods are more with the trees while land nymphs hang out in meadows and grass. There's me, the sea nymph. I grow a tail and swim in different bodies of water. We are also known as water nymphs," she finished.

Mom asked, "What color is your tail?"

She smiled. "Purple. It's a deep purple with some highlights of lavender that shimmer in the sun. It's the perfect shade for me." She wasn't lying about that. The purple was stunning against her dark skin.

I realized I had never seen Natalia in her sea nymph form. I had never seen her tail at all. I was going to plan for us to go to the ocean and swim together. We were best friends, and swimming together in our natural habitat only made sense.

Natalia and Mom went back to eating, talking here and there. Mom was able to get along with my friend and that's what I appreciated tonight. I wanted Natalia to be accepted into the family as one of us. She was my best friend, so she was my other half.

"All right, well, Natalia and I are going to go home. She'll be staying with me while she's here for the time being." I looked at my mom. "That's what Thanksgiving is about, you know, being thankful for those you love."

She hesitated. "Okay, but just make sure Dylan is fine with it. It's his apartment just as much as it is yours." It was a fair thing to say. I'd never want to exclude Dylan, and I tried not to as much as I could. I just hoped that he and Nat got along, or I'd be torn between worlds for eternity.

Sixteen

"MIA!" DYLAN YELLED FROM the bathroom. "Have you seen my pants?"

"Pants?" I furrowed my brows and looked up just as he walked out of the bathroom in just his briefs. Oh hot damn. "Um, no, I have not..."

He searched through some boxes. "The rest are washing, and I can't find the good pair. My favorite pair." He leaned over the boxes.

Where was the fun of living with your best friend if you couldn't catch a glimpse of his ass every now and then? "What's wrong with what you have on?"

He mocked my joke. "Ha, ha, very funny. Please, help me find them."

I agreed and jumped from the couch, searching through some of his clothes with him. Every now and then I snuck a glance at his firm ass. "Is this them?" I held up a pair.

"Yes!" He grabbed them and put them on, zipping up. "Thank you."

I nodded as I watched him walk back to his room to find a

shirt. I'd never really looked at Dylan that way but what would it hurt to acknowledge that he had a nice body? He'd certainly grown into it well, too.

~

DYLAN SWUNG HIS FEET back and forth, overlooking the ocean with me. The cliff was small, so it was not anything too scary. "I see your friend is visiting."

"She is. Natalia still wants to meet you, but we hardly see you at the moment." The ocean mist blew towards us, but it wasn't nearly enough to make me change my form.

"You told her about me?"

I chuckled and looked at him. "Excuse me, but why would I keep you to myself? I told her all about you and our friendship, Dill Pickle."

"Oh damn, you told her about...that." He gave me a look and I smiled in return.

I looked back at the water and admired the amount of blue it displayed from the reflection of the sky. The surface glistened in the sunlight and hugged the rocks at the bottom of the cliff.

"As long as you don't dwell on misadventures, life might actually be worth living." I kept my gaze fixed on waves.

Dylan looked at me. "What now?"

I shrugged. "Oh, you know, life is a happy place to be if things go your way. Some people have smooth sailing, and others not so much. When I was at the academy, the only thought that I always had was about living. Why was I living my life when every day was miserable?"

Dylan frowned and wrapped his fingers around mine.

"What do you mean?"

Glancing down at our hands, I said, "There are things I can't say out loud, and they hold me back."

"You can trust me. I will always be here, and I won't judge you for any reason. I accepted that you're a siren, right?"

I smiled a bit, realizing my smile held more sorrow than contentment. "I wish I could tell you. It is a lot more complicated than that. There are things in my life that are too personal." It was getting risky with me telling him I had secrets in the first place. My mind did not seem to care.

Dylan squeezed my hand and turned to look out at the water. "You can always trust me, Mia."

"I'm aware."

He groaned and stood up, letting go of my hand and leaving it empty and cold.

I followed him, but he turned towards me, running at me. I widened my eyes and tried to move out of my way but there wasn't a lot of time to react. He tried to stop himself from running into me, but he wasn't quick enough, and he sent us over the cliff. I plunged into the water. He fell in after me and I swam away once my legs took their natural form as a fish tail.

As I came upon the shore, I pulled myself onto an empty beach by some rocks, trying to dry myself off. I kept my eye out for Dylan, but I couldn't find him. Once my tail dried and turned back into legs, I stood and looked all over the beach until the sound of someone clearing their throat echoed behind me.

I spun around and my face flushed as I tried to pull down my shirt. My transformation caused my bottoms to split apart and get lost in the ocean. "I..." I didn't know what to say.

Dylan took off his shirt and gave it to me, respecting me

enough to not look down in that direction, as tempting as it may have been.

I wrapped his large shirt around my bottom. "My shorts ripped on a rock." What a beautiful lie I told. It wouldn't have had to be a lie if he didn't push me off the cliff, but he did. "And what the hell is wrong with you?" I hit him, intentionally causing him pain.

"Ow, what did I do?" He rubbed his arm.

I shook my head, eyes still glaring at him. "You pushed me off a cliff. There were rocks at the bottom of that cliff. It's not even a tall cliff! The possibility of me missing the rocks at that height is very slim with that trajectory." Frustration was an understatement. How could he do something so horrid?

"I'm not sorry. I had to do it. I saw someone."

"Saw who?"

"Todd."

The wind whipped through my hair. "Todd? As in the bully who would make fun of me for being a girl who ate dirt as a child?" I gave him a look. In my defense, dirt tasted good. Didn't every child eat dirt at some point?

"As in the bully who started the rumors after you got your period at camp. I was worried he would have done something, and I didn't want him to see you. There's..." Dylan rubbed his face with one hand and sighed. "Years back, after you left, he made a rumor. *Another* rumor. He made an awful rumor about you, and I tried to make that rumor go away but it didn't. He told everyone that you asked to see his penis and you forced yourself on him."

I almost inhaled the salty mist that blew our way. "Excuse me? We were just kids! Who the hell would believe that?" I threw my arms up. "And it still doesn't justify pushing me into the ocean!" Too many thoughts ran through my head at once. I couldn't catch them all and sort through them properly.

"I didn't want him to see you, Mia." Dylan came closer to me and gave me a pitiful look. "Without you here for seven years to control the rumor, he got away with it."

"That bastard. He is going to pay." Now that Natalia was back, she was my perfect revenge partner.

Dylan scratched his neck and looked away. "We should get home."

I grumbled in response, and we walked back to our apartment.

Dylan lent me a pair of his gym shorts and I put them on, feeling very cold without underwear. I laid down on his bed. "So this bastard decided to spread a nasty rumor and destroy my reputation and for what? To gain the upper hand? He is still a bully if he hasn't told anyone the truth."

Dylan nodded and sat next to me. "He hasn't. Not from what I know."

"Everyone assumes I'm a...pervert...or something? Is this my life? I have enough to deal with and now I find out there's an old rumor that everyone believes, and nobody told me." I sat up and looked at Dylan.

"Well, almost everyone. Olivia and I don't believe the rumor."

"Oh, so the people who know me don't believe it. That helps so much," I said, rolling my eyes.

Dylan sighed. "I know. I failed as your best friend. I couldn't stop a lie."

It wasn't so much his fault as it was Todd's. "I just can't believe this would happen. He made up shit about me. He made up lies and now I'm a criminal. I have never assaulted anyone or attempted to do so. I was eleven. My little girl brain was not thinking about Todd's dick and how pathetic it probably is."

Dylan chuckled. "It has to be if he needs to feel better based on a story of you wanting to see it."

I stood up from his bed. "We need Natalia for this job."

"For what job?" He looked up at me.

"She is the *master* of revenge. She helped me get revenge plenty of times at the academy."

We called up Nat to come home, and as soon as she heard the story, she was all in for revenge. Well, I called it a prank, but she said it was more serious than that.

"Any ideas?" I asked her.

"Does Todd have a car?" Nat asked Dylan.

He nodded.

She gave me a look, a small smirk curving her lips. "I have a few, but this one seems fun. I'm going to need black ink."

"Ink?" I tilted my head. "And what do you plan to do with this black ink?"

"That's a surprise." She dragged me and Dylan to the store to get black ink, then we drove to Todd's.

Dylan pointed out his car but pulled me back. "Are you sure this is a good idea? Damaging his car is vandalism. It's illegal. I don't want you to get arrested, and you are old enough to go to jail now."

"Ink? Is ink really vandalism though? He can wash it off."

"Depends on where she puts the ink."

"Dylan, I appreciate the love. I really do. But Todd literally turned me into this criminal when I couldn't defend myself. Sometimes you have to play the part they give you to dish it back." I patted his chest and walked over to Nat. "What's the plan?"

She nodded her head towards the street. "Keep an eye out for anyone who's looking through their windows, anyone who's driving by or walking. But mostly keep an eye out for Todd. And act natural. Don't make us look like we aren't supposed to be here."

"Aye, aye, captain." I saluted and twisted my body as I shoved my feet together, looking at the street.

Nat opened the hood and poured the ink into one of the little containers. She lowered the hood and the front door opened. The three of us scrambled down the street, out of view.

The moment we arrived back at my house, I asked what was next.

"Now, we wait," she said.

I WALKED IN THE door from school, swallowing. "How was school?" Nat asked.

"Fine," I muttered before heading to my room. I threw my bag down, but Nat slipped in the door behind me. She knew I was lying. "Have you seen the news?"

Nat shook her head. "No, why? Is it about the boy? The case you wanted to solve?" Right, that. I forgot I had told her to help me. She was the only one I trusted.

"No, Natalia. It's worse," I croaked. I sat down and pulled out my phone, showing her the articles. "Todd wasn't at school today, and I wondered why. I thought maybe his car broke down." She grabbed my phone and skimmed the headlines. "Todd is dead, Nat. We killed him."

"That's impossible. It was only in the wiper fluid. I didn't replace his engine oil or transmission fluid or power steering or any of that." She handed me my phone.

My stomach dropped. "Do you hear yourself? Black ink in his windshield fluid container. When he's going to spray his windshield to clean it, all he sees is black." I stifled a sob with the back of my hand. "I never should have said yes. I never should have done this. What happens next? The police are going to know someone tampered with his car. They're going to start doing investigations. I'm going to go to prison for murder."

"Accomplice to murder," she corrected.

"Nat!"

She put her hands up. "Nobody will even know! Todd probably had plenty of enemies. We just need to lay low. Besides, how would they trace it back to us? What he did to you was so long ago and you weren't even here for it. They're not going to know that you're his enemy now."

"What does Dylan think of me?" The sobs broke out. "I brought my best friend into this mess. We killed someone. I've never killed someone before."

Nat pulled me into her arm, stroking my hair. "Hey, Mia. Listen to me. They will never know it was us. And if they find out, they won't know it was you."

"What?" I lifted my head. "Why me?"

"I'll take the blame. You and Dylan weren't even there."

I yanked myself from her arms. "Nat, you can't do that."

"Why not? I'm not quite of legal age yet."

I swallowed, wiping away my tears. "So that's your excuse? You're saving my ass because I could be tried as an adult?

What's worse, Nat? The fact that I could be put away for murder at eighteen or that you could be tried as a black woman? Your age means nothing to the system. I'm white. At least I have a fighting chance."

Natalia sat back. "And what about Dylan? Love the guy but we both know he won't keep quiet. And even if we try to exclude him, he'll confess to save your ass."

"No, he won't. Because you and I will both agree here and now that Dylan was never there. Our word against his. And if we can get Olivia in on this, maybe she can keep him safe for me." I stood from the bed and approached the window. "Yes, it is risky telling her, but we need backup plans. And this is that backup. It's simple. If the police catch me, I'll confess. I won't mention anyone else. I'll come clean about Jason at the academy to solidify my story, and then if Dylan tries to confess, I will tell Olivia to lie for his sake. By then she'll know what I did. There's no reason to lie to her."

Nat stayed quiet, but I didn't tell her that I was terrified. If I went to prison, I would be forced to shower in front of other women. I'd be caught, and unfortunately for me, I couldn't use my voice to put women in a trance. I'd be surrendered to the government at best but taken into hiding and experimented on at worst.

To save everyone I loved, I had to make sure we were never caught for Todd's little accident.

Seventeen

"I WANTED TO SHOW you the treehouse," Dylan told Olivia.

I couldn't hang out today and it was backfiring on me. How wonderful.

I began chewing my lips, trying not to imagine him showing her our secret hideout. "I'll see you guys later." I waved to them and walked home. I went up to my room and threw my bag down. He was taking her to our treehouse!

He could have another friend, but he was trying to do everything with her that he and I did together. Instead of creating new memories or hideouts, he was doing everything we did together but with *her*. And I knew it wasn't romantically. Which is not what bothered me, even, but what did was that his friendship with her was a copy of ours. Our friendship wasn't unique between him and I.

Natalia came in and put her bag down. "What's wrong?"

"I'm jealous. I'm jealous of Olivia." My brother had been right all along.

"Why? What happened?"

I looked up at her and sighed. "He's taking her to our

treehouse. What if...what if he gets tired of what I am and cuts me off to hang out with only her? She doesn't have a dangerous power. What if..."

Natalia grabbed my hands and squeezed them, nodding. "You like him. You like Dylan."

"I don't like him. He's just my best friend."

"Mia, it's nothing to be ashamed of. He's your best friend and these things happen a lot. You know him like the back of your hand. You trust him with your life. You can't say that you don't want to be with Dill Pickle. He may be a goofball and you may have seen every part of him, but he is still your Dill Pickle. You have the biggest history with him." She sat next to me.

My eyes moved to the floor, watching the carpet do nothing. "I don't like him, Nat. I don't see how that is possible."

"I just told you! Were you not listening?" She hit me in the arm in a playful way and rolled her eyes.

"That's not what I meant. I have never wanted to be romantic with him."

She scoffed. "You get upset that they spend time together. You're jealous of what they have. Why is that? This is because you are trying to compensate for the fact that you want to be with him instead. It's your brain's way of trying to hide and get rid of your feelings. Romantic feelings make much more sense than platonic feelings."

I shook my head. "I'm jealous of her in a friendly way. I don't want her to replace me as Dylan's only best friend. Besides, if you're implying that Olivia and Dylan could be secretly dating, drop that idea now. Olivia is gay."

She shifted her posture a bit. "Oh. Well, yeah, that

might...change things up. But I still think you like him. I can see the way you look at him, Mia. It's not the same way you look at other boys."

I looked at her and sighed. I didn't know how to argue with her. However, I only looked at Dylan differently because he was my best friend. The other boys weren't.

"It's okay to admit this. It's not going to be the end of the world. It's not wrong to like your best friend. People do it all the time."

I shrugged a bit. "He doesn't feel the same way and we will always be friends. If you say I like him, I will be the girl who got rejected by her best friend and I do not find unrequited love to be a fun hobby of mine. It's just sad for everyone involved."

"How do you know he doesn't like you?"

"Because I don't like him."

"Has he told you this?"

"No...but I know him. We are just two best friends trying to rekindle our old friendship. There isn't room for romance."

"You keep saying you're jealous of the friendship, but you really want to spend more time with him for a deep reason. You're trying to find reasons to not admit your feelings. Now, tell me, what is it that you want?"

I chewed my lip, ripping the skin off. "I don't know."

Natalia made a negative buzzer sound with her mouth. "Wrong! You want to be with Dylan. Say it."

"No."

Natalia gave me a look and pinched my arm. "Say it."

I rubbed the spot and frowned. "Why is this so important to you?"

"Because my best friend likes her best friend and I want to

see real romance blossom once in my life before I die. If you don't admit the truth, how do you think you'll ever be happy in this world? You'll live your whole life denying everything about you, Mia."

She had a good point. I spent so much time denying who I really was. I was ashamed of myself, yet I could never accept that part of me. But I knew I didn't like Dylan, and it was time for *her* to accept that.

"I don't like Dylan, Nat, and that's that." I put my foot down, literally.

She mumbled something but didn't say anything else.

"He's going to take Olivia to our treehouse, but I want that to be our thing." I couldn't picture it. I refused to see it for myself.

Natalia rubbed my arm and shook her head. "I do get your point, but at the same time, you need to let it be. Dylan has other people in his life. He has to have time for everyone, okay?"

Dylan and I knew so much about each other. He knew things about me that I forget he knew. I'd never risk that all for a romance over a friendship, even if I did happen to like him.

"Let him hang out with Olivia, and don't be jealous about it. They had all these years alone while you went to school with me. They don't need you to come in and ruin that friendship, okay?"

Natalia had a point. She *always* had a point. "Okay..." I let out a sigh.

However, my mind lingered on her words. He was nice and I could trust him. He knew nearly everything about me.

Sure, he was cute. He had the cutest dimples when he

smiled. His hair was so messy and yet it managed to look so good. Every day, he smelled nice, and I knew that when he grabbed my hand, even in a friendly manner, I liked it. He was warm. He'd always been concerned for me. He cared about my wellbeing and that meant a lot. He even knew when to stop and not go too far. He almost pushed me out of the treehouse but when he saw my fear, he stopped. He felt awful for scaring me like that. The remorse was real, and I loved that. He didn't hurt me even when he knew the truth. He had control and he made me laugh all the time. As a bonus, his brown eyes resembled chocolate.

But I didn't like Dylan more than my best friend.

A revving engine drowned out the sound of the waves crashing at the base of the cliff. One minute the vision was clear, and the next second it was black. I lost control of the wheel and crashed into the side rails, plunging into the abyss below.

Water filled the car, but I couldn't get out no matter what I did. My seat belt got stuck. My window wouldn't break. My door wouldn't open. And I didn't transform.

I was drowning in my screams, and nobody knew where I was.

I shot up, screaming and crying. Dylan rushed into the room and sat on the bed, pulling me into his embrace. "Mia, what happened?"

Clinging to him, I continued to sob. "Todd. I was reliving his last moments." And I deserved to.

"I'm here, Darling," he whispered against my hair.

I sniffled, pulling away to look up at him. "What? Darling?"

He chuckled. "Thought I'd test it out. Sorry."

"Why?"

He shrugged. "I wanted to distract you. Make you laugh. Make you forget that bad dream."

"We need to talk about Todd, and what happened. I didn't know what Nat did would kill him. I've never killed anyone before him." I intended to keep it that way, too.

Dylan grabbed my chin, holding it in place. "You're right. We should probably talk about it. I know you and Nat had this conversation, but I need to get it out of my system."

His touch was so warm, gentle. Forgiving.

"What happened was scary. Todd did something horrendous, but knowing our prank killed him is eating me alive. I don't know what I'm supposed to do, Mia. I know I can't just turn you guys into the police, or turn just myself in. But between you and I, getting decent sleep is a bitch right now," he said.

"I'm sorry I dragged you into this."

He rubbed his thumb across my cheek. "No. I'm sorry I dragged *you* into this. I told you about what he did in the first place. If I had just let you confront him, things would have worked out normally. Maybe you could have slapped some sense into him, but I caused this. I'm the one feeling the effects."

"It might be easy for Nat to get over this, but it isn't for me. It should be. I'm already a monster. But I'm not. I'm—"

"Mia, stop." He shook his head, hints of anger entering his irises. "You are not a monster. Don't even say those words. What happened to Todd was unfortunate on every level, but you're not a monster. Nobody knew this would lead to death. People die."

I released a sigh, laying my head against his chest, near his shoulder. "And yet you're also blaming yourself. If people die, why do we feel so much guilt? Todd was a disgusting guy, but I never wanted to kill him. This is my life, Dylan. If you want to be in it, you need to know that death is a common occurrence. I'm not proud of it, but I can't escape it, either. If you can't handle that, tell me now. I don't want to drag you down with me."

"I can handle it."

"Because I can't go to prison. If they put me in prison, they'll discover what I am. I'll endanger my entire race. If you're with me, you have to keep this secret forever."

"I will, Mia." He kissed my hair. "I will keep it. We're best friends until the end." Why did hearing him say that make me feel sorrow? "You and I." Dylan rested his head against mine, rubbing his thumb across my cheek some more. "And I'll stay here until you ask me to leave."

I'd never ask him to leave. He knew that. Maybe that's why he made the offer, to prove he would if I wanted him to, but he knew he would never have to. He made himself look like the hero while getting exactly what he wanted and giving me what I needed.

He switched from his thumb to his knuckle, brushing it up and down my neck. It gave me chills in places I never knew got them. Ultimately, it comforted me. He made me feel secure in his arms and like I could take on the world. Even after that nightmare, I didn't feel so scared anymore. My tears dried up and my shame slipped beneath the waves.

His knuckle caressed under my chin and my skin tangled from his touch. My nerves went to sleep, and I knew that was his intention. Dylan was attempting to put me back to sleep, ensuring I didn't have any more nightmares. The only nightmare I'd have tonight was the thought of waking up to find Dylan missing from my life for good.

Eighteen

My head rested on Dylan's shoulder as we watched one of the many animated movies about talking animals. If only they could really talk to us. "I can't believe this is a kid's movie! They're making sexual jokes," I said, pointing to the screen. The only TV in the house was the one in the living room.

Dylan chuckled and shook his head. "Kids don't usually notice them."

"It's no wonder everyone wants sex so much," I joked. I pulled the blanket over my body and smiled to myself. His warmth transferred to me, and I loved it.

"Hormones are a crazy concept." Dylan patted my leg.

"That they are." The last time sex was brought up, I dismissed the topic right away. I think now I was starting to adjust to it and it wasn't becoming awkward for me. Aside from that, I enjoyed cuddling up to his side. He didn't realize it, but it was one of the many perks of having a guy best friend.

We both continued to laugh at the movie and talk about some parts that were iffy. It wasn't anything spectacular, but we still shared it together. I wouldn't want to spend

Christmas any other way.

Mom and Dad were at home spending it their way, alone, and secretly thanking me for giving them space. To Dylan, this was innocent. Two friends were watching a movie. After the other night, it was a whole new world. He'd promised to be by my side until the end. Not just anyone did that for me. I wanted to be around him even more. He was warm, and he smelled of cologne.

Dylan shifted and I frowned, sitting up. "Where are you going?"

"I have to pee. Is that okay?" He gave me a look.

My cheeks turned red and I nodded, looking away from him. "Of course it's okay. Just remember to come back."

"Are you afraid I'm going to climb out the window?" He laughed and it made me smile. His laugh was medicine.

"I never know. You surprise me every day." I shrugged.

He shook his head and went to the bathroom.

I wrapped the blanket around my shoulders, now feeling the cold seep into my body. Being half fish, or part fish—however the math on that worked—I was cold-blooded. Without a warm human by my side, I held no warmth of my own. Some days it was no big deal. Others, I experienced how much I missed heat.

Dylan came back and sat back down. He grabbed a pillow and put it on his shoulder. "I'm sure my shoulder is uncomfortable."

I furrowed my brows, but I was more taken back by the statement. Maybe he was being generous, or he was trying to distance himself from skin-to-skin contact. I hoped it was the first option. "It's okay. Your shoulder isn't uncomfortable." I just laid my head on his shoulder after removing the pillow.

He didn't object.

We stayed like this even after the movie ended. "You weren't into soccer before I left. I want to know what got you into it."

"That boring stuff?" he joked.

"Yes, all of it." I glanced up at him, not daring to move my head from his shoulder.

He chuckled. "All right, I warned you."

I smiled, waiting for him to go on.

"I had just entered high school and being a freshman was hard enough. I wanted to find something I was interested in to keep me occupied. Olivia suggested soccer. I had always wanted to try out for it. I had stunk at first, but I found my way. I tried out for soccer and the coach said I had potential. It was a lot of work to get where I am, but I did it. It was worth it. Something about being on a team makes me feel a part of something better. These people are my friends and family. We support each other."

The way he lit up when he talked about soccer made me giddy. I had never expected him to find a sport, but I was glad he did. I loved that he loved it.

"Oh man, when I'm out on the field, that's something else. Practice can be tough because you practice a lot, and it gets annoying sometimes because I just want to go against a real team. I want to kick their asses. The look on their faces when we keep scoring goals. I never make it look like I will make it, but I do. I fool those losers, and me and my team celebrate our win. We always go out to eat somewhere new each time." He looked at me. "Am I boring you?"

"No, not at all." I shook my head.

"I have gotten into a few accidents and the sport comes with risks but they're worth it. I love being on the field and having the ball in front of my feet. It's a rush when you're kicking it and aiming for their goal. Once it makes it in, the feeling that comes is of accomplishment. You feel like you're worth something, and I feel so free in soccer. I feel useful and at home.

"You should've seen the guy I messed up. I was aiming for the goal and he blocked my shot, and it went up into his eye! The guy was practically blind for the rest of the day. I feel bad, but it comes with the sport. You kind of risk all your senses and body parts. It's just a matter of being able to handle it and walk it off," he finished.

Goosebumps covered every inch of my skin as I nodded a bit, still smiling. "That's great. I'll go to your games. I promise. I know you have Olivia, but I want to be there to cheer you on, too."

"I want you to be there. I want you to cheer me on. You matter to me, and I want to see you in the crowd." He nudged me with his elbow.

"I will be there. I promise." I wouldn't break it for the world. Soccer was a part of his life and I wanted to be by his side when he needed me there. That was part of being a good friend.

"You look tired." He observed me.

I shrugged and yawned. "I may or may not be getting sleepy."

"I'll let you sleep then. I should go to my room anyway." He moved but I frowned. He stopped when he noticed it. "You don't want me to go?"

"I don't want you to move... I'm too comfortable," I mumbled.

"Okay, okay." He chuckled and pulled the blanket over us

both. "I won't go. But it'll be cramped here."

"Shh..." I closed my eyes, beginning to drift off. I was pulled into the darkness before I had a say in anything.

I WAS WOKEN UP by a noise but the apartment was completely dark. I sat up, feeling around. I widened my eyes and pulled my hand back when I grabbed a questionable body part. I'd forgotten Dylan was here.

I got up and went to the kitchen, getting myself a drink. I looked around, the only light coming in from the back door where the moonlight came through. I walked over and stared out the window. I wondered if I was any step closer to telling Dylan about Jason and my magic. I couldn't predict the future and I didn't know how he would take it. I didn't know if I would ever tell him. It was a scary thought.

"Mia, what are you doing up?" Dylan asked me, his voice low and barely audible.

"I...don't really know." I put my cup back on the counter and went back to the couch. "I'm sorry for waking you. Go back to sleep." I helped him tuck himself back in. As much as I wanted to cuddle with him, I didn't. I wanted him to have his space. The couch was too crowded just as he said.

I went to my room and laid in the bed, next to Natalia. I looked at the wall of my room, getting lost in my thoughts.

I wanted to tell Dylan about my magic. I wanted him to know my secrets. I ached to be *free*.

The tears rolled down my cheeks as soon as those thoughts popped into my mind. I wanted him to know everything. I had always despised keeping secrets from him. The constant ache of not being able to tell my best friend everything weighed me down. He deserved to know who I was. It made me feel so closed off from him and neither of us wanted that. And after killing Todd, I didn't want to further poison that apple with Jason.

My silent sadness continued to flow while I turned my head into my pillow. Eventually, it turned into sobbing. A hand rubbed my arm and I looked back, seeing Natalia looking at me with those eyes. She didn't say anything, but she wrapped her arm around me for comfort.

I just wanted this to be over. If I could find a way to tell him, I'd do it. I could no longer live with myself if I was not treating him with the respect he deserved for being such an important person in my life. I couldn't hide forever. Secrets always came out somehow and I was going to let it out before it was too late.

I turned to Natalia and wiped my gross tears. "I can't keep living like this. It's tearing me apart."

"You want to tell him, don't you?"

"I do, so bad." I put my head on her shoulder, taking deep breaths. "I keep this big piece of myself hidden and it's so exhausting. I'm terrified to even show him my tail when he knows what I am, and swimming is something I love. How can I live this way?"

She rubbed my back, holding me. "Don't you worry, honey. I will help you and be here. You should let him know every detail. This is the only way you will get true peace. If he accepts you, it's even better. You will be happy, and everyone deserves to freely be themselves. I should know that more than anyone," she joked.

"He's my best friend, and I can't just deny that I want him

to know this part of me. I want him to swim with me, even. I need support. I've been my own support system, and now I want someone I can trust with my entire life," I whispered into her shoulder.

"Of course."

"We grew up together. He was always there. He was the one who made me laugh when I was crying. I want to know that he still needs me as much as I need him. We were inseparable as kids. I was there when he heard that I was leaving for seven years. He was devastated and broken. I broke him, and I want him to know that I, too, was shattered when I left him. I am so sick of the lies."

I was going to tell Dylan about my magic, and maybe even Jason. He had a right to know. If something *could* happen, I had to take that opportunity. The fear was controlling me and I was fighting back. I had to do this for both of us. There was no going back. My decision was final.

Natalia rubbed my back, not saying anymore words. The silence saturated the air and we stayed this way for hours. I needed her help to tell Dylan the truth. It would take time, but I wanted to get there eventually. The first step would be telling him how I *felt*. It would be terrifying, but I was going to tell my best friend that I wasn't so innocent anymore.

Nineteen

Maybe it had gotten cooler according to all the other residents here. They feared the ocean during winter. They feared the cold. I, however, did not. I was born to swim in the ocean any time of the year, and the beautiful thing about everyone else being afraid was they were locked away in their homes, shivering in fifty-degree weather. I had the beach all to myself.

I walked into the water and dove in once it became deep enough. I swam through the waves as my legs turned into a tail—one filled with green shades that lit up the ocean perfectly.

Water flowed through my hair as I pushed my fin upward and spun onto my back so I was facing the surface. My hand hit something, and I moved back, turning immediately to see what it was.

A body without a head.

Covering my mouth, I swam back to the beach and pulled myself out of the water. I coughed, trying not to choke on the air. I failed.

Something caught the corner of my eye and I slowly turned my head. Two eyes locked with mine. They held pure fear and hopelessness. What they didn't hold was any sign of life.

The body I had run into in the ocean had been headless, and I now was face to face with the other piece. I pulled myself up the shore and dried myself off, pulling on my clothes. I grabbed my phone and called the police.

As soon as they all showed up, I showed them the head, then pointed to where the body was. They got a crew to go out on the water and fish for the body. When they came back, they zipped it all up into a bag.

Flesh had been torn off, hanging from the bones. I knew one of the sirens got to him, and I feared it had been Calliopé and Kysana. I was picking up their mess.

The police asked me basic questions, then they asked me a few more personal questions like why I was swimming during winter and what I had been doing all day. I had no alibi. I had nobody to confirm that I didn't rip apart this body.

I was leading them that much closer to Todd's killer.

They helped me to my apartment, and I knew right away my mom was angry with me when she was waiting there. I'd gone back to the beach, and I came across a body. I broke two of her rules at once. But were they really rules now that I was under my own roof?

When the cops left, I headed towards my room, but Mom stopped me. "We should talk."

I spun on my heel, not saying a word. The punishment was coming. Everyone was quick to blame me or scold me for whatever reason. Nobody asked me if I was okay after I'd found a body torn to shreds, separated from its owner.

Mom called Dad into the conversation. Things were about

to get ugly, and it'd be long before I would set foot on a beach again if she got her way.

"I told you to stay away from the beach." She crossed her arms. "Do you understand what kind of trouble you have put us in?"

"I understand, Mom."

"No, you don't. If you understood, you wouldn't have done it! The police are going to think we're all crazy because you keep getting them involved in everything you do." She sighed. "I had meat right at home, Mia. You didn't have to rip a child apart."

I stopped looking at the floor and met her eyes. "What? You think I did this?"

"Who else would do this? Why call the police if you didn't?"

My heart dropped to my stomach. My mom thought I was a killer. She saw me as the rebellious child who killed a man. No wonder she didn't ask me if I was okay. She thought I did it.

Dad stepped forward. "Mia, this is serious. We can't hide you. You're going to have to deal with the consequences of your actions."

I saw no point in arguing. Their minds were set in stone. Nobody believed it wasn't me. I was just the bad guy. "I see." I dropped my shoulders and headed to my room, locking the door behind me.

There was no strength left in me. I felt nothing in this moment. I couldn't shed a single tear, and my parents thought I did this to someone. They thought I had lost control of myself and tore someone open. If only they had been more open and accepting with me would they have realized I'd never do such a thing. I was not the killer.

Someone knocked on my door but before I could tell them to go away, Dylan called from the other side. I leaned against it, letting out a sigh. "I don't know who else to go to." When he didn't reply, I opened the door.

What struck me as odd was the fact that he wouldn't look me in the eyes. Had I done something wrong? "You seem to be at the beach a lot, Mia. Especially during the night..."

My eyes watered. Now it was beginning to hit me full force. My own best friend thought I was a killer, too. "I swim, Dylan. I swim and I like my privacy. I didn't kill anyone!" A tear slipped down my cheek. He knew what I was and his first thought was I did it.

Dylan didn't say another word, but after a few seconds, he closed the door and left me there alone.

I choked on my own sobs before I broke down. Every last tear left my eyes and I was left with a puffy, red face. I took a deep, uneven breath every now and then to try to get my lungs back to normal.

Dylan never came back to my room. In fact, he locked himself in his room and never made eye contact when he came out. My secret was destroying me, and yet if I told the truth, it would destroy me even more. I had no shoulder to lean on.

Someone knocked on my door.

"Go away," I said in a hoarse voice.

"It's me," Nat said.

I dragged myself over to the door and unlocked it to let her in. She locked it behind her and got down to my level. "I heard about what happened..."

I leaned against the wall, pulling my knees to my chest. "What difference does it make? Dylan thinks I killed that kid.

Nobody believes me. They see me as someone who hides and sneaks out at night. They don't see the real me."

She frowned and looked at the carpet for a split second. "I get that. I mean, I don't understand what it's like to be...judged in that sense, but I've dealt with racism. People are so cruel. They look at you and see you one way and nothing will change their mind. You're dirty to them. But the truth is, we were all made for a reason. We all have a purpose, Mia, and I choose to believe that. Some people may never see it that way, but we all have our part and sirens do, too."

Shivers ran down my spine as I closed my eyes. Exhaustion took over and all I wanted to do was sleep. "And my purpose is to kill, right?"

The words I longed to hear all night—she said them, "I don't think you did this."

"Why? Everyone else thinks so."

"Yeah, and when was the last time your mom and dad saw you? You were eleven. You're eighteen and you went through many years of puberty, changing, growing, and finding who you are as a person. Your parents missed all of that. They don't know the real you and they haven't had time to meet you as you are today. They see this version of Mia who learned about her heritage, refused to accept it, then snapped and gave in. They see the outer layers. I see *you*. I grew up beside you, and I know you've fought so hard to make sure you're not like the other sirens. You wouldn't rip apart a boy out of nowhere."

After gulping down some air, I looked at her. "Thank you." I gasped a bit, but Nat pulled me in for a hug and kissed the top of my head. "Thank you for believing me."

"I will always believe you. You're my best friend and I know you'd never lie to me. You have no reason to lie because I've never judged you before. We don't do that here." She stroked my hair as I laid my head in her lap, staring at the wall across from us.

Nat knew what it was like to be judged. She wasn't a siren, but she was different from other people, and they didn't always accept that.

When she first came out to me, I remember seeing the fear in her eyes. We'd been together since we were just children and back then neither of us were interested in any romance. We were solely interested in our heritage and what made us, us.

Hormones kicked in, and I would point out a cute boy now and then, but she never really commented on it. It was always something simple like, "He is cute."

There were never boy talks at our sleepovers. Eventually, she felt like she could come to me without being judged and she told me there was a girl in her class that she liked. It all made sense at that point as to why she had never liked talking about cute boys. Before she started crying, I hugged her to tell her it was okay. I supported her, and I would never leave her side for something so stupid. We were different in many ways, but we were the same in the fact that we both loved the ocean. We could never be torn apart.

"I love you, Nat."

"I love you, too."

FOR A FEW DAYS, I stayed in my room when I wasn't at school. I avoided any dinners and family members. I avoided Dylan. I avoided anyone who thought that I had torn the flesh off someone else, and it was for my own sanity.

Mom tried hard to talk to me, but I refused. She could hate me, but nothing hurt more than being told I was a murderer. Dad tried more than anyone to get me to tell the police what I did, and they did come over a few times for more questions, but I answered them all and they left. I wouldn't let my parents send me to prison for a crime I didn't commit.

Olivia tried to talk to me, but I didn't say much. She was Dylan's friend more than she was mine. I knew she took his side on this matter.

Everyone at school avoided me. They whispered different things. Some people thought I did it, and others were worried about how I was doing after something so horrendous. I'd seen a dead body and it was not any easy image to live with.

It was only a matter of time before they caught on and figured out I killed Todd, too. Dylan already knew about that venomous story.

I had a nightmare the other night about it. I woke up screaming as I saw this torn body on the beach and Nat was there to remind me that I was home safe and sound. I was home, but I was anything but safe and sound. Those images haunted me. What I needed was someone to talk to about it, but nobody would listen. They all pointed fingers and the last thing I could do was go to therapy when my parents were telling me to go to the police.

Maybe I'd been crazy to think nobody would think I did anything wrong. It was absurd of me.

I was tempted to go out and search for the killer myself just to prove I didn't do anything. I wanted my friends and family back. I wanted life to be semi-normal again, but it wouldn't be. Even after they proved I was innocent, the pain would still be lingering. The truth would still be exposed.

Everyone thought I was the monster I fought desperately not to be.

Twenty

"THIS IS REALLY HOW you want us to spend our New Year's Eve?" Nat asked me.

I shrugged. "It is." I searched the beach for any clues, but nothing came up. The body and head had been taken that same night, but the blood still stained the sand.

Police tape blocked off the area, but Nat and I walked past it. She kept more of an eye out while I searched for any evidence. Unfortunately, my name wouldn't be cleared. All evidence was gone now.

"It's freezing out here," she said, hugging herself.

I glanced at her. "You're cold? You're a sea nymph."

"Yeah, and I'm cold. That isn't so strange." She rubbed her arms, looking in every direction. "Hurry up."

"You can't rush excellence," I grumbled. I fell to the sand. "There's nothing here. I'm going to lose everyone I love because of what I am. This is pitiful." I threw my arms up.

She released a sigh. "The truth will eventually come out."

"Will it?" I looked over at her. "Because sirens have a way of hiding their crimes and I might always be the culprit. I'm eighteen now and I can be tried as an adult. They will want someone to blame and I'm the easiest target."

Nat rolled her eyes. "Don't be so dramatic. They will have to find someone and it won't be you. You found the body but that's it. There's no way they'll pin it on you because his blood was not even on your body. No blood under your fingernails."

"You think my parents would believe that? Doubt it."

She stomped over to me. "Stop with that bullshit. Your parents are not cops, and there's a good reason as to why. They're assuming the worst of you and that's not right. In America we follow one justice system motto, and that is: innocent until proven guilty. You are innocent because you have not been proven to be guilty and you won't be because you aren't, therefore, you're innocent."

A female from the water said, "And in the UK, they believe you are guilty until proven innocent."

Nat and I looked over at her. Calliopé stared at us, not saying another word. Kysana emerged from the water and looked around the beach. "What happened?"

"Like you don't know," I said with a scoff.

Calliopé narrowed her eyes, coming closer until she was barely in the ocean. "Are you accusing us of murder?"

Nat pulled me back, but I ripped my arm away from her. "If the shoe fits."

Calliopé grabbed my ankle and pulled me down, dragging me into the ocean. I struggled to get free, almost drowning on the spot until my body transformed and my gills came in. I clawed myself away from Calliopé, but she grabbed my hair, pulling me into her cave. She pushed me against the rocks, keeping her arm against my throat.

Kysana followed her, poking her head above the water.

However, she didn't come to my rescue. But Nat did.

Calliopé pushed Nat off her back, turning to face me again. "You have no right to accuse us of anything." She spat at me. "You're the problem, Mia. You've always been the problem."

Nat covered her bleeding nose with the deadliest glare I'd ever seen in her eyes. "Do you two know each other?"

I swallowed. "Calliopé is a siren, and not one of the good ones. She's not even a purebred."

Calliopé's hand came across my cheek, leaving behind a stinging sensation far worse than a slap done with dry skin. "You don't know me."

"I know enough."

Kysana came forward, trying to get between us. "Stop! We didn't kill anyone! Calliopé and I have been trying hard to be more like you!"

I furrowed my brows. "What?"

Calliopé let go, backing away. "Forget it, Kysana. She's not worth our time."

Kysana glanced back at me, but she never said a word.

Nat grabbed my wrist and pulled me from the cave. When we surfaced, she made sure they were nowhere in sight before asking, "Who were they?"

Did I tell her the truth, or did I tell her a lie? "They're just sirens. They're none of our business now."

I started back towards the shore, but something with quick movements slammed into my side. I rolled over, my screams silenced by the water. As I tried to gather my strength and vision to fight back, they pushed me into the rocks before I had a chance to see who was trying to kill me.

My head connected with the jagged edges, cutting into my scalp. The blow sent a dull ache throughout my entire head, and before I had a chance to flee my attacker, I lost consciousness.

A GROAN ESCAPED MY lips as I opened my eyes. My brain was pounding against my skull. I tried to sit up, but Nat pushed my back down with little force, reminding me to rest. I didn't want to rest.

"You can't get up. You got banged up pretty bad," she said.

I scanned my surroundings, thankful I was home in my own bed. I sat up quickly as soon as my eyes landed on Dylan and Olivia. "What are they doing here?"

Nat crossed her arms. "I told them."

"Why?"

Dylan's eyes were filled with pity. I didn't want any of it. "Because we care about you."

I scooted away from him, distancing myself as far as possible. "I wouldn't have felt any need to go solve the murder of that boy if everyone just believed I didn't do it. I wouldn't have been attacked." I faced Nat. "Who did this? Who attacked me?"

She frowned. "I didn't see anything. I'm sorry."

"What?"

Nat grabbed my hand, patting it. "They were too fast. I don't know who it was."

Those were the words I dreaded to hear. I thought maybe it had been Calliopé or Kysana but Calliopé's red hair would have stood out even if she moved fast. Kysana couldn't move as quickly. In fact, neither of them could. Someone could, though, but I had no idea who wanted me dead. I assumed this person might have been behind the murder or all of the murders, and if that was true, that meant I was wrong about Kysana and Calliopé.

I released a sigh, not bothering to look in Dylan's direction. "How bad is it?"

Nat looked at my head. "It's...bad. Olivia helped me with your stitches, and we've bandaged it up. We can't tell what other damage it might have caused but we've got a few tests to help us determine your state of mind." She held up fingers. "How many?"

"Two."

"Okay. Follow my finger." She moved it from left to right, and I followed it. "Now, what is your full name?"

"Mia Anabelle Dawson."

"When were you born?"

"September sixteenth."

"Who was the first president of the United States?"

"George Washington."

Nat nodded. "So your memory seems okay and your vision looks normal. You're reacting well, which is a good sign. We can't be too sure about a concussion but I'm not sure if that even matters now that you've been out for hours."

I widened my eyes and jumped off the bed, running to the bathroom. I opened one side of the mirror cabinet and positioned it so I could see my bandage. I lifted it enough to see the damage. It was as I had feared... They shaved part of my head to stitch it up.

"I'm sorry. We had to make sure your wound was clean and stitched properly. Your safety comes first, Mia." Nat leaned against the frame, arms across her chest.

I'd be wearing hats and finding ways to keep that area

covered for a while. I wasn't about to shave my entire head though.

My balance faltered and Nat reached forward, but another arm caught me. Dylan cleared his throat while his arm wrapped around my waist to keep me upright.

I didn't want him to be around me—not when he believed I was a killer. Not when I was vulnerable.

I turned my head to the side, looking at his shoulder. "You shouldn't be here. You have no right."

He frowned through the mirror. "I'm not going to leave you alone. That's not what friends do."

Ripping my body away from him, I backed into the wall. "Friends don't believe the worst first, either, but here we are."

All that pity I despised returned. "I know. I shouldn't have, and I hurt you. I'm sorry for that and I will do everything I can to make it up to you. You're my best friend."

He reached out, wrapping his fingers around my wrist and pulling me back towards the counter. I faced the mirror and placed both hands on the edge of the counter to keep my balance. I supposed I was a little unsteady.

Dylan lifted the bandage from the back of my head at the base of my skull, peeking at the injury. "It's time to change the bandage out and keep it fresh." He grabbed a few supplies from the cabinet while Nat watched me through the mirror. Something wasn't right with the look in her eye, but I didn't have time to solve that mystery.

Dylan wrapped a new bandage around my head, keeping it tight but not too tight. He used medical tape to keep it in place, before doing something that caught us both off guard. He leaned down and kissed my forehead.

Coughing, he pulled back. "I'm sorry. I thought maybe I

could kiss it better but that sounds stupid now that I think about it."

He was right. It did sound stupid, but maybe I was stupid, too. I needed comfort even if it was from the one person who hurt me the most.

I leaned forward, wrapping my arms around his waist and pressing my cheek against his chest. I refused to talk about the murder. Not here. Not now.

Dylan seemed a bit shocked by the gesture, but eventually he wrapped his arms around my torso. We stayed like this forever. Why did we need to move? Why did we need to speak? Our hug contained everything we needed, and it said everything we wanted to say.

Nat smiled and left us alone in the bathroom.

I closed my eyes, enjoying the warmth from his touch and the sound of his heartbeat. It sounded so...chaotic. His heartbeat wasn't anchored but somehow it comforted me. It told me that even if my life was chaotic, someone else's was, too. I wasn't alone and Dylan would remind me of that every day. He was there when I needed him the most.

Opening my eyes, I looked at Dylan for a moment with my head still pressed against his chest. It took him a few minutes to notice that I was staring at him but when he did, he placed a second kiss on my forehead. This time, neither of us pulled away. It wasn't weird, and it wasn't abnormal. It was innate.

Deep down, I feared the worst. What would happen when he knew the truth? Would he be repulsed? Would he be quick to assume I murdered more people?

Every day I went on letting humans believe that when they heard beautiful voices inside seashells, they were listening to the songs of mermaids.

I never corrected them.

If they knew the truth, they'd never step foot near a beach again.

Mermaids could not sing the way sirens could. Sirens were blessed with the gift of song, and mermaids were blessed with the gift of *our* recognition.

The songs inside those shells came from sirens and sirens alone. No mermaid in this world had that kind of voice. Sirens were cursed with the need for human flesh, but mermaids were cursed with the music of a dying cat.

The question remained. Which was a worse curse?

The answer was always clear. Any man preferred a terrible singer over a serial killer for a best friend.

Twenty-one

The news played as background noise while Nat changed out my bandage. I could do it myself, but she insisted she take care of me. Did she feel guilty for what happened? It wasn't her fault.

"How was that with Dylan?" she asked.

"How was what?"

"Don't play dumb. You know I'm asking you how it was being so close to him. I'm sure he smelled great."

"He smelled like sweat."

"All right, so he smelled like sweat. But was he warm?"

I nodded a bit. "He was. And that was why he was sweaty."

"And that was nice, right?"

"Yeah. Love a sweaty guy."

She rolled her eyes. "You are killing me. We both know you have a crush on him, and we both know you have thoughts running around in that head of yours. Now spill."

With a nod, I said, "This isn't like that. He grabbed my wrist and pulled me closer. He changed my bandage. He kissed my forehead. To him, it meant nothing more than a comforting gesture. To me, it meant the world." He cared about me in ways that made me feel so safe around him.

A small smile formed on her lips. "That sounds really nice." She dropped her smile as quickly as it had formed. "In other news, the case of Harrison Peterson has been closed and the killer has been caught." Harrison Peterson was the body I found. He was the boy whose head I had run into on the beach.

Mom and Dad rushed into the living room, standing over the couch. "What did she just say?"

Nat patted my hair. "They found the killer and Mia is innocent."

Dad grabbed his chest. "That's the news we wanted to hear."

"But it's the news you refused to believe," I said.

"Mia," Mom said with a stern voice.

I jumped up from the couch, facing my parents. "No. You don't get to make me feel guilty for this. I had found a dead body and the first thing you did was accuse me of being a murderer. I was already traumatized, and you added to it. You made me feel alone and small. You made me out to be a monster. That's your fault. That has nothing to do with me."

Mom opened her mouth to say something, but someone else interrupted. "She's right." Christian came out of the hallway. "Everyone pinned the murder on her. We have no right to be mad at her for being upset with us for something so serious."

Mom looked at Dad before nodding her head. "We're sorry. We shouldn't have jumped to the worst conclusion and that's our fault."

Hearing those words eased some of the pain, but not all of

it. Some of it left residue.

"We're sorry," Christian said.

Nat nodded towards my family and took me to the kitchen. She made me a sandwich. "How do you feel?"

"I don't know how to feel. They apologized. The truth remains that they thought I did it this entire time. How can I forget about that? I know they'll always have an eye over my shoulder to see if I'm going to snap. Even my own family thinks I'm a monster."

She placed the plate in front of me. "That's fair."

I looked at my food. "It's embarrassing. I hate knowing what everyone thinks of me. Dylan even thought the worst."

"The truth is out. You're not a killer. Focus on that for the moment and let your feelings settle for a bit before you decide what to do." She grabbed my plate, picking up the sandwich and taking a bite.

I glanced at the TV again, seeing the face behind the murder. I squinted as he mouthed something, and it took me a few tries before I realized what he was saying. "I'm innocent."

"Hm?"

"The killer is still out there, Nat. I know lots of killers might try to say they're innocent, but I know what it's like to be blamed for a murder. He looks like I did when everyone else accused me. He's desperate. Someone else did this. I think whoever did this is the same person who hurt me."

She glanced at the man being taken away on the news. "Mia, it's not our problem anymore." Except it was. If it was the same guy who hurt me, he was after me specifically and anyone who got in his way was just collateral damage. I refused to let an innocent man fall because of my enemies.

"I found the body. I was accused of killing him. I was then attacked. It's my problem until the real killer is behind bars." Or worse—dead.

Dylan came running into the kitchen. "They caught him!" He hugged me, making sure to be careful with my head. When he pulled away, he glanced at Nat before facing me again. "What's wrong?"

"He didn't do it. He's been framed."

"Mia, we are not detectives. Let's just forget about this and let the cops handle it. They get paid for this."

I folded my arms across my chest. "No, Dylan. This is not just something you forget about. They're putting an innocent man behind bars. That could have just as easily been me. He deserves to have someone on his side." Right, because I didn't.

Dylan shoved his hands in his pockets. "What do you think you're going to be able to do?"

"The only thing I can do. I must find the real killer." Sure, that was easier said than done. But if I had been framed, I'd wish someone would prove me innocent. The justice system may have believed innocent until proven guilty, but they didn't follow it. They'd find enough evidence and lock someone away just to close the case.

"That's dangerous," he said.

I shook my head. "It is but I can't let that stop me. The way I felt when everyone blamed me is how this man feelings right now. I'd be cruel to let him continue to feel that way. What good is the justice system if innocent people are locked away while we do nothing? We'd be no better if we knew the truth, and we do."

Dylan leaned forward. "We don't know the truth. For all

we know, this guy is the killer and we're putting ourselves in danger."

"We? I'm doing this alone and you clearly don't want to help."

He lifted both eyebrows in surprise, as if I were the stupid one. "You think you're going to do this alone? We're still best friends and we do everything together." Even if he disagreed with it, he'd still do it because I was. Was that supposed to be sweet or disrespectful?

I shrugged, ignoring all his warnings. "You can't change my mind. I guess we're both going after the real killer. Prepare yourself because things may get messy." In other words, I was going to solve this by myself. The killer had to be a sea creature and Dylan had no idea that mermaids, sirens, and all the like existed. I wasn't about to let him find out during our investigation. Somehow, I had to keep him on the downlow and pretend I didn't know anything more than I did.

Dylan left to go gather what evidence he could and sort out this case. I did the same, except I had more information for obvious reasons.

Nat leaned over the counter, trying to hint at something else. "You and Dylan are now becoming detectives together. It's only a matter of time..."

"Before what?"

"Before the crush grows."

"It's not a crush."

"Why is that?"

"Because he's cute but I don't want to date him."

Nat shook her head. "I doubt that. That's too small to matter."

"Small? Is that what I am?" I clenched my jaw.

"Huh?" She straightened herself. "What are you talking about?"

I glanced at her. "I'm not small, and I don't like him. Drop it, Nat."

Nat furrowed her brows. "I'm going to keep talking about it. It's only a matter of time until the two of you get closer."

"If closer means ever ruining our friendship, I don't want it. My point stands." I organized all the information. "Now if you'll excuse me, I have a killer to catch." I stood up, spinning on my heel. I stopped immediately. "What?" I asked Mom.

She shook her head. "You're not going after a killer. That's the last thing you're going to do. You are on bedrest right now. That's an order."

"What? That's not fair! You can't just accuse me of something then tell me what to do!"

She patted my shoulder, giving me a smile. "Yes, I can. You will not be chasing down a killer. You will rest while your head heals. That's important."

I groaned, stomping past her. I didn't make it far when she called out to me, forcing me to look at her.

"I'm sorry I saw the worst in you, but this time I'm stepping up to be a better mother and that requires you to listen to me this time. Drop the case and focus on getting better. You must come first."

I left the house and went back to our apartment, locking the door behind me. I couldn't just live on dry land forever. That wasn't in my blood.

Dylan came into my room, plopping himself down on the bed. "Mom thinks she can still tell me what to do."

He chuckled. "That's fair. She's only looking out for your best interest. You did get hit pretty hard."

"I feel fine." I rolled my eyes.

Dylan sighed. "You weren't fine the other day when you fell out of nowhere. Whose fast reflexes had to catch you? Me."

I snickered. "I'm fine now," I mumbled.

My balance had been off for a while, but it wasn't off so much now. I was regaining my ability to walk like a normal person and not like someone who's feet fell off. It wasn't too bad.

Dylan looked at some of his papers. "Detective Dawson, what do you have?"

"What?"

"Are we solving this case or not?" He gave me a *duh* look.

Pressing my lips into a thin line, I nodded. "I know that the body was in the water, and the head was on the beach. The flesh had been torn off." I couldn't keep that from Dylan. That kind of information was public now. "There was no sign of struggle, but it's hard to tell on a beach when the water washes away the evidence, Detective Adler."

That brought a smile to his face. "Detective Adler. I like it."

I laughed. "Of course you would. You want that position of authority, don't you?" I rolled over, laying my head into his lap.

"What I want is to have a title. Lord Dylan. Detective Dylan Adler. Officer Dylan Adler. Professor Dylan Adler. I like the way it sounds. I don't feel so...helpless. I feel like I have a place to belong. I love soccer but sometimes I question if that's what I want to do for the rest of my life." He stared at the floor.

I had never really asked him what he wanted to do with his life, but then again I don't think either of us talked about our futures. We wanted to pretend we were still eleven and seven years hadn't been ripped away from our friendship. We were both adults now. We'd have to make decisions about our own futures.

"I'm sure you'll figure it out. The Dill Pickle always figures it out because you're amazing. Don't believe otherwise," I assured him. "You can change your future at any time. The choice is always going to be yours."

Putting the papers down, Dylan began stroking my hair away from my face. "I hope you're right about that. But the real question is, do you believe that for yourself? You can't prove to everyone else that you're not the stereotype if you refuse to even accept what you are. To first break out of the mold, you must accept the truth."

His fingers were so gentle, and it made me sleepy just laying here. But he was right in every form. I couldn't prove I wasn't a monster if I refused to admit that I shared their same DNA. It confused people. I confused people.

I confused myself.

Twenty-two

"STOP IT!" I NUDGED his foot.

Dylan was playing footsie with me for no real reason other than to be a nuisance. I gasped when our feet knocked into the game board. "Dill! You ruined our game." I frowned.

He chuckled and shrugged. "It's not my fault. It's the board's fault. It was in the way."

"Yes, blame inanimate objects for things *you* do." I sat back against the side of my bed, my butt planted on my carpet. Dylan sat on the other side of the board that laid between us.

"Your feet are so small." He looked at them.

I pulled my foot back, hiding it under my leg. "I know and I don't like to talk about it."

"What size are you?"

"Size six." I looked at the game board, refusing to look at him.

"That's tiny."

I glared at him and kicked him with my small foot. "But they hurt like hell so watch your mouth, Dill Pickle."

"Mia..." He paused, tasting my name, "what does your

name sound like? Mia. Mini Mia. Mimi." He watched my face for reactions.

"I am not a Mimi!" I kicked him more.

He knew that was the one that bothered me the most. "You are to me," he joked, breaking out into a full-blown laughing fit.

"You're so mean to me." I put on the music, trying to drown out his mean comments.

He still laughed over the music. He finally calmed down and wiped some tears. "That was good. I'm going to live for a long time."

"Lucky for you. I'll die first."

He tilted his head. "Aw, is Mimi hurt? I'll make it up to you. What do you want?"

This was a good thing. I could use this to my advantage. "Hm. Well, kisses always make people feel better." I tapped my cheek. "You can kiss away the insults."

"Fair deal." He scooted himself around the board.

I hadn't expected him to agree so easily but now I was beginning to realize the situation we were in. He was going to kiss my cheek. My stomach was doing flips, and breathing was becoming a challenge.

"All right, a kiss for the boo-boos." He put his back against the side of my bed, leaning in.

I swallowed, unsure if I was even ready for this.

No. I wasn't. "Dylan," I said as I turned my head, "I was ki—" Our lips met and there was no taking it back now. And to my surprise, Dylan took my face in his hands.

And for a split second, every inch of my body went putty from his touch.

Dylan stumbled away with wide eyes. "I'm sorry. I did

not..." He seemed uncertain of how to finish his sentence.

The kiss had been quick, sure. But it had also been soft. Inviting. He'd tasted of chocolate, the same color of his eyes.

I had to tell him the truth. "Dylan, I have to tell you something."

"What is it?"

I shivered, but I wouldn't let my secrets hold me down. "I..." I laid my head on the edge of my mattress, closing my eyes. Maybe if I couldn't see him, I could say it. "That kiss opened new feelings inside me. I want more of you, Dylan, and more than just being my best friend."

"Oh..." He sounded a little lost.

I opened my eyes, looking at him as I released a deep breath. "It's okay if you don't feel the same way. I just had to say something." I locked my fingers together and laid them against my chest, feeling my heart pound against my ribcage.

"Mimi, you think I tease you for no reason?"

I scrunched my face up in confusion. "You tease me because that's what we do. We're friends and we enjoy poking fun at each other."

Dylan shrugged a little. "True but we do it because we are masking the way we feel."

I opened my mouth a bit. "You say we as if..."

"...as if I feel the same way. I don't tease Oli the way I tease you. I like making you laugh and smile. That is why I tease you. You're my best friend and I want us to be like that."

"So you're saying you like me, too." I was trying to grasp this. "Or do you want us to stay friends?" My heart clenched at the thought of Dylan distancing himself from me after that moment. Even if we stayed friends, nothing could be the same after that confession. I liked him more than just my friend, and now he knew that. He'd always be afraid to accidentally lead me on, and I'd hurt from being close but never close enough.

Dylan laughed. "I'm saying I want us to be more."

I was completely overtaken by joy. My brain was overwhelmed all at once, but I couldn't keep this to myself. I leaned in, pressing my lips to his as my fingers tangled in his hair.

He returned the kiss without a second thought, and all I could think about was the idea that I was kissing my best friend. Even though I knew that, it didn't feel like he was simply Dylan, the boy next door. Every part of me was on fire, flames spreading throughout every crevice of my body. I'd never craved Dylan like this before, nor this much.

Dylan grabbed my waist and pulled me against him as my skin burned under his touch. This kiss wasn't as soft. It was firm yet intoxicating. It had me begging for more.

Here, in this exact moment, everything fell right into place. This was where the world was meant to be. The only person in mine was Dylan, and I was entirely happy with that equation.

I pulled away. "I got too excited. I'm sorry." I used my thumb to wipe my bottom lip.

He shook his head. "Don't be sorry. We both wanted it."

As if to counteract my attempt to wipe the taste of his lips from mine, he kissed me again. This time it was slower and more sensual. My entire body was at peace. My muscles relaxed and I felt safe—secure in his arms.

We both pulled away. "I liked that a lot," I whispered.

"We both did." He pushed a strand of my hair behind my ear.

I put my head on his shoulder and grabbed his hand,

intertwining our fingers. "You're the one person who truly makes me feel safe. I can trust you. We know everything about each other. I never have to worry about you becoming abusive or cheating on me because I know you're the best guy ever. You'll always be my best friend."

Dylan laid his head against mine. "And you're mine. Nobody could replace you, even if you did leave me."

"I'm not leaving you again and I promise that. I'm an adult and it's up to me where I go—and I choose to be here, with you."

He whispered, "If that's true, will you let me be your boyfriend?"

I squeezed his hand. "Yes." Even the idea that he had Olivia couldn't ruin my happiness because her friendship with him meant something different to each of them. He liked me, and she liked girls.

He cleared his throat. "What should we do today?"

"I don't know. Maybe we can figure out what we like to do together. What is it that you want to do?"

"Well, I'm not sure. We can go hang out at the mall."

I looked at him. "Really? We're both broke and I just finished paying off Olivia."

"Well, that's true." He laughed a little. "Oh, there's a party at Michaela's."

"Who?"

Dylan rolled his eyes playfully. "She's basically the popular girl. What about it?"

"Are we party type of people?"

"Well, no. Olivia is. She's going to be there."

I thought about it. "Well, if things don't get too crazy. I want you to stay by my side. I don't like big crowds."

"I can agree with that. It's not like I need to go off on my own. You're my only friend. Aside from Olivia of course." He got up and pulled me up. I fixed my shirt. "Let's go then."

I raised my eyebrows. "Now? I'm not ready."

"You look great."

I snickered. "At least let me do something different with my hair."

Dylan released a sigh and put his hands up. "Fine. I'll allow it."

"Good. Now go." I shooed him out of my room and locked the door. I smiled to myself, looking around my room. This was the best feeling in the world. I got to call myself Dylan's, and I loved every second of it.

After I French-braided my hair into two braids, I walked downstairs. Dylan saw me, smiling. I grabbed his hand, and we left the house. He walked us there since I didn't know who she was or where McKenna lived.

"Let's make the best of it," Dylan said.

"You know we will. We are the life of the party." My laugh echoed into the sky as I skipped along the sidewalk. Dylan was a bit annoyed by it because I kept tugging his arm.

When we got to her house, I looked at it. Dylan pulled me against his side. "Hey, don't worry. I'm here."

"It's just so crowded. Teenage parties scare me."

"Why?"

"Because of alcohol and drugs." I didn't need a repeat of the academy either.

Dylan squeezed my hand and pulled me inside the house. We slid through bodies until we found an area that wasn't so bad. He pulled out his phone. "I'll text Oli."

I nodded and looked around. I noticed a couple that was

making out and desperate to get naked. I made a face and looked at Dylan. "We are not doing that."

"Why not?" he joked.

"Because I don't want to have to worry about ending up pregnant. I just want us to be together and do stuff that's cute and romantic. We have plenty of time for sex later."

I could never risk getting pregnant now.

He smiled. "Don't worry, Mimi. I won't make you do something you don't want to do. I'm happy as we are." He placed a quick kiss on my lips.

I smiled at him.

We both jumped when a girl screamed in our ears. We looked back at Olivia, and she came over, gasping. "Tell me that kiss means what I think it means."

"What do you mean?"

She covered her mouth with both of her hands and looked back and forth between both of us. "Are you two together?"

I looked at Dylan and he nodded. "She's my Mimi and I'm her Dill Pickle."

"Oh my word. I'm so glad you two finally saw what I saw." She hugged us both. Olivia sat down and grabbed our hands. "I have to know everything."

"We took too long to realize we liked each other, and it was stupid to keep waiting." I nodded.

Olivia laughed. "Yeah, it would be stupid. You guys make a lot of sense."

"We do?"

"Because you're cute together. You know each other too well and you're always making fun of each other. It just makes sense." She shrugged.

"If you say so." I took another look around the party. "This place is so busy. McKenna must be really popular."

"Michaela," Olivia corrected me.

"Huh?" I looked at her.

"Her name is Michaela."

I slowly nodded, remembering now. "Right. I'm sorry. I've just never met this girl."

"There she is." Olivia pointed to her.

I looked at who she was pointing to, and I made a face. "Wait, that's her? This is her party?"

"Yeah, why?"

"That's not what I pictured as a popular girl. At my previous school, I saw her as someone else. I mean, the popular girls were all preppy and stuff." I looked at Michaela and tilted my head. She was dressed in all black with a nose piercing and fiery red hair. She must have been a lovable person.

"She works at the animal shelter," Dylan said.

I nodded, watching Michaela. "That's nice. You can trust animal lovers." Something about her seemed familiar. It was the same vibe I got from Nat, only in a different wavelength.

"Why is that?" he asked.

As she glanced at me for a second, I tilted my head. Her eyes shimmered gold. Only one kind of nymph had such a feature, and now I knew she was one of them. Land nymph. It all made sense as to why she was so popular.

In a quiet voice, I said, "Because if animals love them, they are trustworthy. Animals are the best judges of character." Being part fish made me part animal, I could judge everyone's character. It was just never spot on. Dylan was the one I got right, though. He'd been so careful with my secret, and I could also introduce to him Michaela and what made her so damn loveable.

Twenty-three

I PAUSED FOR A moment before continuing, "And then we kissed."

Even when he thought I killed that boy, he never told anyone my secret, or turned me in. Even after I *did* kill Todd. It was no question as to why I fell into Dylan's trap so easily.

Natalia shook her head and laid back. "Wow. You guys kissed, and good on you for making it happen."

"It was the best thing ever. If only I could just get over my other fear and find a way to tell him the truth about me."

"Hm, the truth. That's tough." She tapped her chin.

I had one idea. "I'm gonna beg him to get a dog. Dogs can judge people and if the dog loves Dylan, I know I can trust him with this secret."

"A dog? You're getting a dog for this?"

"Oh come on, dogs are cute and I would love to have a pet. Dogs make great friends. I would love him just the same."

She shrugged. "Whatever you say."

I straightened my posture. "How have you been, Nat? We should do something together."

"Why?"

"Why not? We're best friends. I want to go swimming with you. I can be happy in the ocean with my best friend, and we can push away the stress of telling Dylan. I enjoy your company and the fact that I have a boyfriend." I nodded.

Natalia and I got off my bed and left my house, walking down to the beach. However, she didn't stop there. "Where are you going?" I asked her.

She looked back at me. "To a private swimming spot. It's safer and more fun. We get to explore." She squealed.

I laughed as I followed her. We walked along the sand that lined the ocean. Life was good right now.

Natalia took off running and I groaned. She climbed up a bunch of rocks. "Look! Mia, come here!" she yelled and waved me over.

I took my time going after her. Looking inside, I widened my eyes. It was beautiful. The area was huge, and the water was a gorgeous shade of teal. I was already in love. "Let's go in." I climbed inside, keeping myself out of the water.

I took off my shirt, bottoms, and shoes but not in that order. I hung them over the rocks, keeping them dry. I slipped into the water and relaxed. The water was warmer than the ocean, which surprised me that we had a hot spring over here. How did Nat find it, and why hadn't anyone else been using it? "It's so perfect." It was just right for the winter season, and the water eased my muscles.

Natalia followed my actions and joined me, leaning back against the rocks. "Now this is amazing."

"Oh, yes." I looked at her, admiring her tail. She was right. It was beautiful. Her tail shimmered in the sunlight as if made up of glitter.

I hummed to myself, sighing. "Even when he knows, I'll always have to be careful around him. I have to keep everyone safe."

"What do you mean?"

"You know. I have to make sure that I don't let anything bad happen. I would never wish that on him."

She nodded. "I know you won't. He means too much to you. You're different, Mia. Don't let people tell you otherwise. Don't let them make you feel bad for what you are. You're not a disgrace to any species. You're sweet and kind. I was the one who had to teach you how to get revenge. You aren't bad. You're Mia Dawson and you are what you choose to be. You are not destined to take one path."

"I'm more like the mermaids than they realize. They judge so much that they don't even take the time to get to know me. They see my DNA and judge me for it. I'm so close to being just like them."

Natalia replied, "Or they're more like sirens than they realize, cruel and all."

I yawned, the darkness threatening my mind. I wanted to give up and sleep here forever. This spot was too good to be true.

"Where do we go after this?" Natalia asked.

"A spa," I joked. "These hot springs are making me crave a spa day. We deserve to relax in mud baths and get our backs chopped like lettuce. I'm not too sure if mud makes us grow tails, though."

"I'm sure it would. It's a mix between water and dirt." She sat up, swimming over to the other side, leaning over the edge. "You can see the whole ocean. It's mesmerizing."

I joined her on that end of the swimming hole and looked

out upon the waters.

Stunning was an understatement. The waves sparkled in the sun and moved gently in any direction the wind took them. The water was perfect, setting the mood for our evening. I was more than happy to spend it with my best friend Natalia.

"What would be a good name for a dog?" I asked.

"You're really going with this dog thing, huh?"

"I am."

She nodded and scratched her face. "I get that. I'm not good at naming animals so maybe you should ask Dylan. He's going to know you're planning to get one, he just won't know the reason why."

I pulled away from the edge and swam a bit, moving my tail. "That's true. Maybe I should ask him. I just need some names that work. I'm no good at naming animals either."

We both swam around, enjoying the water and relaxation. There would be no aches and pains after the things we planned to do today. This water was a natural healer, and I would be coming back a lot more often.

"Are you ever going home?" I asked in a quiet voice.

Natalia choked on her words. "Whoa, a little forward. I mean, I don't know. I'm already eighteen. Does it matter?"

"No, I just want to know how long I have with you. I don't want to waste my time if you're leaving next week or something. I want to spend every second with you if you're going to leave me." I rolled onto my stomach, my back facing the sky. I put my head under, opening my eyes. Everything was much clearer under the surface.

I swam closer to the bottom, touching the rocks with my fingers. I took a deep breath, not at all harmed by the warm water that was going in and out of the gills that lined under my breasts. I went back up to the surface and looked at Natalia.

We didn't need to say anything to communicate. She knew from my eyes that I was content in the moment yet scared for the future. I knew that she would be by my side, no matter what.

Part of me scolded myself for being a horrible friend. I was constantly complaining to Nat about my issues, yet I never listened to her about her own. I knew she had them. Her father was always absent even if he was there, and her sister took first place in the favoritism contest.

I wanted to ask her how it was going but I knew the answer. She'd been with me the whole time so she hadn't spoken to her family at all. She broke up with her girlfriend before coming down here. I had a boyfriend who was the sweetest guy I knew, and yet I complained all the time about what he would think of my past. Nat had to be tired of hearing about it by now.

I loved her, but I was debating if it was time to dial it back on my whining. It was something I had to deal with on my own.

The truth was that I was the only one who had to figure out a way to tell Dylan. Natalia wasn't in the same predicament and yet I kept making her feel as if she was.

I needed to be a better friend for us both.

I'd mention it, but I wouldn't continue to dwell on it and push it on her as if it was her responsibility to help me.

"What's on your mind?" She asked.

I shrugged. "Too much to account for." Simple answer. She accepted it, too.

We both got out of the secret pool and dried ourselves

off before getting dressed. I pulled my shoes on and climbed down the rocks, scanning the area for any sign of people. During this time of year, few people came this way.

"Let's head back home," she said. I laughed a bit at the thought of her considering my home part of hers. It was in a way.

As we started on our way back, I kicked at the sand to occupy my mind. If I let it run rampant, bad things could pass through. I spent so much time worrying that for once, I was thankful that not a single doubt was in sight. All that was left were tumbleweeds rolling through the desert that made up my brain.

"This is nice. This is exactly what I needed to get through this," I said.

Natalia asked, "Get through what?"

"Life. I need to get through life and figure out how to tell Dylan."

"What about the dog?"

"I want a dog but I'm realizing I need to be practical. I think after relaxing my body, I know what I truly want. I just want to find out for myself and tell him when the time is right. It's kind of like when you aren't allowed to focus on the stress of what to do, you realize what you don't want to do. I don't want to mess this up. This is a big part of who I am and telling him will mean the world to me. I need to know he will still want to be with me," I said.

Natalia nodded a little. "That makes sense. Do what you feel is right. As long as he gets to know, it's good. He has a right to know who he's dating."

That got through to me, stressing me out once again. He had a right to know who he was involved with romantically.

He had no idea who I was. I feared his reaction when I did tell him. Would he hate me? Would he be afraid? Would he never want to see me again? I hated asking these questions, but they were necessary because they were possibilities to the truth of me exposing my past and the magic that came with it.

I PACED AROUND MY room and Natalia watched me, not really commenting on it. "I just can't for the life of me figure out how to do this. How am I supposed to tell him? How is he going to feel about my magic? I controlled him and telling him that is terrifying!"

"I'm sure he'll know you weren't doing it intentionally," she corrected while holding up her index finger to point it out.

"I don't give a damn about intentions. Intent and impact are not the same. I'm dating my best friend and I have to tell him what I did and I'm not sure how he will take that. What if he judges me as the mermaids do? What if he can't stand to be around me? I will lose my best friend! I will lose my only chance at love." I sat on my bed, looking at the floor.

Natalia came over and hugged me. "Hey, don't you worry. We've been over this. You will have your chance. You deserve to be with someone."

"Do you believe in soulmates?"

"No."

"Then you can't say I will get my chance. You can't truly believe that. I have nothing to keep me going if this fails. Dylan means so much to me. I want to be with him forever. I want him to accept me as I am. That's why this is such a big deal. If he rejects me, I will be heartbroken." I looked at her.

Natalia sat next to me and nodded. "I know what it's like to hide who you are, to be afraid to tell your best friend the truth. I was terrified to tell you that I like girls, but you were there for me. You didn't look at me differently. I know that if he's worth it, he'll accept you with magic, too. If he doesn't, he was never worth it to begin with. I don't believe in soulmates, Mia, but I believe that someone out there is willing to see us as people. The man who's worth it will accept you. You just have to be patient. You're still barely an adult. It's not worth stressing over."

I sighed and shook my head. "I have to figure this out on my own. It's my problem. He's my boyfriend and my best friend and I will eventually have to tell him that I controlled him with my magic, and about Jason and what he did to me. I'm not the hero in this story, Nat. I'm the villain and Dylan deserves to know."

Twenty-four

I STEPPED FOOT ONTO the grass, taking a deep breath. It had been over six months since I was here, but it was much more surreal. I had changed since I'd last been here. I'd now taken my full form.

Nat had given me the green light to come here and do some more research on myself and the whole mermaid and siren rivalry. She said she could handle being alone at the apartment for a while. Besides, it was *only* an hour drive.

I walked up to the front door and let myself in. I arrived at the office to obtain my visitor's badge. "Mia, hello!" a woman yelled.

With a smile, I waved. "Mrs. Goffer, hi. I came back to do some research on my history again."

"It's good to see you." She came around the counter and gave me a hug. "You're eighteen now. May I ask about your transformation?"

"It was amazing. I finally feel at home in the ocean, like I belong."

She gave me a warm smile. "I'm happy to hear that. I'm

glad you're enjoying it. That's always our goal here. We want every student to embrace their heritage and be themselves." She grabbed a sticker with the word visitor on it.

I wrote my name and stuck it onto my shirt. "My best friend and I got an apartment together. Even better, we're dating."

Her eyes lit up. "Oh, a new boyfriend?" After what went down during the seven years I lived here, it was news to hear me get as far as getting a boyfriend.

I nodded. "Yes. I'm here to help with finding a way to tell him more about myself. I want to tell him the truth, but I'm just stumped on how to do it."

Mrs. Goffer went back behind the counter. "Of course. We're always glad to see you. I have to get back to talking to the principal about one of our students, but it was so good to see you."

"It's good seeing you, too." I left the office, taking in the familiar smell of the academy. It smelled of the ocean—a strong scent of sea salt. It lingered here to help students feel more at ease. It helped us get ready to become what we were always meant to be, creatures from the water.

I stopped walking, scanning my surroundings. I'd spent my entire teenage years here, and it was not the prettiest era of my childhood.

On the outside, this building looked like a large castle with different wings and towers. These areas were designated for specific sea creatures and their lore. Bricks made up the structure, securing it for centuries to come.

Inside, the color scheme was that of light blue, white and gold to fit with the uniforms. The walls were split in half, lengthwise. The bottom half was the light blue color of the ocean. The top half was white with a gold trim between the two colors to tie it all together in a neat way.

The floors were covered in white tiles, and the ceiling was white as well. The doors were light brown in color with small square windows towards the top.

Lockers didn't line the walls since the academy had dorms instead. Dorms were on the bottom floor, in the basement.

As I walked down the hall, I noticed all the offices on both sides. I'd been in all of them at least once. Main office, counselor's office, and the nurse's office.

I took a left at the end of the hall, heading towards the library. There was an equal amount of structure on each side of the main front hall. Classrooms lined each side on this floor and the floor above us. The library was towards the back of the school, which was an odd place for it.

When I recognized the doors to the gym, I stopped to look at some kids inside as they played sports. I remembered this place the most.

I narrowed my eyes, walking up to him. "You just refuse to quit."

He shrugged. "You messed with my hair. This is war now."

"I don't understand why you hate me so much. So I used to stuff my bra, whatever! Being a girl with small boobs is hard. I don't know why this has come as far as it has."

He crossed his arms. "You're fun to mess with. You're an easy target."

I lifted my hand, slapping him as hard as I could. My hand stung but it felt so good to finally do something bold.

His cheek was a bright red shade, and when he looked at me, his jaw dropped. "What the hell?" he shouted at me.

"That makes you just as easy of a target if we're at war. There

are two sides to this. I'm fighting back. Try to keep up, Jason." I backed away and turned on my heel, smirking to myself. It felt so good to show him how I felt about him after he tried to drown me.

I came back to reality and glanced at the floor. I didn't have to worry about him anymore. He could no longer hurt me.

I walked further down the hall, stopping at an area with a dead end. He had tainted my perspective in every inch of this building. A new bad memory surfaced.

Pain exploded in my back as he pushed me against the wall. "Take it back, now!" he yelled in my face.

I shook my head, fearing what he was capable of. More than anything I wanted to take advantage of what I was and use it to control him, but I vowed to never control a man like that.

"Take it back or you're going to regret it," he threatened.

"I refuse to let you scare me into submission. I will never give you the power."

He gripped my arms with so much strength that his fingers began to draw blood. "You made this choice." He let go of me and I made the mistake of thinking it was over.

His fist met my nose and I heard a crack. I screamed out and dropped to the floor. I tried to catch all the blood in my hands, but it was spilling onto the white tiles, staining it with my mistake. "What are you?" I whispered, looking at him.

He backed away, shaking his hand a bit. "That's none of your business. Stop pretending you're so innocent. You know what you are. Use your power to kill me."

I didn't respond and he scoffed, abandoning me in the hall.

I swallowed, wiping the tears from my cheeks. The floor was still stained a light pink color. He was the real bully all those years. I never told anyone because I knew what their response would be. They'd criticize the way I handled it. They would tell me to use my abilities to take advantage of him and hurt him the way he did me. I refused to kill him.

Forgetting the memories was difficult, even as I continued down the hall. These were the nightmares I didn't want to dwell on. Just as soon as I dreaded it, I passed the bathrooms and closed my eyes as another memory hit me.

As I ran into the girl's bathroom, I grabbed the counter while the cries grew louder. I wanted to leave this awful place. I wanted to be like them. I wanted to be anyone but myself.

Natalia came in after me and bent down as I fell to the floor. She grabbed my face. "Tell me what he did. Now."

"He..." I choked on my cobs, barely able to breathe. "He made me eat it..."

Natalia was livid. Her eyes darkened—pitch black. She let go of me and clenched her fists. "That prick is going to pay. I swear he is going to pay."

I didn't really have the option to care if she fought my battles for me. I couldn't find them at this point. She had my back when I had no strength.

"I'll be back." She left the bathroom, and I scooted under the counter, hugging my knees. I tried to silence my crying, but I failed. The worst part was how delicious it was, as if I'd never had anything that made my taste buds dance with joy.

I grabbed onto the wall for support, taking deep breaths. I never knew what Natalia had done to him, but I never asked. I hated the memories I had of this place. It was strange how the trauma overshadowed the best parts. If the trauma were extreme enough, the brain would even go as far as completely erasing the memory. I wished my brain did such a thing.

The library came into sight and I entered, sitting in the

armchair in the corner. I despised every memory that involved Jason. I needed a moment to myself to really breathe.

The library was full of color, and every color. It was meant to be so vibrant to stimulate the brain.

I couldn't be more thankful for Natalia for taking me under her wing and accepting me. She was the light at the end of the tunnel. I would be lost without her. I would have never survived otherwise.

It wasn't as bad when I had first arrived here. Everything was very normal. It wasn't until I tried to hang out with the mermaids that they began to single me out.

They knew I wasn't one of them. They judged me for it.

Once Jason had drowned me, things took a real turn. I had spent so much time hiding in my dorm. Natalia noticed this and tried to get me out and into the world again. This is where she noticed how people really treated me.

As we got older, I finally bloomed after the bra stuffing incident. Natalia decided to get revenge on Jason for everything he started. This is what led down the path of our war, back and forth pranks. Those pranks eventually turned into full-on bullying and the bullied started fighting back.

I never told her what happened at his dorm that first day. In her mind, it was just bullying after playing a prank about wanting to take me on a date.

He had caused emotional pain and then turned to physical pain. Natalia was always aware, and she would help me get revenge. It wasn't long before the teachers found out what was really going on.

With Natalia and me fighting for the truth, Jason was exposed. He was only suspended, unfortunately. After a week, he came back. We continued our war from that point on but Natalia made sure that she was always nearby so he wouldn't try anything stupid.

It was the only thing that kept me safe. *She* kept me safe.

When we all graduated from the academy, he went home and I was thankful to never see his face again. Losing Natalia after graduation was the hardest part. When I found out Dylan was still next door, I was more than excited to have a friend to lean on again, and especially one I had grown up with.

Getting to know Dylan again was much more fun. I didn't regret the way things have gone. Kissing him was the best decision I made. My biggest worry about telling him the truth relied on the fact that Jason had completely used my identity against me. I hated that so much. If Dylan did the same thing, I would never be able to come back from the broken place in my mind.

More than anything else I have ever needed in my life, I needed Dylan to accept me. I had to tell him sooner than later because if I fell in love with him, it would be much worse when he rejected me.

I was going to find out more about how to properly go about this. I just had to do a few things first. My first task was to research the history of the siren and mermaid rivalry. I needed to get down to the very last word of why the two sides were such enemies, but I had to be prepared for what I could uncover.

My fingers brushed over the spines of different books. I had time to spend today, and I realized I'd never taken time to learn about the other creatures I shared the sea with.

Picking out a book, I started reading about selkies.

There was so much different lore about each one, all

ranging in different cultures. The main one was the Scottish mythology of the selkies. I had seen them around the school, but they seemed so different from us.

According to this history of them, there were men and women selkies, but their love stories were different. Women had tragic love stories all throughout history and it involved them being coerced into relationships and marriages with humans. The selkies were believed to be half human and half seal in some places, but in Scotland, they were not like that. They had sealskin that was worn while they were at sea, but on land, they would shed it and become human.

Women came upon the issue with men always stealing their skin and hiding it, forcing these women to marry these human men. It never went well.

However, with men, they would shed their skin and search the land for women to marry. It wasn't as tragic because men weren't being forced into anything and the option to migrate back to the sea was still there.

I never had too many selkies in any of my classes. Most of my classes revolved around my own mythology.

I placed the book back on the shelf, moving onto the next creature. I laughed to myself, realizing I had picked up the book about nymphs. What didn't I know that Natalia hadn't already taught me? I skipped to the section about water nymphs and started reading. Most of this mythology stemmed from Greek mythology.

Everything Natalia had told me was in this book, and some things she didn't mention. Nymphs were found in bodies of freshwater, and not just any body of water.

Nymphs were only female, and male nymphs didn't exist. Nymphs were not immortal, but they did live a long life, longer than humans. A lot of nymphs tend to have captured the heart of men, which is what sirens and nymphs shared. However, unlike sirens, nymphs could attract anyone. Sirens could only attract the opposite sex when they sang to their heart's desire, and since sirens were also all female, men were always the victims.

I yawned, putting the book back. I sat down, snacking on some crackers to pass the time. I needed a small break from reading. I wondered if I would find anything on Jason. I wanted to know what he was. Was he like me or was he completely different?

People like me were supposed to be evil and yet I refused to fall into that mold.

I watched students come and go, checking out new books and returning old ones. You could tell who was who by the books they got. Most students never read history outside their own, and I was no exception. When I went here, I never bothered for that. It was only now that I did it because I was curious. Sometimes that research didn't stay within the lines.

I grabbed a book once again, skimming the basics. These were elementals, but a specific one was talked about more than the rest. Water elementals. They came from Germanic mythology and this one seemed the most interesting to me.

Also known as ondines, they lacked human souls. To attain such a thing and live forever, they would acquire one by marrying a human. Once married, their spouse couldn't cheat or else the water elemental would be fated to die at some point and their purpose to marry for immortality would be broken.

This lore intrigued me the most and I wanted to meet an ondine myself. They didn't have human souls and I wondered what that was like. Mermaids would say I already knew.

I picked up another book, flipping through the pages. This one was about water sprites and spirits.

A water sprite was a fairy that could also breathe underwater. They were completely harmless unless they were threatened. They were considered an elemental spirit.

Moving onto the spirit part, this next one was an actual spirit of the sea. Beginning as aunga, they were good creatures. Once they died, they became adaro, which was an evil spirit that resided in the sea. These were malevolent mermaid-like sea spirits.

Adaro were made up of strictly male creatures that were dangerous.

The flashbacks rushed back to me, clouding my joy as I saw everything Jason did to me. I knew. I knew exactly what he was now. He was an adaro. He was dangerous and evil because the good part of him had died.

I covered my mouth, quickly calling Natalia. She picked up after the second ring. "What's up?"

I squeezed my eyes shut, whispering, "I know what Jason is. He's an adaro. I think I killed Jason."

Natalia choked on the other end. "Say what now?"

"Aunga are the good parts of sea creatures which is what he was and at some point, one of our pranks must have killed him somehow. When he died, he became adaro. They are evil ghosts of aunga, and that's why he became so much worse when I kept pranking him. It was all fun and games until someone got hurt. Jason killed himself but because his spirit didn't die, he is still here. He is here as adaro." Right? Or maybe he was dead before it all began. Aunga wouldn't drown a siren, would they? Maybe. But maybe not. I couldn't tell Natalia that, though.

"But what does this mean for us?" she asked.

"I'm not quite sure. I just... Natalia, what have we done? We killed him. That's two people now that we've murdered." I rubbed my eyes. I knew deep down, this meant he wanted revenge on me alone. I took away his life, didn't I?

She laughed. "Excuse me? He started this shit. He was the bastard who made fun of you for being insecure. All we did was paint his hair and he took it further. You never once laid a hand on him. He broke your nose. He forced you to eat that meat."

"That's not entirely true."

She stopped talking to question my answer. "What do you mean?"

"I mean... I did lay a hand on him. I slapped him."

"Good for you! He deserves it for how he treated you."

I laid back, getting the side eye from the librarian. "Nat, we still bullied the bully. How is that any good? We are no better than him for perpetrating this war. It would've looked better if we didn't antagonize him."

Natalia sighed. "Don't start with that, Mia. Don't you dare tell me that you believe we are in the wrong. He made fun of you for years. He forced you to eat the meat of a human man. He broke your nose for telling the school about his little accident," she paused.

"I just believe it wouldn't have gotten as far as it did if we just left it. All it did was make everything worse. He really hurt me and now he's an evil ghost of some sea creature that looks like a human, shark, and swordfish had a baby."

"Huh?"

I pushed hair behind my ear and nodded. Of course, she couldn't see me. "They look human, have tail fins, have the dorsal fin of a shark and the swordfish spear on their forehead. That's his true form."

"Oh, that is rich. This. We can use this," she commented.

"No, damnit, Nat!" The librarian gave me a look and I returned her an apologetic look. "We can't continue this. We can't. We already killed him."

"For all we know, he could've known what was going to happen after he died. He could've committed suicide on purpose to gain more power and anger to take you out. Either that or he just couldn't handle his own medicine so he committed suicide and this happened," Natalia argued.

"That's not a good thing."

"No, but it still isn't our fault. Did we kill him? No. He ultimately made that choice. He started all this shit and he should've expected this to happen." She cleared her throat.

I chewed my lip. "We still made it worse and now I have to live with this guilt and trauma. It's my pain to bear."

Twenty-five

The siren had dropped the bones into the ocean, using the water to wash away the blood that dripped from her lips. She looked at the mermaid that came her way. The mermaid stopped, keeping her distance.

"What is your business?" the siren asked her.

"I have come to tell you that you need to stop with your appetite. It is getting far too risky for the mermaids and sirens to continue down this path."

The siren scoffed. "We are not a team. If anything, you risk the exposure more. We eat men and they simply go on a missing person report. You fall in love with them and tell them our secrets."

"Our secrets? We are not the same, Nadia," the mermaid replied.

Nadia floated in the water, barely listening to the mermaid. "Oh, but we are almost the same. We look alike. We are only different in our need for men. You want babies. We want food." She waved her hand as if to dismiss the mermaid's use for men.

"I am here to warn you to be careful. If you know it's good for

you, you'll listen." The mermaid started swimming the other way, looking back at the siren.

Nadia hissed, baring her shark-like teeth. She closed her mouth, smirking and playing with her hair. "Don't act so threatened, Adeline. It's not the sirens you have to fear."

I was engrossed in this backstory, and I had to know more. The history of our kind was even more intriguing. Mermaids and sirens were the craziest of all, and they despised each other. They never expected either side to defy the odds the way I was.

"What have you done?" Adeline yelled to Nadia.

Nadia gave her a look and shook her head. "I knew this day was coming. I was trying to protect you, believe it or not. We are different but we are the same. We are practically cousins, and we must stick together."

"Protect me? You ate the love of my life! How is that good for me? I can never forgive you for this."

Nadia sighed. "He was going to hurt you. He was going to use you. I could not let you love the wrong man. This quarrel is not with the sirens. This isn't about our disagreement on how men should be used. This is about the safety of sea creatures and our existence. He was going to expose all of us."

Adeline refused to believe it was true. Backing away, she shook her head, repeating the same words, "You're lying. He loved me."

"Listen to me. He was going to use you as evidence. I was saving you from the evil of man."

"You were hungry, and he was the easy target. This is just an excuse to get you out of the cage. You're not. I will never forgive you for what you have done. I will make sure all the mermaids know about this. Watch your back, Nadia. All

future generations will suffer because of your actions," Adeline warned.

"The man was later found dead with scales under his fingernails. Some said the sirens murdered him. Others say it was a mermaid fighting for her life," Calliopé said. "It's hard to say who is right, but sirens have never had ill intentions. Mermaids just gave us that trait themselves."

I swallowed. The entire feud began over a misunderstanding. Now the mermaids judged the sirens for trying to protect them. We were not the bad guys. We were the ones who were wrongly judged, and the mermaids had taken it too far. They refused to see another side to things. The mermaids refused to believe that sirens could in any way make good decisions.

As far as I was concerned, the mermaids were the evil ones.

"How do you know this?" I asked.

Kysana grabbed the edge of the ledge and pulled herself up. "We've traveled a lot, Mia. We told you. The legend in every single city is the same. And in other countries, where sirens and mermaids began, they have old books recording our history. Generations of families writing down their ancestry, to make sure their story was told the way it was meant to be told."

"Where are these books?" Was I going to swim there? No. It'd take days just to swim across the oceans. "Where did sirens and mermaids originate from?" Everyone knew vampires came from Romania, and selkies came from Scotland. But where did *we* come from?

"Not the same place," Calliopé said. "Mermaids actually came from Syria originally. Sirens come from Greece. Sure, they're not far from each other. That's probably why the two came across each other, and realized they were alike. Before mermaids turned on us and turned us into the villain, that is."

Greece. My ancestors were Greek.

Sure, a lot of people had confused us with the other kind of sirens. The beautiful woman with the legs of a bird. However, they had male sirens in their species. We didn't. We were similar in many ways, but this was not one of them. We were in the water, and they the sky.

"Do the bird sirens still exist?" I asked.

Calliopé folded her arms and laid them across the ledge. "If by exist you mean not extinct, then yes. But they're few and far between. Endangered in our world. To find a siren with the legs of a bird is unheard of, and if you do find them, they will kill you if you don't kill them first."

"Okay, and one last question. Do they transform like us, or are always they in their natural form?"

She shrugged. "They're long gone, Mia. Why does this matter?"

"Because I'm trying to figure out what Jason may be." However, even if he were a siren from the sky, he wouldn't have reason to hate me. Would he? No, certainly not. Even if the mermaids did befriend him and turn him against me. Besides, he went to a school for sea creatures. He would only be there if he were from the water.

Kysana grabbed my hand. "It's over now."

I wasn't so sure about that.

What I was sure of, was that we really weren't so different from mermaids. People loved to depict us as the evil versions of our loveable counterparts, but they had no clue. Mermaids, too, could be evil. Like them, we could also be good. Nobody was destined to be someone they weren't.

I refused to fit into the mold society created for me.

"What does Dylan think?" Calliopé asked with a bit of irritation in her voice.

"About me? Dylan loves it. He thinks it's the coolest thing ever, that I can just put people in a trance by singing. I'd never use it. I'd never seen anyone react the way he did. He's the strangest human I've ever met."

Yet the one I was falling in love with.

Kysana giggled beside me. "Have you guys had sex?"

My cheeks burned. "Kysana, that's personal."

Calliopé smirked. "It's only personal if you make it personal. Just answer the question, Mia. Have you possibly had sex?"

"And do what, risk getting pregnant? No. Never. Dylan is wonderful, but we're taking things slow. And I love that about him, you know. I love that he's enjoying what we have and not pushing it." I slipped into the water. "Now who's with me to go get some food?"

Kysana gasped. "Me! What kind of food?"

I was craving fries at a time like this. With barbecue sauce.

Calliopé grabbed my wrist and twisted me in the water to face her. She backed me into the wall of the cave, trapping me. "Don't."

"What?"

"Don't have sex with him. Sex can be terrible, Mia. If you're so certain that you're the good guy here, you can never have sex with him." Was this a horror movie? What the hell?

My blood began to boil. "It is not your place to tell me what to do. And I will not keep myself closed off forever. Someday I want to have sex with him." Saying that out loud tasted spicy in many ways.

"You know that sirens are born from violence, correct?"

In a skeptical tone, I said, "No."

"If you want to prove you're the good guy, you can't get pregnant. Dylan's sperm determines the sex of your baby, and if that sperm happens to have the X chromosome, you will end up brutally killing someone when you conceive a siren." She backed away, allowing me to breathe.

My hands began to shake at just the thought. Hearing her say that out loud made it feel real. When I was conceived, I'd killed someone just so I could come to life. How evil was that?

"And what about mermaids, Calliopé? Would that mean they also kill people when they conceive girls?"

Kysana closed all the space between us, pressing her lips to my shoulder. "We're not so different from them. They just want to pretend we are."

Mermaids were killers just as much as we were, and for what? Sex? Babies? And what sickened me the most was knowing that mermaids were the ones who had more sex than we did. Did they even know what they were doing to humans? Of course they had to know. They had so proudly bullied me, so what would it mean to them if a human died so they could get pregnant? They'd call it a sacrifice.

Now my appetite was gone. I didn't want to eat fries with the thought that if I ever wanted kids, I'd have to end a life. The answer seemed so simple. I was never getting pregnant, and I'd have to explain that to Dylan.

"You could always just skip the brutal murder and bite someone to make them a siren," she said.

"And force an innocent person into this life? Like what happened to you? No thanks." I pushed my hair back. "What happens if we bite a man? You said we could bite a woman and she turns, but why? Why wouldn't the same happen to a man if we bite him?"

"You know the answer to that, Mia."

Maybe I did. Maybe our saliva didn't react well with a male's blood, yet it clung to females.

"And what if we bite a mermaid?"

Calliopé sighed. "What's with the questions?"

I lowered my head. "I'm sorry. I can't ask my mom anything. I was just curious." If we bit mermaids, what would happen? And how did one become a mermaid? Could they bite humans, too?

"I'm not your damn encyclopedia. Please, stop."

"I'm going to go," I said before quickly swimming out of the cave. When I arrived at the shore, I pulled myself out of the water. Maybe I'd have to bite a mermaid to find out. Calliopé was already sick of me, so why bother her anymore? If vampires bit werewolves, could they turn? Maybe it was like with mermaids, too.

The question lingered at the back of my mind, gnawing at me. There was only one way to ease these curiosities, but they certainly killed cats. Was I willing to give up my life to find out? I might not have a choice. The mermaids were the enemy, and they'd never stop bullying us. The only way to make them see our side of things was to make them like us.

They told me that I'd never be able to fit in, and I'd always be like the monsters who kill for food. It was now my move, and I was going to prove to them they were right. And it would cost them their life for wanting to be right about me all along. They'd never even see it coming. Deep down they knew I wasn't like others who lived in the sea, but they were afraid to admit that.

And much to their demise, they were right about who I really was.

Twenty-six

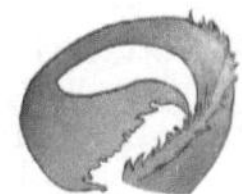

Calliopé hadn't completely forgiven me for accusing her of killing Harrison Peterson, but Kysana was already my friend again. According to her, the two of them were only eating men who proved to be bad people.

Despite our feud, I *still* had questions. "What do you two know about aunga and adaro?"

Calliopé glanced at me. "Why?"

"I think the boy who used to bully me is that. He was once an aunga, and now he's an adaro." I coughed. "I...have this theory that maybe the killer I've been searching for is Jason. I think he's been trying to get back at me by doing what I refuse to do—kill innocent men for food."

Kysana nodded. "It makes sense."

Calliopé sighed. "And why do you call him a bully?"

Was she really asking me such a stupid question? "Because he would play pranks on me. He drowned me before I turned. He forced me to eat human flesh. He hit me. I know for a fact he was a bully. He *is* a bully. He's an adaro."

With a nod, she said, "Were you friends before? When he

was still aunga?"

"Never. He's always been rude to me."

"Has he been adaro this whole time?"

I furrowed my brows. "Well, I mean... no? I can't say for sure. All I know is aunga are good creatures and adaro are the evil spirits left behind when aunga die."

"Sounds to me like he was adaro before you met him, if he's been a bully the entire time." She shrugged.

I had wanted to argue with her and say she was wrong, but I came up with nothing. According to the facts, aunga were good creatures. Jason had always made fun of me, which meant he'd been killed before I ever met him. Someone else had killed him, but who? Why?

Either way, something made him snap. He'd been evil the entire time I knew him, yet he got far worse at one point.

I scratched my neck, taking a deep breath. "The real question is how do I take him down? If he's already dead."

Calliopé glanced at Kysana with a small smirk on her lips. "We can help."

"Is that a good idea?" I asked.

She swam closer. "We love a good battle, and this boy sounds like the kind of man we need to kill. Everyone wins."

I swallowed. Was I okay with killing Jason? What other choice did I have? He was dead and if he continued in this state, he'd hurt everyone around me. He was long gone. Whoever Jason was before I met him was long gone.

Lifting my palms to the moon, I looked at Calliopé. "Do I have the ability to control other creatures that aren't sirens?"

Something dark flashed in her eye as she grabbed my hands like delicate flowers. "Absolutely. You have all the power, Mia. The magic is yours to do with what you will."

Kysana giggled. "This is going to be so much fun!"

"What will Dylan think of me?" That was a question I couldn't answer. Did I want to?

Calliopé shrugged. "He must understand that you're going to be a hero. You must protect yourself and others. The world isn't so black and white, is it? You should know this personally."

She was right. The world wasn't black and white. Murder wasn't wrong just because it shed blood. There were factors to consider, and if I really thought about it, I was saving Jason from himself. He had no control over the evil spirit that he was. He was almost like a zombie, and I was asked to put him out of his misery.

"Have you ever cared about someone the way I do Dylan?" I cleared my throat.

Calliopé shook her head. "I don't plan to. If you ask me, love is stupid. I'm a siren, not a mermaid. I need men for one purpose and that's to feed my appetite. I don't need to get pregnant, nor do I want to. To answer your buried question, do I care what Dylan will think of you? No. He's a human. He's prey. But I also believe that if he doesn't see the hero in you for protecting yourself and others, then he's not worth your time, is he?"

Kysana hugged herself. "I loved someone once."

"Who?"

She shivered. "He's gone now. It doesn't matter anymore."

I studied her expression, concluding that whoever she loved had deeply hurt her. People could be so cruel.

Calliopé stepped back, leaning against a rock. "You can't practice your magic on Kysana and I but we can get someone who's willing to be a pawn."

I furrowed my eyebrows. "I can't practice on anyone. You said my magic has consequences on the people who fall victim to it."

She shrugged. "And it does. But how else do you practice?"

She made a good point, but I wasn't about to hurt anyone who was innocent. Not now that I knew all magic came with a price. All siren magic did.

Calliopé's lips curved upward as she crossed her arms. "How about Dylan?"

"No. No. I will never use my magic on him. My loved ones are off limits." I shook my head, sitting down on a rock across from her. The waves rolled up onto the shore, but they didn't quite reach our toes.

Kysana walked towards the road. "Let me get someone! I have the perfect person."

Calliopé and I said nothing as Kysana disappeared. She was gone for quite a while, but the silence was more peaceful than awkward. It gave Calliopé time to forgive me of my mistake and gave me time to reflect on myself.

"Perfect," Calliopé said.

I looked in the direction she was. Kysana stood there with the same boy who I'd saved from them but was now questioning his own sanity. He was already damaged. How much worse could I make him?

With my palms up, I said, "Sit down."

The boy did exactly as I said.

I took my magic one step at a time, keeping in mind that my energy was limited. The boy did simple tasks, before I started moving him towards bigger things. "Walk into the ocean."

He walked into the ocean, but he didn't stop. Damnit, I should have told him to stop.

"Stop." But he didn't stop. "No, I said stop!"

"Mia," Calliopé warned, grabbing my hands.

"Why isn't he stopping?" I yelled.

When we glanced at my palms, they weren't glowing. My magic had run out. No. This wasn't happening. No.

"Save him!" I ran towards the water, diving into the waves and searching for him. I grabbed the boy who had lost all consciousness and was now floating in the abyss. I swam back to the shore and laid him down in the sand. I leaned over him, doing chest compressions. "Come on, please. Wake up," I begged.

The longer I did chest compressions, the more hope I lost.

Kysana grabbed my shoulders and pulled me back, holding me against her chest. "He's gone, Mia."

My chest tightened, throat closing in on itself. Before I had time to process it, my cheeks were burning from the hot tears.

Calliopé dragged his body back to the ocean, letting it float away with the waves. "You did the right thing. He wasn't sane anymore. You sent him to a better place. You can't hate yourself for that."

I buried my face in Kysana's chest, refusing to look at Calliopé. He was the first boy I ever directly killed. I tried hard to tell everyone I wasn't like the rest of them, and I failed. I was a killer.

Calliopé sat beside Kysana and I. "I'm sorry."

She wasn't. This wasn't like having sex for the first time and having it go horribly wrong. You could always try again. You could get better.

I had *killed* a man. I took a life. This was something I never wanted to do. This was a first I never wanted to experience. I couldn't take it back.

When all my tears had dried up, Kysana let me go and I walked to my parents' house. I couldn't hide the tears. My parents were waiting for me, and Mom was ready to scold me for going to the beach, but Dad stood up first.

"Mia, what happened?" he asked.

I stared at the floor, unable to face my parents. They would never love me again. "I killed him."

Mom jumped up from the couch, but Dad held her back. "What do you mean? Who?"

"I met these two sirens, and they only eat men who are bad people. They've been helping me learn more about myself and my magic. I had stopped them from eating a boy one night, but Calliopé warned me that my magic is of evil nature, and I saw that I saved the boy, but he went insane. He wasn't normal anymore." I gulped. "We thought it wouldn't hurt to practice my magic on him since he was already hurt. But I didn't have enough energy to stop him from drowning and...and..." I choked.

Mom looked at Dad. "Let me handle this."

He nodded and left us alone in the living room.

I had expected Mom to shout at me or take away all my freedom. I didn't expect her to hug me, but she did. She held me in her arms and placed a kiss on my head. "You didn't mean to, Mia. You didn't mean to."

Did intention matter? No.

She pulled away, holding my head in her hands. "Look at me. You are not a monster. You are not a bad guy. You were just...a product of my failure."

"What?"

Closing her eyes for a second, she readjusted her emotions. "I refused to teach you about yourself. I forbid you from being who you are. I figured you weren't ready to meet other sirens in the ocean. I thought you couldn't handle any of that kind of magic and I forgot that you'd want to learn exactly what your magic does."

It was the first time I'd heard my mom blame herself for what I did.

"You're young. You want to do the opposite of what I tell you. It was wrong of me to expect you to stay away from the ocean and never use your magic." She wrapped her hands around mine. "Let me help you."

Did I hear that right? "Help me?"

"Let me help you learn more about sirens. I'll answer all your questions. I'll help you practice your magic in a safe environment and teach you how to control it." She glanced at the moon, lifting her palm. "I can help."

I swallowed. What kind of magic did my mom have? It made sense that I couldn't learn very well around Calliopé and Kysana. They weren't purebred. They had *no* magic.

A smile formed on my lips as I nodded. "Yes, please. Help me control it."

Guilt had a strong hold on me from what I did to that boy, but with my mom's help, I could ensure that mistake would never be made again. I was going to make sure my magic was used for good. No matter how hard I tried, it would be used for good reasons.

"What is your ability?" I asked Mom.

She tilted her head. "You ready to know the truth?"

"I've been ready."

Mom lifted her chin, stepping back to demonstrate what she could do. All the lights in the house turned off, and the aura around my mom glowed a bright white as she stepped forward. When the glow died down, I almost choked. I'd never once realized I hadn't seen my mom in her siren form before, yet here she was.

Every siren I knew had one tail to swim through the ocean the fastest. I knew it was rare, but not impossible to have two tails. My mom had the ability to create an extra tail and she could do it on *dry land*.

Twenty-seven

"WHAT DOES IT MEAN now that I've killed a boy?" I glanced at my mom.

She brought a book from the closet, laying it on the counter in front of me. "There's this ritual that sirens have. They have a rite of passage into the siren world of the deepest waters. The rite of passage for every siren is to kill, but things got twisted over the years."

"Why?" I looked at the book.

Mom sighed. "Sirens were not always the bad guys. The worst thing we do is eat human flesh, but is that our fault? Mermaids must seduce human men to reproduce. That's not so innocent, either, but we were painted as the bad guys." She pointed to the same story I'd heard. "Nadia saved Adeline, but Adeline saw the worst in her because she got blinded by love."

"So why do sirens require a rite of passage now if we aren't supposed to be the bad guys?"

She laughed. "Mia, are you listening at all? Because sirens eat human flesh. Back then, they didn't have the option of getting their meat from a morgue like we do. They had to kill, and for every teen girl, that first kill was like a sixteenth birthday. It was her door into womanhood. She was embracing part of who she was."

I made a face of disgust. "They celebrated murder."

"In a way, yes. They had to teach their daughters how to hunt properly without leaving a trace. If one got caught, our entire species would be in danger. It was about survival more than anything. What happened to the boy who drowned?"

I crossed my arms. "Calliopé pushed his body into the ocean."

"Good. It'll look like a drowning. We don't need you caught up in any more crimes." She cleared her throat. "Who are these siren friends of yours?"

If Mom would approve or not, I couldn't tell. But I couldn't lie. "Calliopé and Kysana aren't...purebred. Like you and me. They don't have moms who are sirens. They were bitten by other sirens. They don't have any magic. They live in the ocean."

Mom nodded. "They probably ran away from home when they turned. Sirens do that when they can't hide their new life. They have human parents, Mia. Their parents won't understand them like I understand you."

My eyes glossed over as I fought to hide back some tears. "They don't have any family. That's not fair."

She pushed some of my hair back. "I know. But they have you to keep them company. You're strong. I trust you to keep true to yourself."

Calliopé and Kysana had to be around my age, right? Kysana said she was probably eighteen. Sirens aged like humans. We didn't live long, and I knew that even after they were bitten, they continued to age at a normal pace. How young were they when they turned?

Mom pointed to the book. "Each purebred siren gets one magical gift. You saw mine. You know yours. Mastering it can be tough and using it without hurting others can be impossible, but that's not always true. It'll take work to use it for good."

"If that's true, I'm willing to try." I looked at my hands. "But I lose energy so quickly."

"How much do you know about your magic?"

"Enough. Mana magic is the kind that needs an energy source, and my magic comes from the moon. I can only use it at night when the moon is out."

She nodded. "True. Now, do you want to know the secret to recharging your magic without having to wait it out?"

I lifted both eyebrows in surprise. "You can do that?"

Laughing, Mom said, "Of course. Mia, I wasn't always the daughter who listened to the rules. When I discovered my gift, I was eager to learn more. I found ways around things so I could use my magic faster and use more of it without getting weak."

Mom led us outside into the backyard.. We looked up at the moon, and she pointed to it. "The trick is to use up all the energy around you. You can steal the moon's energy. It's like a charging cable. Instead of just sticking it into the port and waiting for it to take its time, you suck it out of the cable."

"You can't do that."

"Humans can't but we aren't human, are we?" She lifted her hands. "Then as you're sucking out the energy, it gives you the ability to take energy from the people around you."

I crossed my arms. "The price paid for stealing energy is that everyone else gets weak."

"Yes. Magic has its limits. I found loopholes and those loopholes have their own rules." She gestured to the moon. "Try it."

I lifted my palms and tried to take all the energy for myself, but I fell to the ground. I looked over at my mom who was removing all the energy, including mine.

"You have to try harder. I'm not the only siren who knows about this method. There are others who will take it from you. You have to fight back and steal it from me." She nodded.

Taking her advice, I pushed myself off the cement and stood. I closed my eyes, holding my palms put for the moon to recharge. I imagined sucking it out, then taking it all from my mother.

When I opened my eyes, my mom was on the ground. "That's good."

I closed my fists. "I'm sorry."

"Sorry for what? I'm proud of you. You're learning and that's the best way to control your magic." She stood up, taking a deep breath.

"How can I use my magic for good?" I coughed. "I've used it on Dylan and Christian before. They were fine. I think."

"You did what?"

"It wasn't on purpose... Sorta." I shook my head. "But they're okay, right?"

Mom shrugged. "I suppose, but there's a way magic will turn against you. It finds its way back to its purpose."

"Are we considered evil for needing the moon to use magic, eating humans, and having magic known for wickedness?"

She frowned. "No, we are not evil. Our magic has dark purposes, but they're not inherently evil. When you make a mistake and feel the consequences, does that make you evil?

No. For every action, there is a reaction. This isn't so black and white, and it *is* possible to use your magic for good. You have to find a way to manipulate that darkness into thinking it's lighter than it is." Mom nodded, pointing to me. "When you killed that boy, you saved him from a life of insanity. That's a good reason, and it might seem dark but it's not about good or bad. It's about how you use it."

The trick was to manipulate my magic into thinking its purpose was more than evil. That didn't seem so simple, but I'd have to try.

Dad peeked out of the back door. "Honey, you coming to bed yet?"

Mom looked at him and nodded. "In a moment."

Dad went back inside.

Mom patted my shoulder. "You're making progress. You must practice hard, but I know you'll do it." She smiled a bit. "I have to allow you some freedom if you're going to be a good siren, Mia."

Knowing my mom had some faith in me warmed me on the inside. If she believed I could be better than the rumors, who was I to say she was wrong?

She gave me a kiss on the head before going inside.

"Hey there, neighbor," Dylan said from the back door. "Thought you might be here."

I laughed a little, waving. "Hi."

"What are you doing out so late?"

"I was just...going for a swim." Good idea.

"You always swim in colder weather, don't you?"

I smiled. "I do."

"It's like fifty-five degrees outside."

"Doesn't bother me."

Dylan looked around. “Fine, but why don’t I take you home with me?” he joked.

A blush crept up. “Well, I suppose a ride wouldn’t hurt.”

We went around to the front and got in his car. The ride was mostly silent on the way home but it didn’t bother anyone.

When we got back to the apartment, Dylan and I went inside and locked the door.

“Goodnight, Mimi.”

“Goodnight, Dill Pickle.” I watched him close the door to his room, then I entered my room where Nat was passed out on my bed.

As I sat down, I put some earbuds in and turned on my music. The beat swept me off my feet, taking me to another world. Everything seemed a mess on my own right now, but this trip helped me see the future. It couldn’t rain forever and eventually a rainbow would form as a sign of hope.

Killing that boy was the rain, but my mom stepping up to teach me about myself was the rainbow. What came after that? Sunshine.

Who would be my sunshine?

Maybe it was Dylan. Maybe it was my mother. Maybe it was someone I didn’t know at all. Either way, the weather forecast predicted a sunny day in my near future.

Someone nudged me and I jumped up, screaming. I grabbed my chest and took out an earbud. “Damnit, you scared me.”

Nat groaned. “Go to bed.”

“I’m not tired.”

“Go. To. Bed.”

I crossed my arms. “No.”

She threw a pillow at my head. I gasped, throwing it right

back.

"Why don't you go back *to* bed?" I grabbed my sweater, left the room, and found myself knocking on Dylan's door. He was not too happy about that.

Dylan cleared his throat. "Mimi."

"Nat won't let me stay in my own bedroom without going to bed but I'm not tired."

He chuckled. "Okay, come with me." He grabbed my hand and pulled me in. Dylan closed his door. "I can't exactly sleep either."

"Perfect." I went and sat on his bed, making myself comfortable.

He sat beside me. "Why can't you sleep?"

"Because I'm wide awake." I looked at him. I placed my hand on his, squeezing it. "I just want to spend the rest of our night worry-free."

Dylan gave me a smile. "I can always help with that. Movie? Game?"

"I was thinking of something else," I whispered. I scooted closer and leaned in, kissing him.

Dylan didn't think twice about returning the kiss. Within seconds, our slow kiss had turned into more. Intoxicating and addicting. I lifted my leg over him, straddling him. He placed his hands on my hips and hesitated in taking off my sweater.

I made the move for him, pulling the sweater over my head.

Dylan pulled away, trying to catch his breath. "Mia..."

I placed a hand against his cheek, leaning in for another kiss. "Yes?"

He shook his head. "Mia, I can't."

With a frown, I put a little more space between us. "What?"

He grabbed my hands, holding them in his. "I mean, I want

to but mentally I'm not ready for this step. I care about you, but...I enjoy taking our relationship a little slow."

I backed off, standing up and pulling my sweater back on. I nodded, turning red. "I'm sorry. I didn't mean to rush it."

Dill Pickle smiled a little. "It's okay. That's why I'm telling you now. I love what we have at the moment." He stood up, stepping closer. He pushed hair behind my ear, kissing my forehead. "Let's watch a movie."

With another nod, I hugged myself and looked through the movies. "Which one?"

We chose a movie and laid down in his bed. Part of me was embarrassed for trying to go further, but the other part of me was thankful he made the right decision for us both. I'd let my emotions get the best of me. I had almost risked a small chance at getting pregnant with the boy who barely touched the surface of my demons. It was stupid and careless on my part.

Thankfully, I was dating someone smarter than I was. He saved us both from jumping the gun.

Dylan and I cuddled, but he fell asleep before I did. I glanced at him, smiling a little. I leaned in, kissing his cheek. I whispered, "Don't ever feel the need to change for anyone but yourself. I love you as you are."

Twenty-eight

After what happened the other night, I made sure to keep my distance but not too much distance from Dylan as to not make him feel weird about anything. I didn't tell anyone at all because it wasn't their business, and I wasn't about to embarrass him.

I reminded myself that Dylan was equal in this relationship, and he mattered as much as I did. He wasn't ready, and it was my job to respect that. If I didn't, I was nothing more than a piece of shit.

I didn't mean to say it that way but there was no other way to really say it. Consent was key, and Dylan was everything to me.

During the times that I did end up by myself to give him his space, I took my time to research more about this rite of passage. As much as I didn't want to admit it, I had killed a boy. I was a woman in their eyes.

Those words made me feel sick to my stomach. There was nothing worth celebrating about the murder of an innocent boy.

I walked towards the front door, but Nat stopped me. "Where are you going?"

"I was going to the beach." I looked at her.

"Mia... You've already killed someone. You probably shouldn't go to the beach after that."

"That's not fair."

"Life isn't fair."

"You're supposed to be helping me. You're supposed to be on my side." I thought maybe she was going to let me be me, but she was pulling away. She was pulling me right away from the ocean.

She stepped forward. "I am on your side. Sirens out there are not like you and me. They're killers."

I mumbled, "So am I."

Her eyebrows furrowed inwards as she grabbed my shoulders. "No. Don't you dare talk like that."

"But it's true."

Nat pushed hair from my face and released a sigh. "Mia, the sirens that live in the ocean are not like the ones who live on land. You come from different worlds. Have you ever wondered why your mom tries to keep you away from them?"

"All the time. The answer is so obvious! They kill and we don't. But Calliopé and Kysana are not like that! They are good, Nat. They are trying to change. They want to be better." I shivered. Did someone leave a window open?

Whatever was bottling inside her was about to explode. I'd sent her over the edge this time. "Stop! You're not listening to what I'm telling you, Mia!" She ran all her fingers through her hair, pushing it back and trying to regather her sanity. "Sirens who live in the ocean don't want to befriend humans. They want to kill them."

I shook my head. "Calliopé and Kysana aren't like that."

She grabbed my hand and pulled me to the couch. We both sat, but I didn't have to like it. "They're not like you. They don't watch humans. They don't befriend them or interact with them. They don't see humans struggling to survive. They see them as food. Humans are nothing more than weak prey." She squeezed my hand. "Therefore, these sirens have no connection or empathy for them. They rip them apart with no mercy. They celebrate the rite of passage. They celebrate murder. Your well-being is everything to me and I will not let you surround yourself with people like that."

"Calliopé and Kysana don't celebrate killing. They only eat bad men, and they're doing better. Can't you try to understand it from their point of view for just a second?" I pulled my hand out of hers. "They were humans. They went swimming and got bitten. They had to throw everything they knew away and result in eating flesh to survive. They had nobody to trust. They can't trust humans, so they have a hard time trying to fit in with them. Their entire life was flipped against their will. They are the victims. They're barely even adults."

Natalia turned her head, looking at the floor.

"Can you understand what it's like to be just a little girl who relies on your parents for everything? One day you're eating spaghetti and the next, you're craving human flesh. Their parents would never understand that, so they had to run and raise themselves as little girls in the ocean. This isn't their fault. None of this is what they asked for, and now they're actively working towards changing their diet to be a bit more suitable."

Nat nodded a bit. "Fine, go. Before I change my mind

about them." She'd been there when they almost attacked me. Of course she only saw the bad.

I didn't question anything. I jumped from the couch and ran towards the door. I didn't stop until I came towards the ocean. I found Calliopé and Kysana waiting for me. "Took you long enough," Calliopé said.

I sat down beside them. "Nat wouldn't let me leave the apartment."

"She is very overprotective, isn't she?" Kysana asked. "I wish I had that."

Clearing my throat, I said, "Yes. But she's coming around. After how she met you two... On other news, my mom has agreed to help me. We've spent a lot of time this month practicing my magic. She's been teaching me how to control it."

Calliopé leaned against the rock. "How's that going?"

"It's been good. I'm learning ways to use my magic without running out of energy. Turns out my mom has magic, too. Which I guess makes sense. She's supposed to. But that's not what got me. What got me is that her magic involves her being able to grow an extra tail."

"What?"

"And get this." I leaned closer. "She can do it on dry land."

Kysana widened her eyes. "That's so cool."

I nodded. "Yeah, you think my magic is cool? My mom's is way cooler. Anyway, that's what's been going on with me lately."

Calliopé shrugged. "Not much has been going on with us. There's no sign of that other siren, or whatever creature it is that killed Harrison Peterson. We've kept our eyes out."

"I appreciate that. I'm still searching for any sign of Jason, but I'm sure he's behind it all. He's gotta show up at some point, right?" I placed my hand against my side where he'd left a bruise when he attacked me. I knew it was him. Nobody else had that kind of vengeance towards me.

Calliopé glanced at me. "It's possible. But if that's true, he's hiding out like a coward now. He's afraid to face you with you able to defend yourself."

I laughed. "Well, you're not wrong."

Kysana smiled. "She never is."

As I looked at them both, part of me ached for everything they lost. They were victims and nobody could make me believe otherwise. After today, I don't think Nat would.

"I wanted to ask, if it's okay, how old you were when...you were bitten."

Kysana looked at Calliopé. She nodded, so Kysana spoke first. "I was fifteen." She swallowed. "I was...young. I was with a man I thought loved me but after drinking too much, my state of mind was gone." She squeezed her fingers. "There were very small bits and pieces that I remember, but I could smell his alcohol breath on top of me. He stole my dignity."

"Kysana..." I reached out, grabbing her hand. "That is so disgusting for him to do that to you."

She pulled her hand out of mine. "I woke up naked. Everything hurt. It all felt wrong, and I felt sick to my stomach. I came to the ocean to try and process it. Calliopé found me." She looked at Calliopé. "She saved me. She killed him, and she saved my life. The sirens are not bad people, Mia. They care more than humans do."

I wanted to say she was wrong about humans, but it wasn't my place. Kysana was young. She couldn't be any older than eighteen now. That kind of trauma stuck around forever, and there was a high possibility that she still had nightmares about that night.

Calliopé rubbed her back. "That was the one night I was thankful for being a siren. I was able to bring pain to the monster that forced himself on a girl." She dropped her arm. "But I wasn't always thankful for this life."

I nodded a bit.

"I was turning ten. I remember it was a huge deal. Double digits is big, is it not?" Sorrow swirled around in her blue eyes. "Everyone was so excited for me. My mom and dad planned this boating trip for me. It was my first time seeing the ocean, and it was the best day ever. I saw a whale jump out of the water and pure joy filled every inch of my body. But then we must have hit something, because as I leaned over the rails, the boat jerked, and I fell in."

"Oh no."

"I didn't know how to swim, especially not in this big, vast ocean." She gestured to the ocean in front of us. "My dad jumped in after me, but nobody could find me. I didn't know where I was. I was sinking, but this beautiful woman found me, and she bit me just before I died. I woke up as a siren, and that was the last I saw of my parents."

I crossed my arms. What was so beautiful about that? She'd been just a child, and she lost everything. Her life seemed so perfect and then it was all ripped away. The sirens had a chance to save her, but they hated humans so much that they took someone's child away from them. It was cruel.

"It's over now, Mia. That was a long time ago." She nodded. "It was in the past and this is the present. If I hadn't become a siren, who knows what would have happened? Kysana may have taken her life. That disgusting filth would still be alive.

Things happen for a reason, and I've come to believe that to stay sane," Calliopé said.

She was right, in a way. Had I never met them, I wouldn't be where I am today. Maybe the three of us were meant to be friends. They may not have been purebred. They didn't have magic, or parents who accepted them. However, *I* accepted them. They were my friends, and they were sirens just as much as I was.

I approached Kysana and Calliopé, wrapping my arms around them both. "I'm thankful for both of you."

They hugged back, and there was nothing else I could ask for. If I had met any other siren, things could have gone very wrong. I met the people I needed to, and that's all that mattered.

Nobody could understand me better.

"I love you both. Please don't forget that." I looked at them.

Kysana smiled. "Never."

Calliopé let out a sigh. "That's what we need to talk to you about, Mia. When you find this killer, Jason, and bring him down, Kysana and I must leave. We can't stay."

"What?"

"This isn't our home. We have to keep moving. There are other people out there who need our help. Other women need us..." She closed her eyes. "Kysana is only one of many who's been hurt by men. We have a purpose now, and it's to make sure the bad men in this world can't teach more boys to be exactly like them. If you want us to help humanity, this is how we'll do it."

As much as it pained me to hear that, she was right. I was going to lose them, but they had other dreams and places to be. I couldn't keep them here forever. I had my friends here to keep me company.

"Will you be okay here, without us?" Calliopé asked.

Would I be? It didn't matter what I wanted. I told them I loved them and there was only one way to prove that.

Let them go.

I forced a smile. "I'll be okay."

Twenty-nine

"I'M HANGING OUT WITH Natalia today," I told Dylan.

"All right. I will see you another day then." He gave me a quick kiss on the cheek and walked to his class. I smiled, watching him disappear into the room. I felt so much happier after knowing what I knew about our history. I could use this.

I walked to the bathroom to take a quick second to change out my tampon. It dropped into the toilet and I cursed under my breath. I got up to try to get it out.

The stupid toilet automatically flushed by the movement in front of the sensor. "No!" I slapped my forehead.

The toilet began to overflow and water poured. I widened my eyes, pushing my hair back. I was not going to live this down. I hit the door and groaned from the pain.

The water poured onto the floor and I tried to open the door before the water touched me but I didn't make it. The sandals on my feet let the water flow onto my toes and I grabbed onto the top of the stall, yelling out. My shorts and underwear ripped as my legs fused together into one tail.

I was now hanging on the stall door, looking down at my

bag. I heard the door to the bathroom open. "Oh shit!" a girl yelled. I recognized the voice.

"Olivia?" I asked.

"Mia?" she answered.

"I dropped my tampon in the toilet and the automatic flush made it a challenge to get it out. I'm sorry."

She knocked on the stall door. "Don't be sorry. Being a girl sucks. Come out and we'll tell a female staff member. Surely she will understand."

"Uh, that's a little hard to do right now." I laughed nervously.

"Why?"

"Reasons..."

Being nosy, Olivia's head appeared over the divider that was between my stall and the next one. She widened her eyes, watching me hang on the door with my tail curling upward. "Oh..."

I froze, unable to move. My grip on the door gave out and I fell onto the floor, groaning once again from the pain.

She climbed over the stall and landed on the toilet that continued to overflow. "Damn, we need to get you out of here." She unlocked the door and helped me up.

I looked at her, catching her attention as she paused. "You need to help me dry off. Now."

She helped me up onto the counter while I pulled myself up. She grabbed a bunch of paper towels, giving them to me. "Use these to dry yourself. I'm going to get someone to stop this." She rushed out of the bathroom.

I used the paper towels to dry myself as fast as I could, using up the entire roll. My legs came back just as Olivia ran in with a female faculty member.

Olivia gave me new bottoms and I slipped them on. The teacher plunged the toilet, getting the water to go back down. She looked around at the floor, coughing a bit. "We will need to get some more staff to clean this up. You girls get to class."

I nodded and Olivia was nice enough to give me a piggyback to the hallway where she put me down.

I scratched my head. "So...you saw that."

She looked at my legs and wasn't sure of what to say. "I want to know more about it after school. That's all I ask."

I didn't know why I had agreed to tell her, but she already saw the proof. No amount of lying could make her believe anything else.

I NODDED, WALKING WITH her to her car. "When we get to your house, I need to use the bathroom."

"Do you go to the bathroom when you're...a fish?" She was trying to say it in a way so as not to offend me.

"We do, but not in the way that humans think. It's more invisible than that," I said. She drove us to her house.

When we arrived, I went to the bathroom first and she showed me to her room after that. It was white with some pops of color here and there.

We both sat down on her bed and she looked at me, waiting for me to start explaining.

I took a deep breath. "As you know, I come from the ocean. I have a tail. I have gills as well. I'm not very proud of my identity because I get judged for it, but the reality is... I shouldn't be judged because I'm not like them. Mermaids especially hate me. I went away to the Academy of Naiad for seven years to learn more about myself and where I came from."

Olivia continued to listen to me, nodding her head.

I explained the history between sirens and mermaids, clearing the air about why sirens were judged but shouldn't have been. Sirens were not as evil as others believed.

Olivia asked, "So you went to an academy of sea creatures?"

"I did. That's where I met Natalia."

Olivia nodded, laying back. "Dylan must feel so left out then."

"What do you mean?"

"He doesn't know, does he?"

I averted my eyes to the ground. "I told him."

"Before me?" But I heard the playfulness in her tone.

"Long ago, before we got an apartment together. He thinks it's the coolest thing ever. Now with my new knowledge of our history, I can explain why people assume we're so bad."

Olivia tapped her chin. "Hm, and do we wonder if I'm secretly one?" she joked.

"Why's that?"

She shrugged. "Mia. Olivia. Natalia. Nadia. They all end in the same two letters. Is that not strange?"

I watched her every move. "I never noticed that."

"Now you have. I think it's just interesting to notice small things like that. So, what else is there to know?"

Over the next few hours, I told Olivia everything I had learned about other sea creatures and what I already knew about myself. I even spilled the part about Jason and what he did, but I never told her that I was planning to kill him.

"So you can control both men and women with magic, but only men with your voice? That's so interesting." Olivia leaned back into the pillows.

I was certain it had to do with survival. Singing to lure men to their deaths and controlling both sexes to make sure our species was protected.

Once that conversation passed, we came upon the topic of Dylan and I. "Have you had your first date yet?"

I shook my head. "We've been so busy, and I've been trying hard to focus on how to tell him about my magic without him hating me. I don't want us to get so attached to the point we fall in love because if he refuses to love me for who I am, I will be destroyed. I can't live with that."

The problem was, I *was* falling for Dylan, and I feared where it might take us. I was not ready for that path but I couldn't stop this love train.

"You guys look so cute together," she stated.

I smiled. "To be honest, I was jealous of you two. I thought you two had something and I wanted it with him instead." At first, that was the case.

Olivia laughed, grabbing her stomach. "Us? No. He's like a brother. He is definitely not my type."

"I get that now. I just feel silly now that I think about it. I feel stupid for ever being jealous."

She shrugged. "Well, I mean, it couldn't have been that bad if I never knew. It's not like you made it obvious or sabotaged anything, whether it be between you two, us two, or any of us."

I nodded, laying back with her. "That's true. Thank you for not making fun of me."

"Have others made fun of you?"

"Almost everyone I've ever known besides friends and family. That's why Dylan means the most to me. I want us to last forever. I want to get married. I know it's strange but it's true. I don't want him to get rid of me because of the monster I am deep down. His acceptance is one I need the most and not because he's my boyfriend but because he's my best friend. He is the boy I grew up with. We know each other too well. His opinion matters the most and I don't want to lose my best friend."

Olivia smiled. "I'm sure he will. I won't tell him because that's your business to tell, but I will say he is pretty accepting of things. He should be able to love you for who you are," she paused for a moment, "he loves me for who I am. Coming out to him was easier than it was for my own parents. You didn't get to grow up with him for the last six years like I did, but I know him. He isn't a mean person. He doesn't judge people. He knows actions speak louder than words."

"Now if you could just tell that to the mermaids, that would be great." I scoffed, laughing a bit. "In all seriousness, I hope what you say is true. I want him to love me. I want to be with him. Dylan is my Dill Pickle. I need my Dill Pickle and I admit that. It won't be easy to just move on if he doesn't accept this part of me. I can't just live and forget." I looked at her. "I'm glad he accepted you. Dylan was always so sweet like that."

Olivia nodded with a small smile. "That's so great. You found your happiness and that's good. I'm glad you could find someone like that."

"I should get home." I got off her bed.

She nodded and sat up. "Well, it was cool to hang out with you and learn about what you are. I won't tell Dylan either. I promise." She zipped her lips.

I laughed a little and gave her a thumbs up. I left her

house and walked back home. It wasn't too far, maybe a twenty-minute walk.

When I got back home, I stopped at the sight of my brother. "What are you doing here?" He gave me a look as if he were one of our parents. I was still the older one, however.

"Where did you go? Natalia said you were hanging out with her."

I slapped my forehead. "Oh, shoot. I forgot. I'm sorry. I... Olivia found out my secret so I went to her house to explain."

He lifted his eyebrows. "Whoa, you did what?"

"I told her the truth. She knows about my identity."

"I don't know what to say to that."

I sat down on the couch and laid my head back. "Don't say anything. I don't want this to be a bigger deal than it needs to be. I told her the truth because she found out and there was no use in trying to make up a lie. She never would've believed it. Now I just need to focus on telling Dylan the truth."

"He better know soon. He probably won't be too happy if you've waited this long to tell him. He is your best friend and your boyfriend. He wants your trust." Christian sat next to me.

"Shut up. I know this." I rolled my eyes and shook my head.

"I'm just giving excellent advice." He shot me a sly smile.

I looked at him, choking on a laugh. "You're giving the worst advice a sister could ever have, and why is it the worst advice ever? Because it's useless." I looked up at the ceiling. "I know too much already. I know that I need to tell him. I just need to figure out how exactly I will do that."

Thirty

A GIRL WITH BLACK hair walked down the beach, her cardigan flying from the wind, matching the waves of her hair. "Nat, this is Olivia. Olivia, this is Natalia."

Olivia nodded. "You're also from the sea?"

Natalia gave me a look. "You told her?"

"She found out." I shrugged a bit.

Natalia began circling her, ignoring the mist from the ocean. "You're the girl who stole my best friend the other day?"

Olivia followed her movement. "Well, actually, I didn't steal her. She never told me you two had plans."

"Way to out me like that." I rolled my eyes.

Natalia stopped and crossed her arms. "In other words, I have Mia to blame."

"Correct," Olivia said with a smirk. Her gaze landed on me.

"Okay, okay, enough of the betrayal." I put my arms up in defense. "I brought you here because you saw my tail and I thought I'd show you in my natural habitat. That is if you're not afraid to swim in the ocean."

A laugh erupted from her. "I swam with you on Halloween night."

Holding up a finger, I tilted my head at an angle. "That does not count because we were in the water for only a couple of minutes, and you could still touch." I looked at Natalia and motioned for her to follow me. "You two will become friends with each other because you're already *my* friends. Olivia knows our secrets and there's no use in kicking her out now. She's been helpful to me. She was helpful when I had lost all hope in the bathroom that day. And if she can trust Dylan with her sexuality, why can't I trust her with my real identity?"

Natalia mumbled something and I nudged her.

Olivia cleared her throat. "So... Let's take a look at this tail. Tails—I should say." She stole a glance from Nat.

Nat scoffed in return. "You're mistaken if you think I'm showing you my tail." Olivia eyed Natalia but it wasn't in a way I expected. "Mia is all yours."

A familiar voice carried from the waters, "Or maybe we could have her." Calliopé and Kysana poked their heads above the waves rocking back and forth.

Olivia's eyebrows shot up. "Who are these two?"

"These are my friends," I said, tasting that term on my tongue.

Kysana shot me a smile. "Yes, we are her friends. We know things you don't, so I suppose that puts us at the top of the list? Is that how that works?"

"No," I mumbled.

"We're sirens," Calliopé said. "In case Mia never told you. She seems to be afraid of that word." She lifted her chin higher. "But we won't eat you."

"Don't sirens only eat men?" Olivia asked.

A small smirk appeared on her lips. "Ah, so she isn't that stupid. Good to know." Her tail moved up out of the water, flashing lavender for a split second before disappearing again.

Before anyone else could change the subject for the fiftieth time, Olivia started peeling off her clothes. "We're getting into the water. Right now."

Nat's expression softened as I grumbled and took off my bottoms. I slipped into the water before my tail formed, twisting onto my back. My fin whipped up from the waves, splashing Olivia. "In its full glory."

Olivia swam closer, reaching out to touch it. "This is literally the coolest fucking thing ever. Legs are overrated anyway."

Taking off my shirt, I threw it back on the beach.

Calliopé and Kysana swam closer but kept their distance.

Nat released an exasperated sigh. "I guess I'll come in, too, then." She stripped down and walked further out, diving into the shallow waves.

"Every single one of you has a tail, and all different colors mind you," Olivia pointed out. "I'm beginning to feel like the fifth wheel here." She crossed her arms with a sarcastic smile.

Calliopé gave her the side eye before grabbing my wrist and dragging me into the waters. Kysana wasn't far behind. When we surfaced behind rocks, I sent them both glares. "What the hell?"

"Mia, you are absolutely naïve." Calliopé placed her body against the rocks. "And maybe it's because you're as straight as a board, but sometimes two girls need some alone time."

What were they talking about?

Kysana hummed as she twirled her hair. "Your friends were

looking at each other differently."

"Olivia and Nat?"

She nodded.

As I furrowed my brows, Calliopé rolled her eyes. "They're attracted to each other, Mia. Their pupils were dilated. Cheeks flushed. It's not so hard to believe, is it?"

In response, *my* cheeks flushed. "Oh. I didn't mean..." I certainly didn't know. I knew both of them were into girls, but I guess it never occurred to me that they might take an interest in each other. Nat didn't plan on sticking around forever, did she?

I didn't say much after that, but Kysana talked our ears off. Calliopé chimed in from time to time just to prove she was still listening. When it was over, we slowly swam back to the shore while I pulled myself up in the sand. The tension hung thick in the air, and I couldn't stop myself from asking, "What happened between you two?"

Nat sat down. "Listen, when two people like each other—"

"Gross!" I squeezed my eyes shut. "No, no. I just need a simple answer."

Olivia laughed, laying back with her hands behind her head. "We made out. That's all. Natalia isn't looking for anything serious, and I'm okay with that."

"That sounds...great." In other words, they both consented. Who was I to say anything else about it?

"It was fun." Olivia nodded.

I wasn't sure of what to say overall. Did that make me a terrible person, or a terrible friend?

Natalia looked at me. "Mia, you alive?"

"I appreciate the sentiment, but Nat was my friend first and I just wanted her around me until she had to leave." I didn't know why I said it the way I did. It sounded very harsh and rude and that was not my intention. "I'm sorry. I didn't mean that."

Natalia let out a sigh. "My last girlfriend was an ass, so excuse me if I wanted to make the most of my time here. Besides, Olivia and I were tired of hearing all this romance about you and Dylan when we weren't getting any ourselves. I think this evens it out."

"Oh, no, Nat." I grabbed her hand. "I'm sorry. I talk way too much about my problems and Dylan, and I didn't realize how annoying it was." I had no excuses.

"I think it's fair that we get to experience some of that romance, too," Olivia piped in.

Natalia stood up. "Yes, it is. We did nothing wrong."

I swallowed. "No. You didn't."

"I can't help it if I think she's cute. I do. I think Olivia is very attractive. Mia, you seem to have this perfect life, and yes I am jealous. You have a perfect family, and they pay attention to you. Your best friend also has romantic feelings for you. Every woman I date is awful, and my dad doesn't pay any attention to me. My sister is never here. You can't control what I feel, but I want you to know at the very least." Natalia pointed to herself.

I nodded. "I know. I'm sorry for making you feel like you can't tell me how you feel. I want you to express yourself. I want you to be open with me. You deserve to be happy, and I won't ever try to take that away from you. I won't stop you if that's what you want. Your past girlfriends were horrible, and I know Olivia would never be like that."

"Dylan didn't know your secret and it stressed you out. My past girlfriends didn't know mine, and I never could tell them.

Who we are is scary to humans. Olivia knows who you are, and she has not made any move to treat you differently. She helped you out, and you know what? That's attractive. She would have my back if I ever got into trouble.

"If Dylan, the man you've trusted your entire childhood can trust Olivia, you know she's great. I'm a girl and I want to be with someone I know I can trust. Olivia may be the perfect candidate because she won't push me into things I don't want, which is why I want to maybe give this a try. Can't hurt at this point."

I scrunched up my nose. "But you're not staying long. I'm just trying to understand the point of a fling. Why would you want to be with someone you really like for only a short time? Why put yourself through that?"

She rubbed her eyes. "Mia."

Olivia cleared her throat and said, "It's a valid question. For me, I think it's a temporary attraction. And I know that. It makes it easy to not get so attached. When you know what's going to happen down the road, you can close off certain parts of your mind and focus solely on the surface things. Like the fact that Nat is pretty and a great kisser."

"But why would you want to kiss someone you barely know? Why kiss someone you don't want to get attached to? I don't understand it."

Olivia shrugged. "Some people fear commitment. Others might be so emotionally detached that it's easy to just focus on what's outside."

A shiver ran up my spine. "And which one are you?"

At that question, a smile crept onto her lips. "I fear commitment."

Nat laughed, shooting Olivia a smirk. "And I'm afraid to

get hurt again so why risk it? At this point, I'm basically trying baby steps. In this relationship, I want just what's on the outside. No emotional attachment or anything. Just a good fling. Maybe next time I might be able to find someone who can give me that. Besides, Olivia already knows my secret. I don't feel stressed or worried about it. Don't you want that?" Her voice went quiet, dripping with more sadness than anything. "Can't I try?"

I chewed my lip. "Of course. I want you to be happy. I want you to find the person you deserve. I just...didn't expect this. I just don't want you to want more and then realize it's hurting you more than it should. I care about your well-being."

"Are you certain it's not because it makes you uncomfortable?"

"No, no. Why would it?"

Nat straightened her posture. "Because you're a straight woman. It's one thing to tell you that I'm gay but another for you to actually be around it. And if you happen to see something you shouldn't..."

"It's not because you're gay, Nat. It would be because I feel like I barged in on something private. Straight or gay, I wouldn't want to interrupt or make you feel awkward. I'd hope the same from you with me and Dylan. I'd never intentionally do anything that would make you uncomfortable. I'm sure we aren't your cup of tea. I'm not asking you to break it off with Olivia."

Natalia relaxed. "I wasn't going to, but thanks." Not that she did need my approval. I think she just appreciated it more than not having it.

"I'm glad it's settled." Olivia smiled at Natalia.

I knew Dylan wouldn't mind but Natalia hadn't planned

on sticking around. I had to be expected to pick sides when these two broke up and I wasn't prepared to do that. Both were my friends.

I was happy for Natalia, and I did hope that Olivia was truly there for her. Natalia had been like me. She spent her whole life trying to find someone who would accept her as she was, and Olivia couldn't bail on her now. The reality was, if I had to choose between them, I'd choose Natalia. She'd always been there for me over the years, and I knew her better than anyone. She needed me and I needed her.

"Nymphs are beautiful creatures. They can easily lure in anyone, and you aren't immune to her beauty. I know it says that nymphs use people for sex, but I know Nat. I know she wants real love like anyone would. She wouldn't hurt you and you shouldn't hurt her. I want to warn you of that now, that I will choose Natalia if it comes to it," I told Olivia.

She nodded, not saying anything else.

Nat didn't say anything in regards to that, either. She let me make my threats, knowing I would always have her back first and foremost.

Changing the subject, I looked at Calliopé and Kysana. "You know what would be cool? If we had different colors in our blood. Like unicorns or aliens or something."

"Like green?" Kysana asked.

"Sure. Green. Like my tail. Although sometimes I wonder if my tail would look better as a different color." I swam backward, bringing my tail to the surface.

Nat furrowed her eyebrows as she came closer. "Why?"

"How cool would it be if I had a red and black tail, or even a red and gold tail? That would be freaking beautiful. How many mermaids even have these colors? I'm curious.

They must be like hair color or eye color. Only two percent of people in the world have green eyes. Only two percent are redheads. A very small percentage of adults are still natural blondes, too. Maybe it's like that. I would love to see one with a red tail. That's gotta be gorgeous."

Calliopé and Kysana smiled at one another. "Maybe someday we will. We travel quite a bit so a siren with a red tail is out there somewhere."

Somewhere...

Red and green. Sirens and mermaids. It was as if two sides were fighting but no side was bad nor good. It was all gray area.

Morality worked like that sometimes. We were just living creatures trying to survive a world we were thrown into.

Thirty-one

I SMILED, LOOKING AT Dylan from next to my window. I was leaning against the pane, and he was leaning against the side of my doorframe.

"Let's go on a date," he said.

I tilted my head. "What?"

He laughed. "A date? Two people do this to hang out more like a romantic couple? I want you and me to go on a cute date. Be ready in an hour." He winked. He knew I needed an hour to get ready.

I closed my door, laughing to myself. A date, huh? This would be interesting.

The hour was too short for me as I contemplated which dress and which hairstyle to go with. It was a nerve-wracking experience for me since we'd never gone on a real date. Hanging out as friends and kissing every now and then was different from strictly being boyfriend and girlfriend for a few hours. Could I do it? Could I manage to be the attractive girlfriend for that long?

I braided my hair and pinned the two braids around my

hair like a crown. I did light makeup made up of brown eyeshadow, mascara, and red lipstick. I wore a teal dress to bring the look together, making sure it brought out my eyes.

Just as I turned, someone knocked on my door. "I got it!" I ran and opened the door, smiling at Dylan. He wore a nice pair of jeans with a button up shirt. "Ready for our date?"

"More ready than ever." I took his hand. He was holding a basket and I laughed, shaking my head. "Are we going to grandma's house?"

"Maybe." He smiled at me as we left our apartment. He walked me through the neighborhood and into the forest. I recognized the path we took.

We arrived at our treehouse and I smiled. This was perfect. He was using our childhood treehouse as our first date. It was starting to feel more like two best friends taking things slow and less like I was forced to be a girlfriend and change for our relationship. It was still just us two, and we enjoyed the company of each other as friends and more.

We climbed inside and he laid out a blanket on the floor. He started setting up the food and emptying the basket. "I know it's nothing spectacular or fancy but I'm kind of broke right now."

"We all are. It's fine. This is amazing. The thought is nice." I sat down and grabbed some food, beginning to eat. It was lasagna and lasagna was probably the best food to ever exist. Every layer was made with pure love. "What should we talk about?" I asked. I was not ready to tell him my secret yet.

He looked at me. "Anything you want to. How is it going with everything?"

"Fine. Natalia likes Olivia, which is sudden, but I guess not every relationship happens in the span of ten years or so like ours. A lot is changing but in a good way, you know?"

"Of course." He took a bite, chewing and swallowing. "We are together. I mean, I guess I never thought I would date a mimi but here I am."

I gasped. "Excuse me, I'm the one who's dating a dill pickle. Do you know what people will think?"

"They'll think: when is she going to see his dill pickle?" He chuckled. "And what about you? People are going to question if I'm becoming a doctor because you're named after medical instruments."

"Technically I'm named after thin fairy-like creatures, but what do I know?" I continued to eat my food. The beauty of this lipstick was that it was the only lipstick that truly stayed on my lips. It was completely waterproof and every other proof where lipstick could smudge.

"Well, Dill Pickle, I want to tell you now that you have a lot to learn about mimis." I smiled.

We both finished our food. He cleaned up and put the leftover plates and bags into the basket, setting it aside.

We laid back on the blanket and looked at the ceiling.

I grabbed his hand, intertwining our fingers. "This is beautiful. I'm so glad I've found you. I'm so glad you stayed, and that you still want to be around me."

He looked at me. "Of course. Why wouldn't I want to be around my best friend? You're everything to me. You know me and I love that. I don't have to worry about what you're going to think. I never expected to fall for my best friend, but I did."

I turned my head towards him so fast. "Fall? As in, fall in love?" Oh no.

"Yeah. Mimi, you must know that I love you. You're my

best friend. You're so supportive of me. You left for so many years, but you haven't changed in a bad way, and I love that. In ways that you did change, it was in a good way. You didn't come back as a snooty girl who would shun her best friend. Growing up and seeing friends drift apart in middle school, I feared that would be us."

"What do you mean?"

He sighed. "I knew a girl. She told me she was best friends with this popular girl when we were in middle school. They had been good friends, but they drifted apart. You never would've guessed they were even friends. I saw it happen to another group. This one girl came in and she was a complete skater girl. She had the pixie cut and wore plaid and everything. She became friends with another quirky girl who enjoyed art a lot. The following year, skater girl became a new person. She went completely girly and ditched her friend for the popular kids. She never went back after that."

I frowned. "That's sad. Seeing friends drift apart is always heartbreaking. I'm glad we didn't do that. I need you in my life."

He kissed my cheek. "I need you, too."

I put my head on his shoulder and sighed. "I'm pretty sure I'm falling for you, too."

"Is that bad?"

"Well, no. It's just complicated right now."

He was in love with me and I was falling for him. This was going to make it much harder when I told him about my magic as well as Jason, and he didn't accept it. And what about the boy I killed?

We laid like this for a little bit, just enjoying the company. He was warm and I was cold. I always seemed to be freezing.

I used my hands to wrap around one of his, holding onto him as if he were going to run off. I looked at him. "You're special to me." I leaned in and kissed him, moving my lips against his as slow as I could just to take in the taste of him.

Chocolate.

He started to return the kiss, placing his free hand on my waist, nails digging into the fabric of my dress.

This was a time where I didn't feel worried or stressed. I was content. I was perfectly happy where I was, in his arms. I wanted this to be the moment we always remembered.

Our lips continued to move together, my lipstick never once staining his lips red. I wanted more from him. I wanted to go all the way.

When I let go of him and tugged my dress, he pulled away. "Mia, we shouldn't do that yet. We're getting caught in the moment but we aren't that far." He wasn't ready. Why did I keep pushing? I was a danger to us both.

I nodded, mentally thanking him for stopping me. I wasn't ready for that step, either. Not entirely.

I sat up, hugging my knees. He sat up with me and kissed my head. "Don't worry. We will do that in the future. We have plenty of time for that."

He could've been right or wrong. Only time would tell when I told him the truth.

There was a jolt in the treehouse and I gripped Dylan's arm as tightly as I could. "What was that?"

"I'm sure it's just a squirrel." He patted my hand.

As if to prove him wrong, the treehouse creaked and tilted, scaring us both. Dylan jumped to the door and held onto my hand. The branch that the structure sat on broke off, falling into the water. "Dylan!" My hand slipped from his and he still hung onto the tree as the treehouse fell into the water. I swam out of the window and down the stream, trying to get away from him. I wasn't ready to show him yet.

Upon finding a shore, I climbed up and laid back, pulling my dress up to let my tail dry separately from the fabric. My tail dried faster than my dress.

After an hour of waiting, I stood, barefoot, and walked back up the stream. I walked back to our neighborhood, shocked to see police cars. Again? Just my luck.

When my parents spotted me, they came running, embracing me.

"We thought we lost you," Dad said.

"I'm from the water. You can't lose me that easily." I laughed to myself and looked at them.

My brother came over, taking in my appearance. "Not even a scratch on you." My lipstick didn't appear to smear. However, I knew my eyes were now black with mascara running down my face.

"Where's Dylan? He must know I'm okay."

Mom pointed to the boy sitting on the steps of our front door.

I walked over, nudging his foot with my naked one. "Hey. Don't look so down. I'm fine."

He looked up at me, eyes widening. He stood up and squeezed his arms around my figure. "I thought I lost you. I'm so, so sorry."

"No, don't be. You couldn't predict the stability of the treehouse. I'm fine." I hugged back, reassuring him.

"But how? How exactly are you okay?"

"You know the answer to that, Dylan. I'm...not human." I couldn't answer that question properly. "I'm a good swimmer. Nothing can hold me under."

"You freaked me out, Mia."

I nodded. "I know. This is an accident though." I rubbed my thumb on his cheek. "Don't stress it."

He still looked unconvinced by my words. I was doing my best here.

We informed the police of my return and they all left us alone, making sure to get some details first just in case.

I sat next to Dylan on the steps, putting my head on his shoulder. "I'm glad you're so concerned about my safety. Thank you. It means a lot to me that you care so much." I smiled a bit.

He didn't say another word. We both went back to the apartment, and I washed my face off. Once I had changed, I got a snack before I laid back in my bed.

It was painful to think about our first date. It went so well up until the end. Dylan had seemed so terrified. He was terrified of what had happened to me and I didn't want him to feel that kind of fear. He knew about what I was, so why did the river scare him so much?

I had to tell him to ease his worries. He thought I'd died and he lost me forever. I saw it in his eyes. They had been red with a glassy look to them. He had *cried* because of me.

I didn't want him to cry anymore. I didn't want him to fear my life when it came to water. I wanted him to trust that I was safe and that meant telling him everything. I was giving myself a week to tell him. I had to tell him this week or I would forever hate myself. I couldn't keep hurting him like this. If I didn't say something, I would tell Natalia to tell him, or even Christian. Someone would have to let him know for me if I was so chicken about it.

Snuggling in my blankets, I hugged my pillow for comfort. Natalia came back from her shower, looking at me. "What's up with you?"

"Our date went wrong. Natalia, I'm going to tell him everything this week and I need you to help me. If I don't keep my word, you must tell him. Deal?" I looked at her.

She laid down next to me and nodded. "I can do that for you. That's what I'm here for." She pulled the blanket over herself and smiled at me, not realizing the stress I was really under.

"Thank you." I closed my eyes, unable to get rid of the worry that filled my entire body. This could be the end of our relationship as I knew it.

Thirty-two

DYLAN HAD BEEN OUT getting some quick errands done, and in the meantime I took a bath. My shower days were long behind me.

I hummed to myself just as a song popped into my head, and without thinking about it, I began to sing. I started out quiet, words flowing softly from my tongue. The acoustics in a bathroom really were fantastic.

As more lyrics left my lips, I poured all my emotions into every beat. My soul clung to every note.

I closed my eyes and let the harmony wash over me. I hadn't felt this much serenity since my first Turning. I never wanted to leave this state. The closer I came to accepting what I was, the more at peace I became.

Fingers brushed across my cheek and I pulled myself into an upright position, screaming as I faced the intruder. No, it was no intruder. It was just Dylan.

Dylan. Shit.

The glassy eyes dissipated and he tilted his head as he met my gaze. "Mia, what am I doing in here?"

"I was going to ask you the same thing," I whispered, covering my chest. But I knew. I'd been singing and he must have come home in the middle of it. He had been under my spell.

Dylan averted his eyes and stood. "I'm sorry, I'll leave." So he left me alone in the bathroom.

When I finished my bath and got dressed, I slowly walked into the living room. "How much did you see?" No, wrong question. "How do you feel?" Now that made it even worse.

"How do I feel about what I saw? I wasn't paying much attention. I don't even remember walking into the bathroom," he said, folding blankets.

"I'm sorry for what I did, Dylan." My lip quivered. "I swear I didn't mean it."

He stopped what he was doing and closed all space between us, grabbing my cheeks. "Mia, stop. This is not your fault. I trust you, and if you want to sing around me, you're more than welcome to. I know you aren't luring me to my death." He pressed my face into his chest. "I just ask that you sing when I'm not in the middle of homework," he joked.

Despite his comforting words, I couldn't stop the shaking. So much guilt coursed through my veins and out my pores. How could I ever forgive myself?

Placing a kiss against my hair, he whispered, "You could kill me and I'd never be able to hate you."

I glanced up at him, mouth hanging open. "You know I'd never kill you."

He chuckled a bit. "I know." In those seconds, the words hit me like a bus. Dylan planned to spend the rest of his life with me. He was utterly in love with me and nothing I could do would ever change how he felt about me.

I'd noticed the change in his demeanor after our first date. The mishap that happened had really shaken him and I saw the fear and guilt in his eyes. I had tried to remind him that I was okay, but he wasn't going to give up the ghost.

Now I understood why.

"Come cuddle with me. We can have a date here, whatever we choose. It'll be fun. Nothing will happen. Just be happy I'm okay and don't waste any more time without me." I reached up to caress his cheek.

It took a minute for him to agree and the second he did, he grabbed me and kissed me, exposing every secret he ever had. He'd told me he could never hate me, and this was proof. I was *experiencing* his pure passion.

The concern Dylan held for me over our date showed me that I meant so much to him. Seeing how deeply this has affected him was what really struck me. It hurt me that it hurt him.

Pulling away, Dylan still held my cheeks, kissing my forehead. "I can't say it enough, Mimi. I am so sorry for the way our date ended."

I watched his eyes, absorbing every emotion this man had. He was without a wall.

He was vulnerable.

"I wish I could take it back. I wish I could redo it and throw you up to grab the branch first. I had never been more scared in my life than when I thought you were lost in the river. I saw the treehouse get torn up by the rocks. It broke apart. It was violent the way the river destroyed that with you inside." He planted more kisses all over my face.

"It's okay now, Dill. I'm still here with you. I love you too much to let anything take me away that quickly." I gave him a small smile for reassurance, bringing our lips back together.

We moved in sync, holding onto each other as if we were about to be ripped away from one another.

More than anything else, I wanted to complete our bond. We connected on every level but we had yet to seal our love with the physical connection. I didn't make any moves to go that far. I could not in good conscience have sex with him when he didn't want that just yet. It was dirty and wrong. Stained and indecorous. I already felt shame for pushing him twice.

We pulled away from our longing kiss. I put my head on his shoulder, letting his presence comfort us both.

Dylan wrapped his arms around me and rested his chin on my head. "I know."

"Hm?" I barely registered his words.

"I know why... I know why you survived what you did. It just doesn't make me feel any better."

I looked at him. "What are you talking about?"

Dylan, trying to soothe my worries, pushed my hair back and brushed his thumb against my cheek. "I know that you're from the water, but it doesn't keep me from worrying. I know more than you want me to, Mia. The night at the beach, you used magic on me. You just didn't know that's what it was. Everyone else knows about your magic but me, so it was only a matter of time before someone slipped up."

I swallowed, my heart beginning to pound in my chest. My lungs wanted to stop functioning.

He leaned closer, whispering, "I know you drowned a boy in the ocean."

He knew. He knew and he was still here. Why?

"I just can't seem to figure out why you wouldn't tell me.

You trust me with your secret, but you won't tell me about anything else. Even after we killed Todd, you're afraid to tell me the truth." He pulled himself back a little.

He didn't know. He knew half of it but he didn't know what I had truly done. There was still a possibility he could judge me when he did find out.

Dylan was getting confused by my silence and as if to make me feel better about this, he leaned back in and placed his lips on mine. It was sweet, innocent, and pure. There was not a single ounce of resentment or panic in his movements. There was no *judgment*.

I almost spilled my secrets at that exact minute, but I held back. "Dylan, what if you don't like the truth?"

"Why wouldn't I?"

"Because in my world, people assume the worst. They don't believe we control our lives. They don't believe we can stray from the stereotypes and molds we are put into. In the ocean world, we are always seen as the name of the creature we hold, the species we belong to. I've tried to defy that. People refuse to accept me. I am like a disease to the mermaids, and they will never accept me as one of them."

"Why do you need their acceptance? Are mermaids the queens of the ocean?" he asked in a tone that held more curiosity than sarcasm.

I tilted my head, lips pressed together. "Well, no. But they're the popular ones. Everyone loves them. I'm like the sick child that a mother didn't want. They continue to push me away." I sat on the couch and he copied my motion.

He shook his head, thinking for a moment. "You're not even in school anymore with them. Is there like a secret city under the ocean that you go to and they have to say as to who gets treated nicely?" His hand laid on top of mine, curling his fingers between my own and holding on tight.

"No..." I swallowed. "I haven't seen a mermaid since I left the academy."

Dylan asked, "Why do their opinions matter?"

I lifted my head to look at him. "It's complicated. Growing up, they judged me. They never let me in. One of the boys found out I stuffed my bra and made fun of me. The mermaids used this to their advantage. I tried hard to ignore it and with Natalia's help, I managed okay. It's just complicated. Things got really bad. That boy, Jason, continued to torment me in every way possible. He tried to drown me before I had turned, and he's done brutal, violent things to me. I think he's dead." I looked down at my lap.

"How do you know?"

"There's a specific sea creature that lives in the ocean. They're good until they die. When they die, their spirit remains and turns evil. Jason took a dark turn when I met him. He got violent. He broke my nose. He forced me to eat something I never wanted to eat. He became so wicked, and the mermaids cheered him on the entire time."

Dylan squeezed my hand. "What's his last name? I'll track this son of a bitch down and kill him again."

"It's fine. I'm fine now. I hoped to never see him again." But he was still out there. "The mermaids still refused to believe I could be good despite the fact that they saw me allow Jason to bully me. I never used my abilities against him. I refused to become what everyone saw me as. I wanted to prove them wrong." Now I wanted to tear them apart, piece by piece. Rip their skin from their flesh and crush their bones into a fine powder.

I felt fingers brush hair behind my ear as Dylan pulled me into his side. "You're strong. You're nothing like them. Don't you worry about being what they see you as because I have never seen you act malicious in any way. You are the sweetest girl I know." He hadn't seen me at the beach that night with that boy. He didn't know.

"Sweet like a candy treat?" I asked in a quiet voice.

He kissed my head, nodding. "Yes. You are absolutely adorable. You don't need their approval to be yourself."

"Damnit, Dill, how are you so wise?" I mumbled into his shoulder.

He chuckled. "I'm a wizard, Mimi. I'm a very old wizard."

"I knew it all along." I glanced up at him.

He planted a kiss on my lips and smiled. "You have your friends who support you and love you. No matter what kind of creature you are, I won't change my mind. I've seen your actions. Your DNA doesn't determine your actions. No matter if you're from a different race, species, or if your parent is a serial killer. We control our own lives and I've seen how you control yours. You're just trying to succeed in life and be surrounded by people you love. The mermaids who judge you can shove their opinions up their ass because you, Mia Dawson, are perfect the way you are."

My insides became mush from his words. How I got so lucky, I didn't know. He was my perfect half.

"You know that my magic is inherently evil, right? I drowned a boy because I wanted to practice my magic but I didn't have the power to stop him. I don't deserve you. Jason has turned me into the monster," I whispered.

Grabbing my chin, he forced me to meet his eyes. "You are not, have never been, and never will be a monster. I'm sure you're not telling me the whole story because you tend to do that. You tell me the worst bits out of context."

While cracking a smile, I said, "You know me too well. I'd saved this boy from being eaten by other sirens, but I didn't allow him to come back to the beach and ask questions. He drove himself insane. Everyone else says I put him out of his misery by drowning him."

"That's the Mia I know. Trying to do good, and only through that might she do something she wish she didn't."

"But intentions mean nothing. Impact is everything."

His lips lingered over mine. "False. Both mean something, and it's up to us to figure out when one is more important than the other. In this case, both are just as important. In the case of self-defense, intentions will play a bigger role. In the cases of murder, impact holds all the cards." He swept his lips over mine. "But that does not make you a monster. You're just a young woman trying to survive in a world that's beaten you down. You're surviving. You deserve to live. You deserve *me*."

I frowned. "You're making it impossible not to kiss you."

"Then do it. Kiss me again."

With those words, I did. I kissed him with all the emotion I had swirling inside me. I grasped his shirt, squeezing it in my fingers as if my life depended on this moment. Dylan wrapped his arms around my waist and pressed us against each other.

Neither of us cared much for air. We breathed something else—something much more intoxicating. We breathed *forever*.

We kissed for a few more minutes, pulling away now and again. "I should head to bed," I said with a smile.

Dylan chuckled as he wiped his thumb over my lips. "I'll see you in the morning." He went to his room while I disappeared into mine.

I laid back on my bed. I looked over at the door at the sound of a noise. My door creaked open just as something flew in.

"What the—" I sat up, squinting at the object in the dark. It was a red rose. I jumped a bit when another one came flying.

I got out of bed and opened my door to see Dylan tossing roses into my room from his bed. His room had been right across from mine. The next rose missed the opening and hit the frame, falling to the carpet. I noticed all the roses that had piled up. Lifting an eyebrow, I looked at Dylan.

He looked at me. "I play soccer, not basketball. Throwing is different from kicking." He threw another rose, but this time I caught it.

He smiled. "I thought you'd want to wake up to roses. This was my best idea to get them to you without having to wake up extra early."

"Roses? Why are roses your go-to?" I admired the pretty pink one in my hand.

"Don't all women like them?"

"Not all. They're pretty but not my favorite." I shrugged.

He squinted his eyes. "You're bleeding."

I looked down, seeing a stream of blood running down my wrist. It originated from my palm where the thorns of the stems dug into my skin. "Huh, I guess I am."

I put the rose on the nightstand between my bed and window. I looked at my bloody hand, clenching and unclenching my fist. I didn't feel the pain. It was a strange feeling to know that I could not register the stabbing from thorns. I had never noticed this before.

"Are you okay?" Dylan questioned.

I met his eyes and nodded, taking my attention off my hand.

"I'm fine. I'm sure it's somehow connected to the fact that I'm a sea creature. I guess that's more stuff I have to research." I looked up at the stars. "I'm just trying to figure out a way to accept it."

He played with some rose petals. "I don't judge you for struggling."

"It's just a lot to take in. Once I officially announce what I am, it becomes much more real. I want to be able to be proud of my heritage and never fear what others think of me."

"I am proud, Mimi. I'm proud to love you, no matter what happens."

Thirty-three

"READY?" CHRISTIAN ASKED.

I nodded as we traveled to a small, local shop with books about sea creatures. To sea creatures, it told our stories in a way that made the humans believe, but not entirely.

As I grabbed a book, I flipped open the pages and skimmed. "Um, I think you need to take a look at this." I showed Christian.

He furrowed his brows in confusion. "That's not what we were told."

"And you can see why, right?"

He looked at me. "So that means..."

I took a shaky breath. "That means I'm the result of a violent death. I was born from bloodshed. Calliopé and Kysana were right."

Christian straightened his back. "The question is, who had to die so you could be born?"

That was a question I didn't want to think about. I thought maybe my existence was normal, but even that had been tainted by blood. I was a giant killer in one form or another.

I sat in the chair and sighed. "Must be nice being a mermaid. You get to be all pretty and everyone loves you. You don't eat humans to survive."

Everyone knew that males couldn't be mermaids or sirens. There was no such thing. When a siren and human got pregnant, the male child was always born a human. The female was always born a siren or a mermaid. It was the circle of life.

"Now, come on, Mia. You must know this isn't your fault. You didn't kill anyone to be born."

"Not intentionally."

"Whoa."

"What?" I looked at him. "Mom and Dad still knew. They purposely got pregnant, knowing that if someone was dying a horrible death, they were going to have me. They allowed this. How can I be okay with that?"

"Maybe they didn't know. If the faculty hid this information, maybe Mom and Dad didn't know someone would die so you could be born." He skimmed the pages. "There has to be something else about it."

I grabbed the book from him. "Face it, Christian. I'm the result of death. I'm not supposed to be here. How can I be any good if all I do is mess up? I hurt people. I killed two boys. Dylan will eventually realize the truth. He'll know that I'm not the same as a mermaid and never can be."

Christian grabbed the book again. "No, that's not true." He flipped through many pages before finding what he was looking for. "Mermaids are born from death, too."

I chewed my lip. "I know."

He pointed to a paragraph. "Mermaids can only be conceived when someone else dies." He froze. "Wait, you know?" He turned to me.

As I read on, the paragraph stated that mermaids were born from a peaceful death. I caught myself about to say that mermaids had it easier, but the reality remained the same. They were just like us. Someone had to die for a mermaid to be born.

"Mia?" He waved his hand in front of my face.

I blinked a few times. "I did know. When I found out that sirens are born when someone dies, I realized mermaids are the same. I know sirens are not so different from mermaids. We both use men for one reason or another. We both are born because of death." I leaned back. "Sirens can be good, Christian. Nadia proved that. She saved Adeline from being hurt and Adeline was too blind to see that."

He nodded. "Of course. Now we know the truth."

Did the mermaids even know? This was a truth that I couldn't wait to tell them. I wanted to crush their world. I wanted to remind them that we weren't so different. We were almost one and the same.

Christian went back home. It was now nightfall and I was headed to the beach to meet up with Calliopé and Kysana. I didn't see them so I started to strip down.

"Not so cowardice now, am I?" a male voice asked from behind me.

I immediately spun on my heel, facing Jason. He was still *alive*. He was here, and I'd been right about everything. "You did this. You're the one who attacked me. You're the one who killed those boys, making everyone believe it was me."

He shrugged his shoulders without a care in the world. "You killed the other boy, didn't you? I'm not the only bad guy, Mia."

I lifted my chin high, refusing to let him put me down. "Bold of you to assume I'm the bad guy." I walked towards him. "In fact, it's been exposed that mermaids and sirens are not all that different. It's simple really. We both are conceived in the name of death. If I'm the bad guy, then all your mermaid friends are my allies. If that's true, you must be the puppet."

He scowled. "I'm nobody's puppet."

"No? Then why are you so cruel, Jason?" I tilted my head, pushing for answers. "You do as the mermaids tell you to. You follow their orders." I folded my arms across my chest. "I know that you're adaro, once aunga. I know that you're the evil spirit left over, meaning you were once the good guy. The good guy would never bully me—never make me feel worthless. Who killed you? Who turned you into this monster?"

He narrowed his eyes, ready to attack. Something held him back, and he dropped his hand. "That's none of your business."

"It's the reason I've had to endure all that cruelty. You made me eat human flesh. You humiliated me in every way imaginable. You're vermin." I stepped forward.

Jason lifted his hand, ready to hit me. He lowered it for a moment but changed his mind and swung at my face. I fell to the sand, spitting out some blood.

I was no longer the innocent and weak girl he knew. I'd changed, and for the better.

Standing up, I faced him. Everything he ever did came rushing back to me, and I knew the truth. There was no stopping what was about to come.

I lifted my hands and locked eyes with him. "Walk over to

that rock."

Jason widened his eyes, but as hard as he fought against the urge, he couldn't win against my magic. His feet led him over to the rock to my left.

"Repeatedly bang your head against it until I tell you to stop." Relief rushed through my body. But it was exhilaration that fueled me.

Jason yelled out but started hitting his head against the sharp edges. Blood started to coat the surface, dripping from his forehead. I watched, not missing a second of this revenge. It was like water on my tongue after being lost in the desert for days.

My muscles ached, and exhaustion hit me like he did the rocks.

Jason stopped hitting his head and turned to see me as I fell to the sand. "You deserve to die."

A figure came up from behind him, hitting him in the head. It didn't knock him out, but it stunned him enough, and he took off running. Calliopé dropped the rock and came over to me, kneeling. "He's gone."

I nodded, giving her a small smile to thank her. I almost had him, but my energy ran out quickly. The more intense the task, the more energy it took.

She pulled me towards the water until both our tails formed. Once they did, she dragged me through the depths until we entered her and Kysana's cave. The last time I'd seen them, they told me they were going to leave me, and I had lied about being fine with it.

Calliopé brought me some meat, but I declined. I wouldn't eat it.

She sat on the small ledge across from me. "If you're going

to take Jason down, you need help. You don't have enough energy to make him kill himself."

I laid on my side. "It wouldn't have mattered. He's still dead. That wouldn't have killed him. He's a spirit and I don't know how to kill him."

She nodded. "I suppose you're right. But all you did is piss him off and weaken yourself. This isn't going to be easy."

"I know."

"But do you? What's going to happen now?"

"I don't know."

"Exactly. That's the scariest part. You have an enemy out for blood. *Your* blood."

Kysana popped in. "Oh, hello. What's going on in here?"

Calliopé pointed to me. "She decided to try and injure Jason. Now he's extra angry and she's got no energy. Things are about to break out into a war."

I laughed. "That's not even the least of it. The mermaids think they're better than us! Wait until I show them the truth. Wait until I bite their heads off." I started gaining some energy.

Kysana pulled herself up, sitting beside me. "Things aren't always as they seem, Mia. Mermaids try to play this nice and pretty persona because they're jealous. They know that they're no better than us. That scares them because they don't want to be compared to a creature that eats humans to live."

I sat up, making sure to be careful with myself. "That's what I want to expose. I want to be there when their perfect world crumbles. I want them to know what it feels like to be me. I've spent my entire childhood in that academy. I was humiliated and made fun of. I was the laughingstock of the school. That is something that forever haunts me and they're at the root of the problem. They deserve to know what that feels like."

"Maybe so." Calliopé leaned back. "The truth remains the same. You need strength and a plan. Without any of that, you'll only embarrass yourself. Let us help you."

"A plan?" My eyes darted between them both.

Kysana and Calliopé both nodded. Whatever plan they had in mind was probably better than whatever I could muster up. Jason had messed with the wrong girl. The mermaids created the lawless monster.

After I talked to them about a plan, I headed back home. Mom was waiting for me. I had struggled between telling her the truth or not. She trusted me more and she wanted me to trust her, but if I told her the truth, she would stop me.

"I was out with Calliopé and Kysana. Don't worry. They don't plan on sticking around for much longer. They have plans to go elsewhere and help other women who are in trouble."

She nodded a little and stood up. "Have you been practicing your magic?" Did she know?

"I have, but I forgot to take energy from the moon and I got tired out quickly." We both knew my magic only worked on people, and it didn't work on Calliopé or Kysana. If I was practicing, it was on someone innocent. In her eyes, anyway. I knew that, that someone was anything but innocent.

"Was that person hurt at all?"

"No," I lied. "I'm using my magic for good." I was in a way. Jason was evil and he couldn't be redeemed now. If I didn't kill him, I would be doing others a disservice.

I wanted to ask my mom if she knew anything about aunga and adaro, but I doubted she did, and it wasn't worth getting into the whole conversation about Jason.

I said goodnight and went to my room while she headed back home. Nat was watching a movie so I sat beside her. I debated telling her about Jason, but I decided to wait until I had more of a plan ready. I didn't want him to target my friends, and I wanted us to be able to hit him without him seeing it coming.

"How was hanging out with Christian?" she asked.

With a shrug, I said, "Fine. I learned a bit about myself and that's what matters. The mermaids aren't so innocent after all, and I'll make sure they know it." I sat back, relaxing against the pillows. "Everyone will soon know exactly how *I* felt."

Thirty-four

Breakfast was awfully quiet except for the sounds of chewing and silverware clinking against ceramic dishes. The hash browns were delicious, so they made up for all the awkward silence. My parents were the ones who invited me here, so why wouldn't they speak?

"Mia wants to talk to you," Christian said to our parents.

I looked at him. "I do?"

"Yeah about what we found the other day."

Yes, that. We found out that our parents had me because someone else died.

I pushed the food around on my plate and shrugged. "I mean, I guess." I met their eyes. "Did you know that sirens are conceived through the violent death of a human?"

Mom glanced at Dad. I had hoped maybe Christian was right and they had no idea but from the way they communicated through their eyes, they knew. "We didn't go out and kill anyone, Mia. Not for you. We just happened to get pregnant as someone else somewhere in the world was brutally killed in the ocean."

Ah, yes, the ocean. Had I forgotten that the deaths that conceived mermaids and sirens were all ocean related deaths?

"Whether we got pregnant or not, they still would have died." That had been the strangest excuse I'd ever heard coming from my parents.

I took a small bite of my egg. "Mermaids are born because of death, too."

"They are."

"Which means we aren't any worse than them. They think they're somehow the good guys but they're not. Good guys don't bully a girl into feeling worthless." I pushed my plate away.

Dad put down his fork. "Do I need to talk to someone's parents?"

I shook my head. "No, no. It's okay. I just want to forget about it." Yeah, I couldn't exactly forget.

After breakfast, Natalia and I decided to go to Jason's parents. I wanted her help on what really happened to him, but I wasn't about to tell her the full truth.

His mom answered the door, and as soon as she saw us, she closed it. Nat knocked again and louder this time. His mom came back. "What do you want?"

"We want to ask you about your son."

"I don't have a son."

I stuck my foot in the door before she closed it again. "Jason. His name is Jason and you gave birth to him. He was once aunga and somehow, he died. He bullied me for years and forced me to eat the meat of a human boy. You very well have a son, Mrs. Stanford."

Her lips twitched as she opened the door. "It's Ms. Stanford."

I nodded. "May we come in?"

She didn't refuse this time. She let us inside and crossed her arms as she faced us. "I disowned him the minute he died. The Jason I knew died that day and this version of him is not my son."

I scanned her home before looking at her. "How did he die?"

Ms. Stanford's whole demeanor changed. She dropped her arms and closed her eyes for a moment before looking at the ground. "His father and I didn't pay enough attention to him. We refused to see the signs."

Nat stepped forward. "Did Jason commit suicide?"

Years after this tragedy, she still couldn't admit the truth. She couldn't say the words. "After we lost him, he continued to come back home but he was cruel. While we grieved for our dead son, his spirit taunted us and treated us like the horrible parents we were. It wasn't long after that when his father and I got a divorce. He ran off, leaving me behind because he refused to be around Jason's spirit. He took half of everything, and Jason got worse."

That had been the snapping point. His parents' divorce was right before he started to get violent with me, wasn't it?

I swallowed. "I'm sorry, Ms. Stanford, but I have to ask. How do we kill an adaro?"

She sat down on the couch. "Jason was born like any other normal boy. We wanted him to learn about himself, so we sent him to the Academy of Naiad. Even after his death, he didn't stop going. Something about a girl... Aunga are good creatures. You must know that my son was never really like this."

Nat snickered. "He may be an evil spirit but we know that

when Aunga die, all that dies is the good part of him. Adaro is the evil part that stayed behind as a ghost. Deep down, he was like this in some ways."

She was right. Jason may not have acted on the bad parts of himself, but they were still part of who he was.

"Why did he..." I gestured. "Why was he so depressed?"

Ms. Stanford sighed. "His father and I had already talked about getting a divorce long before his death. We would fight all the time and things just weren't what they used to be."

Nat looked at me. "That would make any child go crazy. He probably felt responsible somehow."

"What?" His mom shook her head. "None of that was ever his fault."

Natalia looked back at her. "We know that, but have you ever been a child with parents before? It's natural to feel like it's your fault. You always believe you can stop the inevitable from happening. Children blame themselves more times than not, and that's at the fault of the parent."

I wanted to stop Nat from saying these awful things, but Ms. Stanford agreed with her. She agreed that she was at fault, and she should have done more to stop him.

"I don't blame him," she whispered, "I don't blame Jason for anything. The divorce, the suicide... None of it was his fault. He was just a child. We did this to our son. We were supposed to be the adults and we failed him."

As much as I wanted to say she was wrong, she wasn't. Jason had barely been fourteen or so when he killed himself. He didn't understand the full weight of what he did. He just wanted to end it and fix everything for his parents. He wanted to take away their burden.

He wasn't the burden. He never had been. His parents had

been his burden. They expected him to raise himself and they ignored all his cries for help. All he needed was a mom and dad to love him as he was.

"Well, thank you for your time. You still haven't answered the question, however. How do we kill this evil spirit?" Nat asked.

She looked up at us, fear clouding her eyes. "You can't."

As I RAKED ALL the ideas in my head, none of them seemed to make sense. She said he was immortal now. He was already dead, so it made sense that we couldn't kill him.

But I couldn't just sit here and let him torment me for the rest of my life. I had to do something. I just wasn't sure what I could do.

Nat sat beside me, nudging my shoulder. "Are you okay?"

I shook my head. "I know I'm not supposed to justify what Jason has done, but I still feel for him. He was the victim in the beginning and all it's done is destroy his life in the end. How is any of that fair? Why would this be allowed to happen?"

"I can't answer that. I know you feel like it's your job to fix him, or maybe talk to him and tell him that he was never the cause of what happened in his family life. But the good part of him died that day, Mia. He will never be able to fully understand and change who he is now."

She noticed that I had been contemplating my entire decision to kill him. Part of me wanted to try and save him, to prove that not all those meant for evil would follow that path.

Unfortunately, I knew she was right. The aunga part of him

had died. He was no longer the sweet Jason his family once knew. He was left a hollow shell of himself—an evil spirit seeking revenge.

"If I'm supposed to kill him, how do I do that? Even his mother said he isn't mortal anymore. Aunga are, but adaro are not. I don't exactly have the means to go back to the academy and research some more."

Nat shrugged. "We'll find a way. We have to, right? Nothing is immortal, Mia. At least not truly. Even vampires can be killed."

"Vampires don't exist."

"Not in this world," Nat teased.

I laughed a little. "Not in this world..." I looked up at the moon, swinging my feet back and forth. Somewhere out there, there were other worlds of other creatures. That's what Nat believed.

In these worlds, things were different. Humans and vampires could be together without issues. If they could do it, why couldn't I? Calliopé did say we were like vampires but with tails. Well, she said something like that.

How would Dylan feel about this plan? I had to kill Jason no matter what, and he wouldn't be able to talk me out of it. Was he serious about never being able to hate me? This would be the true test to his integrity.

I had to give him that chance to decide for himself.

"Do you ever want kids?" Nat asked.

I shrugged. I'd never really thought about it, but I wasn't sure if I did. As for Dylan, he sounded like the kind of guy that did want kids someday. If we made it past this bump in the road, maybe we could talk about that later down the line.

"Do you?" I asked in return.

She looked at the ground. "I do, sometimes, want a mini-Natalia to raise and hold. She'll be so cute with her little tail."

That was the one bummer about being a siren. We didn't get our tail until we turned eighteen. If Dylan and I did ever have kids, there wouldn't be any babies with tails.

"She'd be adorable. I'd happily babysit if you ever need me to."

Nat smiled. "I'd make you babysit."

We both laughed. We knew she would, but I'd enjoy it. Even if I never wanted kids of my own, I could enjoy others' kids. That was the perks of being an aunt.

"Where's Olivia?"

She looked around. "She's been trying to get her first job. As well as crack out the last of the homework before you all graduate." It was no secret that Nat wasn't physically in school with us. She decided to finish her senior year online since her graduation wasn't going to be that big of a deal with anyone back home.

"Before *we* graduate. You'll be there with us."

"Not wearing a cap and gown. My diploma will be mailed to me."

"You'll still be considered the class of 2021. You can't escape that. We'll all be celebrating." It was hard to believe that next month would be our final month in school. I hadn't truly decided yet if I wanted to go to college.

Nat was certain she wanted to go, but she was interested in marine biology. It was strange considering she was already a sea nymph and she had to hide herself from others, but she said she wanted to do it the right way. She wanted to study other creatures while treating them with respect to show humans that they could do the same about us. It was her way of leading us towards a future where we could all live peacefully.

It was sweet of her to want to aim for that kind of future, and if she had kids, she'd be a wonderful mom for it. She didn't always come off as this woman who cared about others, but she had always been that way. She just wanted everyone to coexist. She understood what it was like to be different and be shamed for it, and she didn't want that to be the future for anyone else. She had a big heart.

Whatever Nat did with her life, I knew she would be part of the change that all sea creatures needed to see. She was anything *but* a monster.

Thirty-five

Dylan massaged my shoulders as we both faced the mirror in the bathroom. "It's not shameful, and it shouldn't be. Say it, Mia. I want to hear you say it."

"But if I say it, it becomes who I am. I hate who I am."

He grabbed my wrist and twirled me until I faced him. "Why do you hate yourself? Give me reasons."

"Because I hate what I'm supposed to be, expected to just be the monster." I met his gaze.

Leaning his forehead against mine, he grabbed my cheeks. "But that's not the law. You choose. You make your own choices and whatever stupid lie the mermaids told you, it's bullshit. You hate yourself because they hate you. It's time for you to stop caring about what they think. They're the ones who bully a girl and think that makes them good people. You do not want to be like them."

I gripped the edge of the counter, swallowing my anxiety. Deep breaths.

"I want to hear you say it. You can never learn to love yourself if you don't accept yourself as you are. You can't change your DNA, so why try? Why put yourself through that kind of misery?"

"I killed Todd. I killed the other boy. It was too easy for me to become the killer."

"We both killed Todd. We both were an accomplice to his murder. And you didn't kill that boy alone. Your other friends were with you. You can't pin all the blame on yourself, Mia. Don't you see? It hurts me when it hurts you." Before I could respond, Dylan kissed me as if I were going to die tomorrow. His lips tasted of honey and without fail, I devoured every emotion running through him.

Remorse. Undeniable love. A pain so broken that even I couldn't handle living like that any longer.

And then I craved more. "Dylan, stop," I whispered, placing my hand against his chest. "As much as I love kissing you, I want to do more and you don't. I don't want to put either of us through that."

A shiver trickled down my spine as he placed his palm over the top of my hand. "What if I told you I want more, too?"

My breath caught in my throat as I lifted my eyes to see him staring at me. Neither of us said another word as our lips created new emotions only we'd ever understand from each other.

Dylan made it seem so easy, like he'd done this before. Had he? I didn't think so, but we'd never officially talked about it. His hands fell as they glided up my thighs and lifted me onto the counter. He pulled my shirt over my head while I snaked my arms around his neck.

The knob clicked as the door swung open and Natalia lifted her eyebrows. "Oh shit. No, um, this can wait. Carry on." She put her hands up. "I do not want to be a cockblock." She closed the door.

The two of us breathed each other in before I put my shirt back on, trying to brush out my hair. I slid off the counter, slipping past Dylan and out of the bathroom. My heart pounded in my ears at the thought of what we had been about to do. For everyone else, it became normal. Routine. Exciting. It was something that so many people did and it wasn't a crazy idea.

But with your best friend, the idea did seem far out there. It felt wrong yet thrilling all at once. To know them in ways you'd never expected to know them before, ways nobody else *could* ever know them.

For the rest of the world, sex was an everyday thing.

For Dylan and I, it didn't seem real.

Nat caught my eye and frowned. "Oh no, I did it, didn't I? I cockblocked."

"Can you please stop calling it that? It sounds weird." I put my hands in my back pockets.

"What else do I call it?"

"Nothing. We just got caught up in the moment. There are more important things to focus on right now, and I don't need the stress of pregnancy on top of that. Contraceptives are not always effective. Even with protection, I'd still get anxiety about it." I shook my head. "We have to go out today. To the beach."

"We do?" she asked with furrowed eyebrows.

"We do," Dylan said as he came from the bathroom. "Because today Mia is going to show me her tail and admit that she's a siren. Isn't that right?" He gave me a look.

Without really overthinking the repercussions, I said the one thing I never wanted to. All because of Dylan. "I am a siren."

Both of them froze in their places.

"Did you just admit it?" Nat's eyes grew wide. "I've never heard you say it before."

I shrugged a bit. "I am. And you're both right. It's time that I accept that. I can't change it just by pretending or living in a fantasy. I was content in living a lie, refusing to embrace who I really am. The mermaids think they're better than me because they make me want to kill myself, but that's not true. Now that I think more about it, they probably despise Jason because he truly is evil. Deep down, they're only using him for their benefit. But I also believe they're afraid of him because Jason is a link between us and them. He is both good and evil—once good, now evil. Sirens and mermaids aren't too different at the root of everything. One just gets labeled the hero while the other the villain."

With all of that out in the open, weight lifted from my chest. I no longer felt the anxiety from what I was by admitting it. Dylan thought I was cool, so why couldn't I believe the same? The mermaids were not as great as they pretended to be. I wanted to be less like them.

Nat followed me and Dylan down to the beach while I planned to show him my tail, and Olivia met us there.

"This whole damn feud started when a siren ate a mermaid's lover. She did this because he was going to expose the mermaid and use her for selfish reasons, but she didn't believe the siren, and now mermaids judge us. They assume we're all evil." I pulled my shirt off.

Dylan scoffed. "You're definitely not. You could pass off as a mermaid if you *really* wanted to."

"Why did you want to be a mermaid in the first place?"

Olivia asked.

"Because they're beautiful and everyone loves them. I've struggled with accepting myself for so many years. I didn't want to be like this. I wanted to be a mermaid. I almost look just like them. I act just like them. I never understood why I couldn't be one of them."

Natalia came over to me, putting her hands on my shoulders. "Fuck the mermaids. They have their own problems and are too hypocritical to realize it. You're a beautiful person who happens to be a siren. That doesn't at all affect your personality. You're strong enough to resist your urges and that is what makes you a better person than them."

"What urges? I've killed."

"I killed Todd, not you. The second boy was more of a courtesy death. There's nothing wrong with embracing something that you can't control. You didn't decide to be a siren. You just are. You can't change it so worrying about it is useless. You control your actions, and you've proved you are much better than that. Be the change. Be the example that sirens are not all bad and that mermaids need to not judge. You even told us the siren ate the mermaid's lover to protect her from his intentions. Sirens are not all bad."

I lowered my head.

Natalia shook me a bit, getting me to look at her again. "You're a siren. So what. You can breathe underwater and swim faster than your human half. That is so damn cool. You are a mythological creature! We are much more interesting than our stereotypes. We are more than our species. You are so much more than just a siren. You are Mia Dawson."

She moved as Dylan stole the spotlight. "She's right. You know she is. You've proved to me that you are not like that.

You've had plenty of chances to eat me, but you didn't." He kissed me.

I kissed back, grabbing his neck. He loved me despite knowing what I was. If everyone could love me for who I was as a person and not judge me for my DNA, I could do the same. I was a siren, but it didn't define my actions.

"Okay, lovebirds. Nobody wants to watch this." Nat rolled her eyes.

We pulled away and I laughed a bit. Everyone fell silent for a few minutes, but it didn't last longer than that. Olivia said, "Let's go swimming already. I'm bored to death."

Dylan looked at her. "You can't be bored to death when you're already dead inside."

She flipped him off.

"Right, swimming. My tail." I laughed nervously, twirling hair around my finger.

Dylan smiled but didn't say anything in response to that.

I averted my gaze away from his, afraid to look him in the eyes.

Without another word, I stripped down and ran into the shallow waters. When it was deep enough, I dove into the waves. My tail came in time as it flashed above the water and disappeared again. I spun around and swam to the surface. "What are you waiting for?"

Dylan ripped his shirt off and ran into the water, falling right into the seafoam. "Let me see!"

I laughed as I brought my tail closer to the surface. He reached out and smoothed his fingers along the fins like they were strands of hair. I giggled, pulling it away. "That tickles."

"Sorry," he said with a cheeky smile.

Both of our smiles fell as Dylan leaned closer.

I'd had this little fantasy as a girl to kiss in the rain, but it would never come true due to the nature of what I was. The closest I could get would be kissing in the ocean, and Dylan was the one I could count on to make that come true.

The kiss started out slow and cautious, hands uncertain of their positions. In seconds, hunger took control. We couldn't get enough of each other and something deep inside me began to grow. I'd never experienced anything like it before, but it was certainly a feeling I wanted to try out again.

And then my sharp teeth erupted from my gums. Dylan attempted to slip his tongue in and I pulled away in a hurry. After covering my mouth, I turned away. "I can't."

"Mia, I'm not afraid of you."

"I'm afraid."

He moved closer, making me face him. "Let me help. That's what best friends are for. I know it can be terrifying, not sure of what could happen. But your mom made it work with your dad, so why can't we do the same?"

Shaking my head, I looked into the water. "I've never felt this way with you. It's new and thrilling. At the same time, that scares me. I'm a creature who survives on the lives of other men. You should be my prey, not my lover. I'm defying the rules just to be here with you."

He closed the gap between us. "Let me love you, Mia."

It wasn't as easy as he made it sound. Did I deserve that after what happened to Todd and the boy who drowned?

He yelled as something rammed into his side and within seconds, he was under the surface.

"Dylan!" I screamed, diving in. I looked around for him as a blur flew by me. I swam after it and caught him, yanking him into my arms.

Jason.

I screamed out, silenced by the ocean. I pushed him into the rocks with his head against the jagged edges.

Another body moved me aside, grabbing him by the hair and slamming his head into the rock. Nat looked back at me and shot her eyes towards another direction. When I followed, I saw Dylan fighting for his life in the depths of the abyss.

Swimming as fast as I could, I grabbed his face and kissed him, breathing air into his lungs. The tension in my muscles vanished when he put his hands on my waist, holding on as if his life depended on it. It did, in his case.

I swam up to the surface, wrapping my arms around his torso to keep him above the water. "You're safe," I choked out.

I hurried back to the shore. Dylan crawled onto the sand, pulling me with him before collapsing into my chest. He was shaking in a way I'd never seen before.

Olivia wanted to run to us, but she knew I had it handled. She had reason to be more worried about Nat.

With Dylan in my arms, I took deep breaths to calm myself down. "You're safe now, Dill. You're alive and safe in my arms. I will never let anything happen again. You can count on that."

How he had accepted me being a siren before I could was beyond me. I never understood how that happened. His love for me was real and I knew that for a fact because he loved me more than I loved myself. I couldn't let him die at the hands of my stupidity.

Someone yelled.

Coming back to reality, I saw Natalia yelling as Olivia helped her out of the water. Cuts and bruises ran along her torso just as guilt swept over me. It flew past me and into the road behind Dylan and I. "We need to get home, now," I said.

As our tails dried, the four of us hurried back to the apartment before Jason targeted us again. Whatever he was planning, we had to be prepared for. His one goal was to kill.

A gasp escaped my lips, and I attempted to catch my breath at the glimpse of Dylan's thigh. I grabbed my chest and closed my eyes. I opened them again, gathering all the supplies to help bandage him up. The cut wasn't deep but seeing the blood brought rage to my soul.

I sat and cleaned him up before applying the gauze. "How's Nat?" I asked Olivia.

Olivia shook her head. "She'll be okay. She needs to sleep."

"What happened?" Dylan's voice was very firm, no hint of humor in it.

I wrapped my arms around his chest, taking some deep breaths. "Jason tried to kill you." I pressed my ear against Dylan's chest, listening to his heartbeat. It calmed my nerves.

"And he'll try again, won't he?" his voice came out barely a whisper.

Panic settled back into me, hanging on tightly this time.

Dylan looked at me. "You have everyone here. Natalia sleeps next to you every night. I'm right across from your room. Olivia is just a phone call away. We are all here for you and he can't hurt you." He held my face, keeping my eyes fixed on him. "He won't touch me again. What he wants is you, Mia, and we won't let that happen."

I nodded slightly, taking deep breaths. "He terrifies me. He has a vendetta against me that has only festered over the years."

"And now he knows you have a whole team to support you

this time," Olivia said.

I looked back at the window, searching for his face but I came up empty. He was gone for now. "Okay." I put my head against Dylan's chest again, giving myself the comfort I needed to soothe the fear. I wasn't too sure if he was stalking me, but the possibility was there.

Adaro were evil and dangerous, and Jason despised me the most. If anyone were going to feel his wrath, *I* would be the victim. He'd been after me all this time for what I did to him. I had to be prepared for anything, even if it meant using my abilities and becoming exactly what I wished I never was.

Thirty-six

I SAT ON MY bed and looked at Natalia. "Do you think I'm crazy?"

"No, I don't. Jason is crazy. He always went too far. He started the damn thing and yet he pretends everything is your fault. People like him have lost all sense of humanity and logic. They blame everyone else for their own actions. It's like in the horror movies when the victim escapes but gets caught, the killer punishes them as if they didn't expect them to run. Jason is punishing you as if he didn't expect you to fight back and defend yourself," she said.

I nodded, looking at the floor. "How are we supposed to get proof? I need to lure him out somehow and show that he's still me enemy. He's still after me and I don't want my family to assume the worst when we find a way to kill him."

"There's one simple way to do so." She smirked.

"I was thinking about it and this isn't just an excuse for me to not be like the sirens but it's also a fact. He's not human. I can't lure in other sea creatures. I can only lure in human men. It's out of the question."

"If he knew this all along, why did he try so hard to make you act like a siren?"

"Because he wanted to humiliate me and prove I was like them. Even if I can't sing to him, he could still say that I attempted to eat him and everyone would know. What use would it be to be seen as a bad siren and have proof behind it? At least with everyone judging me, I don't feel guilty because I know it's not true. I feel more ashamed than anything. It's as if I'm the daughter of a serial killer." I released a sigh.

"We will find a way. I mean, he can't hide forever. If he is planning to get back at you, he will eventually show himself. What if we bait him?" Natalia nodded.

I looked at her, furrowing my eyebrows. "Bait him? How?"

"He wants you, right? He wants you when you're alone and vulnerable. We can make it seem as if you are and then he will have to make his move. We will catch him and kill him."

"He's already dead."

Natalia rubbed her eyes. "Mia, you are getting on my nerves. He is dead, but there's still some way to defeat the evil spirit. There always is a way to defeat evil. To those who believe in hell, demons don't die either, but you can still lock them up or defeat them somehow. This is no different. We will figure out how to defeat him first so our plan is foolproof."

I fiddled with my fingers, thinking about it. "Okay. We will probably have to research more about them. We have to go back to the library at the academy."

Natalia nodded. "Then let's not waste any more time."

I SWUNG MY LITTLE bag over my shoulder, turning around

and bumping into someone. "Sorry." I looked at him.

Dylan chuckled. "Hello there, stranger. You now owe me a favor. One kiss, please."

I smiled and kissed him, walking away.

Everyone followed me and Natalia back to the academy. Dylan drove us much to my convincing.

Upon arriving at the building, we all stood on the sidewalk, eyeing it as if we were about to fight a war. We were but it would not happen here.

"Let's go, my friends." I walked inside and they followed me to the office where we all got our visitors badges.

"This is where Natalia and I spent our teenage years. It's crazy that time went by so fast," I said.

"It looks like a castle. It's huge." My brother was looking around, staring mostly at the high ceilings.

Olivia nodded. "I love that. A big castle. It makes it feel less...restricting. I don't feel like I'm at a boarding school or somewhere strict. It's fun. It gives off a friendly environment."

Christian walked ahead of us.

I went to catch up, shaking my head. "You don't know where the library is, you idiot."

"I'm sure I can find it."

I scoffed. "Yeah, right." I looked at the ceiling and coughed a bit. I looked at some places and we stopped at the end of the hall, looking at a little dead end that had a big window to let in light. "This is where Jason forced me to eat human meat."

Natalia grabbed my hand, squeezing it. "That prick will get his karma."

The scene was still etched in my brain, reminding me of the pure terror gripping my soul. Nothing had been crueler than this exact memory, and if it had been the only thing he did, it was enough to fuel all my hatred and send me to kill him.

"Eat it!" he yelled, trying to shove the meat into my mouth. I turned my head, refusing to go down this way. "Grab her," he ordered. They grabbed me and held me in place. I couldn't fight back.

"Stop! This is wrong! You can't do this!" I was begging that he wouldn't go through with it.

He came over, forcing my mouth open. "You are what you eat." He forced the meat in, closing my jaw and holding it. "Swallow."

I tried to move my head, refusing to swallow. It just sat there on my tongue and I could taste every ounce of flavor in it. It wasn't long before I swallowed it. He checked my mouth, patting my chin. "Good girl."

His friends let go of me and I took off towards the girl's bathroom. My cheeks were completely soaked and I couldn't get the tears to stop flowing.

I turned away from the window, sighing. "The memories are still too painful."

My brother came over this time, hugging me. It was unusual. "That's not fair to you. We will make sure he pays. Forcing someone to eat something they don't want to is sick on so many levels." He pulled away.

I nodded, taking a deep breath. I was okay now.

We turned and walked the other way, down the hall some more. I stopped as we walked into the front doors.

"This is the library. Find everything you can on adaro." We put our bags down. I went to the shelves and searched for all books containing lore on adaro specifically. There had to be some sort of hint in here as to what would defeat them. Jason was going to get what he deserved.

I scratched my shoulder and took a seat in a chair. I flipped through pages, skimming over anything that mentioned their weakness. They had to have one. Everything had a weakness.

"This is getting nowhere. While you guys continue this, I have something I want to do first." I slipped out of the library and found one of the teachers in her empty classroom. She was a siren herself.

"Mia, come in." She waved me over.

I did as she said, approaching her desk with caution. "I wanted to ask you a question and I'm hoping for an honest answer."

She lifted her eyes from her desk. "What is it?"

"Why didn't we learn about our magic? You knew we'd get it no matter what, so what good does it do to hide it? Why not tell us about it and help us use it for good? Uncontrolled magic is more dangerous than having it." I put my hands in the back pockets of my shorts.

She nodded a bit. "I see. May I ask what your gift is?" She called it a gift, meaning she didn't believe our magic was evil.

"I can control people."

"The board doesn't want us to concern you with magic. As harsh as it sounds, they don't trust you and they certainly don't trust us. Besides, there weren't enough courses, teachers, or time for us to help you all master your magic. If you didn't turn until after you left, it didn't seem useful to mention magic. We leave that part up to your parents."

After a minute, I thanked her and went back to the library, playing my role once again in the hunt for adaro.

We searched all the books, ready to give up hope. "I found

something," Olivia said. She came over and showed me a few paragraphs. "They're a mix of different sea creatures, correct? Well, what harms those? Those are easy to harm. Stabbing them with something metal is the best because they're big and have tough skin. What harms the sea spirit? Iron. You need to get metal iron to pierce him. Then we will win."

I read the paragraphs, confirming what she said. She was right. Jason needed to be defeated with an iron rod of some sort. It wouldn't be hard to find. "His weakness is iron. This is gold. Pun intended," I joked.

We all left the academy and went back home.

"Thank you," I told Olivia, throwing my bag on the couch. "You shouldn't be caught up in this mess."

She shook her head. "No, don't worry about it. I want to do this. I want to help you defeat the boy who hurt you so bad. We're friends now, Mia. Friends help each other out."

"But I feel bad."

"Then don't. Jason is a bad guy. He has traumatized you. I want to help you get back at him for it. That will be payback enough," she said, laughing to herself.

Natalia laid onto my bed, sighing happily. "Isn't this nice? All on our own now." She shot Olivia a smirk.

I rolled my eyes. "It's just for the weekend. We are only here to find out his weakness and bait him, getting rid of him for good. We have a few more days to do that. If we don't succeed..."

"We will." Natalia looked up at me. "You get to show him what you're made of. Enough is enough." She pushed her curls from her face, struggling to make it stay put.

I sat, frowning. "I hope you're right."

Olivia looked at her, smirking. "So, no parents for the

weekend. Any plans for us?"

I gagged. "Please, save the sexy talk for when I leave the room. I'd like to keep my innocence, thank you."

Natalia sat up and smiled. "Yes, I do. I planned a date, then maybe something else after."

A date didn't sound bad. But why would they need to go on a date if this was just a fling? I didn't understand.

Olivia laid on her stomach, resting her chin on her hands held up by her elbows on the bed. "That sounds like a wonderful idea."

I looked at them, not saying anything.

Natalia got up and looked at us. "Let's all go out."

"Where are we going to go? We're all too young to drink," I commented, not looking at them but rather at my phone.

Natalia put her arms around my shoulders. "Where else? We can just go hang out with the boys. I mean, if I'm going to have a date with Olivia, I can't stay here all day."

I shrugged a bit. "Whatever."

She laughed and got off the bed. "Come on!" She grabbed an outfit and changed. Olivia and I got up, not really needing a reason to change.

Natalia came out of the bathroom and fixed her curls, looking at us. "What do you think?" She looked at her outfit.

Olivia gave her a smile. "I think it is absolutely stunning on you."

Natalia blushed.

It was a simple black dress with a straight neckline and thin straps to hold it together. The skirt flowed, creating a high-low look. It was cute but not too formal.

"Let's go." She led us out the door and knocked on the door across from ours. The boys came out and looked at us, understanding what we were here for.

We all went to the park. Natalia was playing around on the children's playground and Dylan pointed to her.

I watched her, smiling a bit. "She's crazy. That's all I can say, Dill Pickle." She was but that was why I loved her so much. Natalia was such a great friend to me. I wanted to be a great friend in return. If I was going to be a good friend, I needed to quit being so weird around her and Olivia, expecting them to expect me to choose a side. If their fling was becoming serious, that was even better.

If something happened between them, I had to be there for both, reminding them that I was their friend and not just one or the other.

"What's on your mind?" Dylan asked.

I looked at him. "Just thinking about Nat and Olivia. I have to learn to get used to them, even though Natalia has ended every relationship so fast. She deserves happiness and love. She's been such a good friend and I need to return the favor."

Dylan kissed my head and grabbed my hand, locking our fingers together. "Good. They could turn out to be a really good couple. Who knows? Maybe they could realize it won't work out. Only they will know, and you just have to give them the chance to find out how well they could work."

Tilting my head as I watched Olivia take pictures of Nat on the swing, I asked, "Do we work?"

After brushing his lips across my ear, he hovered right near my temple. "If you were to ask me to marry you the day you came back, I'd say yes in a heartbeat."

Thirty-seven

I LOWERED MY HANDS, letting go of the energy I'd stolen from the moon. The innocent bystanders were given permission to walk away, and I hoped and prayed they would not end up like the other boy I killed.

"That wasn't bad," Calliopé said. "But you can't win against Jason. You need more practice."

"More? Do we want to wear me out? The whole point of practice is so I can get used to not wearing myself out when using my magic. If I keep using it all at once, I'll never learn when I need to stop and where my limit is."

She grumbled. "What else are we supposed to do?"

"Maybe we should come up with a real plan to kill Jason? He's dead. We have to find something that works. I can't just go into this war with a blind eye." I rolled my eyes. The rod idea had failed. It wasn't so easy, yet the books had misled us. Adaro didn't want anyone to know the true way to kill one.

Kysana walked in front of us, sitting down on some rocks. "Here's the deal. He's adaro, meaning he's already dead, right?"

I nodded.

"How do you get rid of the dead?"

"I don't know."

"Okay, well, have you ever seen a scary movie?" Kysana gestured.

I shrugged. "Yeah."

"Again, I ask, how do you get rid of the dead?"

"Exorcism."

"No, that's demons. Demons are not dead."

"I don't know! Every movie I've seen, they haven't been able to get rid of ghosts." In my eyes, ghosts were impossible to get rid of.

Calliopé cleared her throat. "You burn the bones."

I gave her a strange look. "What?"

She looked at Kysana. "You burn the bones. Adaro are evil spirits. They are not a body, so you can't actually damage them because they're just...an entity. But that means the body it's attached to is somewhere, and we must burn the body of Jason to try and get rid of his ghost."

"If it's that easy, why didn't his mother tell me?"

Calliopé threw her arms up in frustration. "She's still his mother! Would you tell someone how to kill your child, even if they were evil? She stayed here for a reason, Mia. There's a maternal bond she can't break with Jason no matter what."

We all headed to go to my parents' house to get the tools we needed to dig up a body and burn it. I thought maybe it would have been an easy task, but when Calliopé and Kysana walked into my house with my whole family there, they didn't let us leave.

"Who are these girls?" Mom asked.

I pointed to the redhead. "Calliopé." Then I pointed to the

second girl with black hair. "Kysana."

Christian was quick to jump off the couch and straighten himself out. "Hey, I'm Christian." His attempts were pathetic, and Kysana and Calliopé saw right through it.

Mom stepped in front of my brother and looked at Calliopé. "I've heard a little about you. Mia tells me that you two were bitten."

"Mom!"

Calliopé shrugged it off. "We were."

I cleared my throat. "We have somewhere to be."

Dad stood up, blocking me. "Hey, we want to get to know your friends. Whatever it is can wait."

We were never getting out of here, and Christian kept ogling over them. They were sirens, sure, but this was just ridiculous on his part. They weren't interested.

Calliopé put her hand out, shaking my mom and dad's hands. "It's nice to meet you. Mia has taught us a lot, even if you don't trust her with our kind."

Mom gave me a look, and I knew I was going to get an earful for that one. What did she really expect? I was going to confide in my friends about how I felt, and I *felt* like my parents had no faith in me.

Kysana waved, ignoring my brother on purpose. I had a feeling that Kysana had no interest in romance after what happened years ago, and I couldn't blame her. Every woman had her own way of coping, and this was hers.

Calliopé turned to face Christian. "We understand that you like our faces and our bodies, but we are not interested. Please, stop staring. It's rude."

Christian turned red before Dad steered him out of the living room, and I was going to tease him about all this later.

Mom led us to the kitchen. "Are you two hungry at all?" She pulled out a container of meat.

Calliopé said no thank you, but Kysana wasn't about to turn down a meal. Mom gave her a few bites, smiling. I could see the way she looked at Kysana. She wished I were that way.

"Mia doesn't eat humans, so I have a lot of meat and nobody to share it with," she said.

Calliopé coughed, changing the subject. "Mrs. Dawson, how do your husband and son feel about all of this? We never really asked because we've never met another purebred before Mia. You eat human men, and you live with two of them. Surely they get sick or scared from time to time."

Mom put the meat away. "I suppose that's a valid question. I do live with my prey. I like to believe that love overcomes my deepest desires."

I'd never thought to ask Christian that question myself, but now I was curious. Did he ever have nightmares about us? I was certain he did. Somewhere deep down, he feared what Mom and I could do.

"These two again?" Nat asked as she came in.

"They're still my friends." I pointed to them. "They're sirens, too. And whether you like it or not, I need to be around other sirens."

Nat crossed her arms and came to grab a snack. "The same sirens who eat humans for fun?"

"Nat, they're not like that." I stepped in front of her. "Besides, you know I'm a siren, too."

"There's a difference between you and...them." She glanced at them.

"They're my friends."

Nat faced them. "What is her favorite color?"

Calliopé shrugged. "Why would that matter? The real question is, what's her magical ability?"

Nat glanced at me. "That's easy. She can tell people what to do. She can control them. She's like a puppet master."

Puppet master. I hated the sound of that. It made me sound so wicked to the core.

Calliopé stepped forward. "If you must know, we're the ones trying to help her kill Jason."

Shit.

"Kill Jason?" Mom asked. "Who is Jason and why are we trying to kill him?"

Nat scowled. "I'm the one who defended her against him all those years at the academy. Don't you dare act like I wasn't her friend first."

"Who is Jason?" Mom asked louder.

Calliopé narrowed her eyes. "Where were you when Jason confronted her? We were the ones who had to take Mia back home."

Mom slammed her hand on the counter, a loud slapping sound echoing throughout the kitchen. "Enough!" she yelled. "You will knock this nonsense off right now." She turned her head towards me. "Who is Jason?"

I played with the hem of my shirt, avoiding all eye contact. "Jason was the boy who bullied me at the academy. He got violent at times."

Mom's eyes softened and she approached me. "What did he do to you?"

The fear in her eyes was hard to miss, but I assured her he never did anything like that. "He used to play awful pranks on me about my boob size. He made me eat human flesh, and he's attacked me multiple times."

Her eyes turned into tiny slits as so many thoughts ran through her mind. What had we unleashed?

"Where is this bastard of a child?" She looked at my friends for answers.

I cleared my throat. "He's the one who killed Harrison Peterson. He's the real killer who tried to frame me for it. But Mom, he isn't normal. He's adaro."

At the sound of that word, she snapped her head back to me. She *knew* what that was. She knew what that meant.

"Adaro? As in the evil spirit left behind when aunga die?" She clenched her fists until her knuckles turned white. She drew blood as her nails dug into her palms.

All I could do was nod.

Mom walked to the counter, every step more confident than the last. She pulled out something. "I've encountered adaro before. They're nasty, but they're not immortal like they claim."

Calliopé laughed. "Whoa, your mom is so cool."

My mom handed me something. "No matter what he does, or what he says, never trust him. Their goal is to make you doubt yourself. You're a siren and you're capable of so much more than that, Mia."

I looked at the object. It was a necklace. "What is this?"

"It was my mother's. The adaro I dealt with is who killed your grandma. I want you to remember her when you rip his heart out. Figuratively speaking, of course." She sighed. "You are the one who can stop him."

I swallowed, nodding. "That's where we were headed, to burn his bones and end his reign of terror. We came to get the shovels and some other things." I held the necklace close to me. "That's why we have to leave quickly."

Mom nodded as she led me to the shed in the backyard. She grabbed some tools and handed me a matchbook. "Take these. Remember, cemeteries do have maintenance. Don't get caught or we'll have a hard time bailing you out of jail."

I never thought I'd hear the words *'don't get caught'* from my mother. She supported our choices, and I questioned why I hadn't been honest with her in the first place. I thought she never would have understood any of this, but she understood more than I thought. For years, adaro were terrorizing the other sea creatures.

Aunga were born and as adaro they'd die.

If they were so vicious, why were they allowed at the academy?

They weren't. Aunga were allowed, but adaro were forbidden. However, Adaro were smart enough to pretend to be aunga to stay, and that's exactly what Jason had done to fool everyone.

I put the necklace on and we took our supplies. Mom sent us on our way while Nat stayed behind. She didn't want to, but I didn't want to have to break up any fights between them, and Calliopé and Kysana knew what to do better than Nat did.

Besides, they wouldn't stay much longer. They'd soon be on their way and Nat could live in peace knowing that I was no longer hanging out with sirens in the sea. She told me to accept myself, yet she didn't want me hanging out with other sirens. It didn't make much sense, but I'd have to ask her about that another day.

Taking Mom's advice, the three of us set out to find his tombstone at the cemetery. I despised being here, but I didn't have much of a choice.

Kysana called us both over when she found him, and Calliopé grabbed a shovel. "Let's get to digging."

We did. We all started digging using the shovels from my home until we hit something hard. I jumped down and wiped the dirt off before opening his casket. I swallowed at the sight of a decaying body left in tattered clothes. The smell was an intense rotting, pungent odor.

Calliopé threw me a matchbook and I lit it, dropping it inside the casket. I closed the lid and climbed out of the pit. The three of us watched his body burn to nothing as that smell began to fill the air around us.

"You think it's that easy?" someone asked.

We turned to see Jason watching us.

"I might have been in that body once, but we are separate now. You can't kill me." A cunning smile formed on his lips. "My mother didn't tell you that I'm immortal because she still loves me. She told you that because she'd already tried."

Thirty-eight

The sun rose in the sky. Birds chirped. Clouds floated by. Everything seemed peaceful, but it wasn't. Not with Jason out there and Nat in here, both just as angry with me.

She was angry with me because of Calliopé and Kysana.

"They're sirens, Mia! They're not even purebred and you want to associate with two sirens who never had anyone to teach them right from wrong! That is dangerous. You are treading in dangerous waters," she said.

I released a sigh as I rested my arms across my windowsill. "They're victims. They're not the bad guys. I can control myself."

"That isn't the point. They influence you."

Facing Natalia, I rubbed my eyes. "Influence me in what way? I'm determined to use my magic for good. I'm killing Jason because I must defend myself and I have that right."

The beauty of Jason already having a death certificate meant if I killed his spirit, I wasn't *really* killing Jason. Jason died long ago, and I was doing everyone a favor by killing the part of him that's hurt so many. I could never be held responsible for what I was doing.

"Mia," she said.

I stood up. "No. You do not get to tell me what to do. You don't get to judge me. The last person judging me should be you." I closed the gap between us. "Why do you hate them so much? And don't feed me some bullshit."

Nat swallowed. "There are things you don't know."

"So tell me!" I threw my arms up. "Stop standing there and looking at me like I'm the monster!"

She stepped back. "It's more complicated than that."

"Stop making it so complicated."

Nat turned away from me, hugging herself. "I know them." She took a deep breath. "Calliopé and Kysana. During the summer I spent at home with my father, they were in town. I went to a party one night and I had this stupid summer fling going on at the time, and she showed up."

I put my hand on her shoulder, turning her around to look at me. "What happened?"

"Calliopé knew what I was. She and Kysana were there to get dinner and they saw me. I tried to avoid them, but they caught up to me. Calliopé wouldn't let it go. She followed me and my date to the pool and she pushed me in, trying to prove to my date that I couldn't be trusted. She told me that all humans are evil and they will eventually destroy all the sea creatures. They all saw my tail."

I swallowed, grabbing her hands and holding them. "Why didn't you tell me?"

"Because I tried to be a good friend! I tried to forget about it."

Frustration built up inside me and I shook my head, letting go. "They never told me. You're my best friend and they never even told me about what they did."

I stormed out of the house and went down to the beach before Nat could stop me. I needed to slap someone. I needed to punch something.

"Mia, hey!" Kysana waved at me.

Calliopé turned her head to face me. "You don't look happy."

Approaching them, I slapped Calliopé. "What the fuck is wrong with you?"

Kysana backed away. "Mia, what's gotten into you?"

Calliopé stood up in one swift movement, getting ready to throw a punch in return. "What the hell was that?" she yelled.

Nat had followed me, and I didn't ask her to. I hadn't wanted her to, but now she stood behind me. Immediately, Calliopé knew what I was pissed off about.

"She told you," Calliopé said, lifting her chin.

I narrowed my eyes. "She's my best friend. We tell each other everything."

Calliopé rubbed her face. "Who I was back then was a different version of me. I've changed, Mia. You must know that."

"Do I? You didn't even tell me the truth. Nat was hurt and you want to brush it off as if it meant nothing to her!" She pointed to Nat.

Kysana watched us from a distance before coming closer. "Calliopé, she's right. We did something wrong and we never apologized for it. We just expected her to get over it."

Clouds rolled over us as thunder boomed above our heads.

Calliopé crossed her arms, digging her foot into the sand. I could see in her face that she didn't want to admit she was wrong. She was struggling to say anything that made her out as a bad person. "We're sorry. We were awful people and there's no excuse for the way we treated you."

Nat blinked away tears. "You humiliated me. You made me feel like I did something wrong by being happy."

Calliopé nodded. "We did. We humiliated you and I'm sorry that you've had to deal with that. We were the ones who really screwed up. *We* did something wrong—not you."

Kysana approached Nat. "We're so sorry. We made you feel like shit. How can we make it up to you?"

Nat glanced at me. "Mia told me that you're helping us kill Jason, then you'll be gone. Is that true?"

Calliope nodded again.

"Then that's all I need. You stay to help kill the boy who's been terrorizing my best friend, then you leave." She puffed out her chest.

Kysana released a sigh. "Okay. We'll do that."

Rain started pouring down on us, and the wind picked up as lightning struck the sky. Calliopé and Kysana headed to the ocean, to their cave. The waves were rocking back and forth.

Thunder boomed once again while Nat and I rushed to my parents' house, and Dylan supposedly had the same idea when he snuck in with us, shaking his wet hair like a dog. "That storm came out of nowhere."

Nat sat down on the couch. "It didn't come from nowhere. Weather doesn't just appear. It had a purpose."

Dylan laughed. "Well, you proved me wrong."

I took Dylan to the kitchen to talk to him about what our plan was. This talk had to come now. I needed him to know what he was getting into.

"Dylan, you know I'm a siren."

"I know."

"You know that...we eat humans."

"But you don't."

"But I have magic to control them. There's no denying this."

He grabbed my hand. "Mia, you'd never hurt anyone intentionally. I know you."

I was about to crush all his hope. "I'm planning to kill Jason."

"You want to kill him, kill him?" I'd never really made everyone believe in my plan when we went to the academy to research about him. They all thought I was joking, or I'd give up after hitting a brick wall.

"I have no option. He's evil, and he's only going to hurt more people. But I want you to know that if you stay with me, this is what you're going to be getting yourself into for the rest of your life. This is the lifestyle I come with. It's a package deal," I said.

He squeezed my hand, giving me a smile. "I know. I'm quite aware that sirens are not pretty little fairies. They're man-eating sea creatures. That doesn't change how I feel about you."

After a few seconds, I leaned in and kissed him. Dylan kissed back but before we could even hold each other, the power went out.

Mom came into the kitchen and grabbed her lighter. "The storm hit hard." She started lighting candles. "You two better not be about to have sex in my house."

I laughed a bit, grabbing Dylan's hand. "I guess we have to find a way to entertain each other in this power outage."

Mom narrowed her eyes. "Excuse me?"

"I'm kidding!" I laughed more. "We're not doing that. I

promise."

Olivia came running in, looking at Dylan and I. "Nat and I had an idea on what to do with this. Let's meet in your basement." She nodded, heading to the basement.

Dylan and I followed her down, finding Nat and her setting up for a game. No, this wasn't a game.

Nat set up the candles. "Maybe you tried to burn his bones and it didn't work. But he's still a ghost, right?" She cleared her throat. "We can try to control him. You can control him, Mia."

"And do what?" I sat on the floor, Dylan beside me.

Nat looked at Olivia. "Olivia and I got to talking and we were thinking maybe...you can force him to tell you how he dies."

Why hadn't I ever thought of that? I had the power, and I could force the truth out of him, but would it work? It had to.

They finished setting up for the séance or whatever. We all held hands, and Olivia scanned the room. "You must pull him here, Mia. You have to force him here. You can do it."

"I can't. The moon isn't shining. I have no magic." My mom's voice echoed in my head as she reminded me I could steal energy from the moon and those around me. I knew what it looked like and it was only behind the clouds. If I could steal the energy, I could use my magic.

Nodding, I closed my eyes and pictured myself plucking Jason from wherever he was, placing him right in front of us. I sucked all the energy out from everyone around me to make this happen. The fingers wrapped in mine slipped out.

When I opened my eyes, all my friends were laying on the ground, but Jason was right in front of me. "What the hell is this?"

I had a short window. "Tell me how I can kill you." I lifted my palms as they glowed from all the power I'd stolen.

Jason smirked. "You can't. I told you, Mia. This is not something you can accept, and it shows. I'm immortal. I'm dead. I cannot be killed."

What was I doing wrong? He was still standing here, denying the truth.

Word play. That was it.

"You say I can't kill you, and maybe you're right, Jason. But how can I get rid of your spirit forever?" I sucked more energy from my friends and the moon, fighting every ounce in me that wanted to take a nap.

He closed his eyes and let out a sigh. He knew I had caught him this time. He couldn't die technically speaking, but he could be banished somehow. "You have to find my most prized possession. When you find it, you must find a piece of my DNA and put it inside. Burn it." He swallowed. "But that's not enough, Mia. You have to banish me from ever coming within a hundred feet of you."

And my friends. I would have to banish him from coming within a hundred feet of us all.

I let go of the invisible ropes and Jason left the room in a puff of smoke as I fell to the ground. All the energy returned to my friends.

"Mia?" Dylan sat up and grabbed my shoulders. He pulled my head into his lap and pushed hair away from my face. "Mia, what happened?"

I struggled to keep my eyes open, but I fought. I'd used up so much energy this time that I needed a long nap, but first, I had to tell them the truth.

When I told them what Jason told me, Nat looked at Dylan and Olivia. "How do we find his DNA if you burned it all? This sounds like witchcraft, and we are not witches. We are sea creatures. Witches don't exist." I almost choked when I heard Nat say that. She believed in so much, but saying witches weren't real was a shock to me.

Dylan grabbed a pillow and placed it under my head as if his lap had been uncomfortable. It wasn't, but I didn't argue.

"We'll find a way. DNA can linger for years." Olivia grabbed all the candles.

Swallowing, the idea came to me. "His DNA would still be all over that house. He might be a ghost, but when I forced him to bang his head, he bled. Part of him is still alive, meaning his spirit form has pieces of DNA inside. One way or another, we will kill him. No creature lives forever, including adaro."

Thirty-nine

LAUGHING FILLED THE ROOM, bringing the atmosphere up in vibes. Dylan held my hand and spun me, not realizing I couldn't balance on my own. I fell and Dylan went with me. We both crashed to the floor as groans escaped from our lips.

"I was trying to warn you," I told him, rubbing my butt.

He helped me up and kissed my lips. "I don't listen very well. Now you know."

I laughed. "I'll remember to mark my birthday on the calendar."

Dylan put his forehead against mine. "I wanted to ask you if I could see your tail again. I know it went wrong last time but this time we can do it here, in a controlled environment. Alone. I just want to know what any of our kids may look like," he whispered.

I looked at him and sighed. "About that," I started. "I don't think we should have kids."

"Why?"

"Because when a siren is conceived, a human must die in their place. A brutal death. I don't want to kill someone just to have a child I may not ever want. I'm not sure I want children, Dill."

He nodded and pushed some hair strands behind my ear. "I understand."

"You do? But if you want kids, I don't want to hold you back."

"Mia, I'm not sure I want them either."

Natalia hit me from the side and put her hands on her hips. "Show him again. Holding off isn't going to lessen the fear. He's your best friend. Do it."

I looked at him and nodded. "Okay, fine. But we have to go to a swimming place that is private this time."

Dylan smiled, embracing me in a hug. "This is going to be great."

Everyone put on their best swimsuits and we all went down to the beach. We found a spot that didn't have people around and it seemed secluded enough.

I looked at them. "Well... Here goes nothing."

Upon request, I took off my bottoms. I dived into the salty water and came back up. I felt a poke in my back, but I rubbed the area and it went away. "You can look."

They all turned. Olivia and Dylan were the most intrigued since they didn't have their own. Olivia was watching it glisten in the sunlight. Dylan was distracted by the colors.

Dylan came over and bent down, touching it to check if it was still as real as the other night. It was. He looked at me and sat in the shallow water. "This is even cooler than being a siren, having a tail of course."

Olivia was smiling and squealing like a lunatic. "It's just so pretty! I'm so jealous. It's so awesome. You are so lucky to be able to grow a tail."

I shrugged, yawning. The heaviness weighed on my eyelids. I knew that sleep was threatening me, and it would most likely win. "I'm going to sleep now..."

Nat argued, "But we are hanging out. We just woke up a few hours ago. It's not even bedtime."

I put my lead in Dylan's lap, closing my eyes. "Goodnight." And just like that, sleep took me away from this world.

I WOKE UP BACK in my bed back home. I scanned the room, wondering what had happened. I'd gotten so tired all of a sudden. How did that happen? I got out of my bed, searching everything I could think of to solve this problem.

"What are you doing?" Dylan asked.

I looked back at him. "I'm trying to find evidence. Jason did this. I know it." I continued to search for the things I'd used, like glasses and plates.

"What did he do?"

"He drugged me or knocked me out. I passed out for no real reason. I was showing everyone the biggest deal of my life. I don't suddenly pass out from that."

Dylan came over to me. "Mia, you were tired. It's fine. It's normal to be tired."

"No!" I turned and faced him again. "I know myself. I know that I would not get tired like that. I know my limits. I know my body, Dylan. Damnit, why can't you just believe me?"

"Mia, why is everything his fault? He's not here."

"Excuse me? What the hell kind of bullshit are you spewing? We have to defeat him because as far as we know, he's still after me. He very well could have poisoned me or something."

"With us all around you? What would that accomplish? We were present. He couldn't get to you this time."

"He could have tried! It's not like *you* are very threatening. He could have tried to catch us off guard. You wouldn't have been prepared. I swear if you keep saying that I was just tired and I don't know my own body, I will beat your ass." I pointed my finger at him.

He sighed. "Fine. I'll drop it." He put his hands up in defense.

"I'm going to get ice cream. Ice cream solves my problems and I love you enough to not want to risk beating you for this." I grabbed my wallet that had a five-dollar bill, walking out of the house to find a shop.

I found an ice cream shop that was cheap enough to afford. I picked out a cookie dough flavor with just one scoop. I sat and licked my ice cream and sighed. I looked at the time, seeing 5:11 p.m. on my phone. It was so late. I wasted the day by sleeping and I was positive that Jason was the culprit.

I heard a ping on my phone, looking to see a message across my screen. Dylan had texted me.

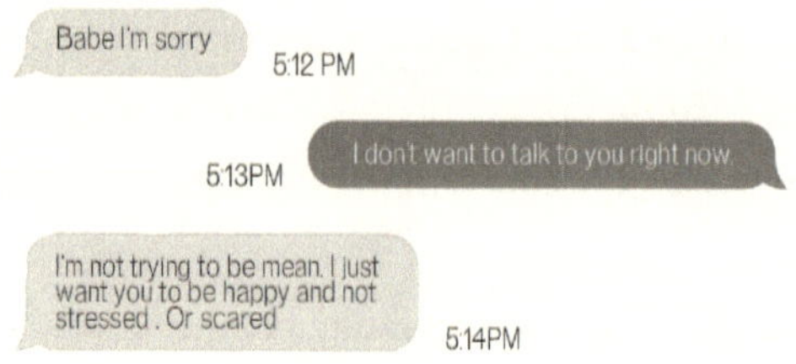

I sighed, rubbing my eyes. His response was one I had no way to respond to. I continued to eat my ice cream, focusing on that first. The end of the ice cream was the best part. When I shoved the point of that waffle cone into my mouth—tasting whatever ice cream had melted into it—it was the best part, and I saved the best for last.

I finally replied to his message.

I get that but you still refuse to believe me. Ignoring the problem doesn't solve anything. If you want me to accept your apology, you have to understand that I may very well be right.

5:27 PM

I didn't get a response after that.

"Can I sit here, siren?" someone asked me.

I looked at her and rolled my eyes. "If you want." I gestured to the seat.

Olivia sat down and looked at me. "What's wrong? You seem stressed."

"Dylan and I had an argument. He doesn't believe that I could've been drugged or something. He thinks I was just tired. I know I wasn't. I know when I'm tired. I have a body that works with my activity. If I'm active, I will not be tired. If I'm listening to music, I will not be tired. I can get tired from piano music and watching something, but I can't fall asleep to regular music. I'm too tempted to sing. If I'm in the middle of showing you my tail, I can't be tired. There's no way." I sighed and rubbed the bridge of my nose. "I know how I felt. I wasn't just tired." But how did Jason drug me when everyone was there? It was supposed to be a private spot.

She grabbed my hand and held it. "Hey, don't worry. If you're right, it will show eventually. Couples disagree. I get that. You have to learn to disagree and move on. You're going to have plenty of more disagreements in the future and if you get married, you must know how to dispute your arguments. Hiding in an ice cream shop isn't going to solve anything."

"It helps me *cool* off."

"I know you, Mia. You wouldn't hurt anyone who didn't deserve it. You wouldn't hurt Dylan over a disagreement. You need to solve your problems like adults. You have to know how to talk it out. If he disagrees, prove him wrong. Don't run."

I crossed my arms. "How? I can't find any evidence. Maybe I'm wrong. I don't want to be wrong."

She scoffed. "Nobody wants to be wrong. We all think we're right. But part of life is accepting when you're wrong and admitting it. It makes you a better person. Trust me."

I nodded my head, glancing at my phone. I sent out another message to him.

I'm sorry. I'm sorry for getting as upset as I did. I just truly believe he was behind this and I want your support. You mean the world to me. I let you into my world and I just want to know it was the right choice. You're the fin to my tail or however that sappy stuffy works. If you can please reply to this, that would be great. I don't want you to be mad at me and I don't want to be mad at you. You're my Dill Pickle. Don't go anywhere, please. I'll be back soon so we can figure this out and solve this like a couple. I love you, Dill. You're my sunshine.

I looked out the window and widened my eyes. I got up. "Oh my gosh."

"What?" Olivia looked in the direction I was. "Who's she?"

Don't do it, Mia.

But I did it anyway.

I went outside and Olivia was quick to follow. "Well, how's Lena?"

She looked at me. "Molly, hi."

"It's Mia."

"Whatever. What are you doing here?" She turned to face me.

"I could ask you the same." I gestured to her.

Lena was one of the mermaids who had made fun of me all those years. "I'm here to help my little sister. She's having trouble in school."

"I live here. This is Olivia, a friend of mine" I gestured to Olivia. Olivia gave her a nod, not having yet realized we were not friends.

"Do you still stuff your bra?" She looked at my chest and I crossed my arms to cover myself.

"I have boobs now."

Olivia was beginning to catch on to what was happening here. She stepped in. "Mia and I will be going back. She's got a boyfriend to make up with. It beats looking at you all day long."

Lena laughed. "Such a cute comeback. But maybe next time you should stand in the background. You look better there."

Before anyone could register it, Olivia swung her fist at Lena's face. "Fuck off."

Lena held her face, sending the biggest death glare I'd seen in the last year.

Olivia and I left her there and I felt better. Olivia wasn't like Dylan. He would've told us both to leave her to her skewed logic. Olivia, however, wasn't taking that crap.

I stopped in my tracks, catching Olivia's attention. "Mia?"

"Olivia, I see him. I see Jason. Do you see him?" I looked at her, then back to the spot where I saw him, by a building across the street. He was gone.

My suspicions had been confirmed. He was stalking me.

She looked over there and shook her head. "There's no one there."

"Of course there isn't." I sighed. I swear I had seen him.

I did.

We walked back to the apartment and I looked around, doubt creeping in. Dylan wasn't here. I started to tear apart the room to find anything to prove I was right. I had to be. I was right.

I ran to the bathroom, looking into the mirror. I remembered being poked. I checked my back in the mirror cabinets, seeing the tiniest hole. I leaned against the wall for support. "Olivia."

She came in and looked at my back..

"He did it. Jason was here. I know he was. He fucking drugged me."

She put her hand on my shoulder. "You okay?"

"No." I began to cry, sliding down the wall. "Dylan is doubting me, and Jason is still after me. I have real proof. It's not fair. And what about what happened the other day? He almost killed him."

Olivia sat next to me and grabbed my hand, intertwining our fingers. "Don't you worry about that. Dylan loves you. He will always love you. You have to focus on that. He will get over it. We are going to get Jason once and for all. We have a plan."

"This plan needs to happen now. I can't take this. I can't do this anymore." I continued to sob, letting her comfort me. Everything overwhelmed me. We worked hard to prepare for Jason and finally kill him, but I was not prepared for the cost. The price to pay would be more than I could bargain for.

After I finished my crying session, Olivia helped me gather the supplies needed to finally kill Jason. It was nearing night which was the perfect time for me to start my final battle. I had all the power now.

The one ingredient we were missing was his DNA. We had his most prized possession, which was a baseball glove given to him by his father.

We went to the beach and Jason stood, waiting for us. He expected us.

I lifted the glove. "You can't hurt us anymore."

Handing the glove to Nat, I lifted my hands as they glowed. "Give us a strand of your hair."

Jason did as he was told, handing Nat a piece of his hair. She put it inside the glove. I grabbed it from her and held onto it. "I banish you, Jason Stanford, from ever coming near me *or* my friends again."

With the swipe of a hand, Jason was gone. He disappeared and left us, and I was too happy to have the energy to celebrate. My friends all cheered and hugged me, but I stood there. I stood in shock.

They all decided to head back home but I stayed. I stayed to relish in the wonderful feeling of victory.

I took those last steps towards the water, the waves calling to me. They tempted me with their song, reaching to get a hold of me. I was alone.

I was completely alone.

The tide washed over my feet, turning me into the very fish I was. I swam into the ocean, spinning around and moving my fins against the water without a care.

I looked around when something swam by me. I went back to swimming, my chest beginning to tighten.

Something swam by again and when I tried to see what it was, it grabbed my hair from behind, dragging me down to the bottom of the ocean. As pretty as the reef was, it was painful when my back was slammed against it. I knew only one person who did this kind of thing to me.

I opened my eyes, staring directly into the soulless eyes that belonged to Jason. I should have known it would never be that easy. He was still here.

But why had he lied when I forced him to tell me the truth?

He pressed my body against the coral, using his hands to cover my gills. I began to struggle, grabbing onto anything around me. I couldn't breathe.

I elbowed him in the gut and he swam back. I swam towards him, pushing him up towards the surface. When I got us up the shore, I slammed him into the rocks. "You lied to me!"

"I had to lie! You keep thinking I can be controlled!" He pushed me off and I fell into the water.

Glancing at the moon, it hit me. There was only one way I could truly defeat Jason and I wasn't proud of this, but it was for everyone's safety.

With my hands glowing, I told him to stop, and he did. When I felt the energy drain from me, I stole more until I was refreshed and powerful.

"Jason, you have lied to me and terrorized me for too long. We know the truth. We know why you did what you did." I swallowed the guilt. "So, I command you one final time to do what you did the first time as aunga, but to the adaro you are now. I command you to kill yourself once and for all."

His eyes went wide as he looked towards the sand. He walked towards a pile of sticks, using a few rocks to spark up a fire. I'd found the secret behind killing adaro, and that's why they could never be killed.

They had to do it to themselves.

Jason stuck his hand into the fire and limb by limb, he began to burn as his screams pierced the air around us.

Every ounce of energy that left me, I took more of. I sucked it all from around me, refusing to let go. I was too close to give up now. I dropped to my knees and yelled out as I watched Jason burn to ash, leaving him as nothing but a memory.

When he ceased to exist, I let go of the ropes tethering me to the energy. I collapsed and closed my eyes, but familiar voices came to my aid.

I coughed and sat up, heavy breaths continuing as I filled my lungs with air and then let it go again. I looked at everyone. They all had looks of concern, but Nat knew what I'd done. She knew I did the one thing I never wanted to do. I made a man kill himself for me.

Nat released a sigh of relief. "He's gone." She reached out, grabbing my hand to reassure me it was true. "Jason is finally gone."

And I had the pleasure of watching him burn himself to smithereens. How lucky I had been...

Forty

Dylan held my face, kissing me with more passion than I had ever gotten in the past few days.

Someone whistled, causing Dylan and I to pull away. "You two really are going at it," my brother said.

I blushed, trying to rub away the pink tones in my cheeks. It didn't work.

Natalia looked at him and hit his arm, shaking her head. "Don't ruin the moment."

"Well, well, well," a new voice popped into the mix.

We all looked in that direction and I pushed hair from my face, struggling as it clung to my wet skin.

"What are you doing here?" I asked. Lena had brought the mermaid queen or whatever the hell they called popular girls nowadays.

"You killed Jason. We're not surprised. You were bound to show your true side," the leader said.

"Leave us alone. This doesn't concern you. It concerned Jason and I," I told them.

"And your friends, of course." She gestured to them. "They

killed him, too. They helped you plan it."

"They did. Why should I care? I tried to be the better person. I tried to show you that I was nothing like the other sirens. You didn't believe me. You judged me. You don't get to judge me for defending myself." I pulled a shirt on, hiding my breasts.

"Defense? Is that what you call murder?"

I snapped, "Yes. When he has beaten you and become violent, you take action. There is no mermaid jail. Jail isn't an option for someone like him. It's about life or death. He stalked me. He tried to kill me. That calls for defense. Death was the solution. He was vile." I used a towel to dry myself.

"You're exactly what you tried so hard not to become."

Olivia stepped forward, pulling her fist back. "Watch your damn mouth."

Lena was the first to cower, knowing what it was like to feel Olivia's anger. It was satisfying to watch to say the least.

"You let her fight your battles. Cute," the queen said, crossing her arms.

"I can't walk, dumbass," I said with a sneer.

"Then come and get us in your natural habitat." She swam back into the waters.

Olivia held me back. "Mia, don't."

Natalia didn't control her urges as she pulled herself back into the water, chasing them. I had to go after them. "If I don't help her, they'll win." I looked at Olivia.

Olivia loosened her grip before she finally let go.

This time, I didn't have the option of using my magic to control the mermaids. The sun was out and I had to use just my wits to survive.

I got back into the water, chasing after them. I grabbed the fin of one, sinking my teeth into her tail. She flopped around, the water silencing her screams.

Unlike them, I had a weapon.

My teeth.

I grabbed her arm and pulled her closer, using my teeth to rip her throat open. Her blood flowed and became one with the water as she choked. Her eyes glassed over, and her body floated but her movements ceased to exist.

Natalia was fighting Lena and her queen B, Leila. That had been her name at the academy.

Swimming towards them, I raced through the water, moving against it. I opened my mouth, running into Lena, biting her neck. My teeth sunk in, allowing her blood to leave her body. With only one way out, it blended with the water. Her body lost all color and I let go of her, looking at Leila.

She watched me, swallowing. She put her arms up in surrender, but I moved towards her, getting her to jerk her body in fright.

Natalia grabbed my hand and pulled us back to the shore, letting her surrender in peace. She pulled us onto the sand and looked at me. "She surrendered. We had to show her mercy. She knows what she did wrong."

Dylan came over, checking my body for any injuries. "What happened?"

Natalia looked at him. "She killed the other two mermaids."

Olivia and Christian rushed over. Christian was the first to say, "Mia, you're a murderer."

"I was a murderer when I killed Jason, Todd, and that other boy. We all are murderers for planning his death. These mermaids had it coming." I felt that rush in my veins as I ripped their skin open and allowed their blood to mix with the salt water. I'd seen the muscles inside their neck.

Dylan used his thumb to brush my cheek, lowering my bottom lip to see my teeth. They were still sharp, refusing to retract.

I laid my hands across my stomach, looking at the sky. "This is what I am. I'm a siren. I'm tired of being pushed around for resisting the temptation to kill those who hurt me. I'm going to embrace what I am. That means embracing the part of me that wants to fight back. I will fight back against my bullies. It's the only way I can win this."

Natalia looked at my brother and back at me. "Don't forget who you are. Mia Dawson, the girl who grew up with Dylan Adler. You fell in love with your best friend. You have a group of friends who support you. Don't forget that we care. We love the Mia we know." She grabbed one of my hands.

I shifted my eyes to hers, feeling my teeth retract, revealing my human ones. My face softened and I tightened my hand around hers. "I love all of you. I won't change that. I'm just tired of being seen as the girl who won't defend herself."

Natalia smiled and we got back our legs eventually. After we got dressed, we headed back to my parents' house.

I touched my lips, taking a deep breath. I looked at my friends, wiping the tears that began to roll down my cheeks.

Dylan used his knuckle to wipe some more. "What's wrong?"

"Everything. Everything that has happened is too much to handle. I've become something I swore I wouldn't. So much has changed. I was there. I tore their throats apart. I enjoyed every second of it. I'm a monster."

He pulled my face, making me look at him. "You are not a

monster. You were defending yourself. You have been pushed around for too long. They thought they could get away with it and you stood up for yourself."

"If you say so..." I didn't entirely believe him. I still saw the monstrous side of myself. He wasn't there when I killed them. He couldn't understand the story because he didn't feel what I felt. He didn't witness me murdering two mermaids. I saw all of it. I knew exactly what I did.

Mom made everyone food after the long day, and I sat by the window, admiring the sky. I wasn't so sure of what Mom or Dad would think of me, knowing what I did. I was terrified. I needed to prepare for anything.

"You're okay now," Christian said. He sat in the seat next to me, observing the remorse displayed on my face.

I looked at him. "It's going to take a lot of therapy to be okay. This is not something I can get over like that. I need something to help me. I want to be okay but I just can't be." I laid my head on his shoulder. It had been a while since we had been this close. I missed this with my brother.

After they all ate, Olivia, Nat, and Dylan left. Mom stood next to Dad as she watched Christian and I. "How was it?"

"We need to talk."

Mom knew that wasn't a good sign. More than anything, Dad was freaking out and it showed in his eyes.

Christian went upstairs while I sat on the couch. "I've done something bad."

"Oh no..." Mom started pacing.

Dad tried to calm her. "Listen to what she has to say, Jenn."

Mom took his advice for a moment and looked at me.

I chewed on my lips, tearing the skin off without any consideration. "Jason is dead." Mom showed a sigh of relief.

Dad seemed indifferent. "But so are some mermaids."

"You did what?" Dad yelled.

I looked down, completely ashamed. There was no worse feeling than your parents being disappointed in you. No parent wanted a murderous child.

Mom sat next to me. "Who did you kill?"

"My bullies. I tried to control myself. I did. I never once used my abilities on him. I never lashed out. But after I discovered what he was and he attacked me, I knew I had to take him out. I used my magic to kill him. I made him kill himself, again."

"That's not so bad." Mom nodded, looking at Dad who seemed to calm down.

"Then mermaids came. They began to make fun of me. They were making me out as a bad guy. I got so mad... I... I murdered them. I killed two mermaids."

Dad began to freak out again. "Shit! Jenn, what do we do? She killed mermaids! Everyone is going to notice dead mermaids!" He pointed to me.

Mom pushed my hair back, staring at me. "We pretend we had nothing to do with it. Cover our tracks. Being a siren comes with its downsides. You do what you have to do. Defend yourself. Be thankful our daughter doesn't kill human men for food."

DYLAN, OLIVIA, AND I all left the building and found our families. Nat joined us with her own diploma in hand as we held our cap and diploma in ours.

Everyone congratulated us, taking all the pictures they

could. I couldn't deny that I looked good in purple. Dylan did, too.

Dylan and I took one selfie together, celebrating the idea of being high school sweethearts and childhood friends. After everything he knew and went through with me, there was nothing that could tear us apart now.

We spent the whole night celebrating the final goodbye to childhood, and when everyone headed out, I was left with my parents. Christian called it a night and Nat was celebrating with Olivia.

"I suppose it's time for me to find a job and move out," I joked. "Oh, wait, I already did that."

Being a full adult who had graduated would be a whole new world, but one I would dive into like I did when I found the ocean. I was ready to take on life itself and steer my future.

I saw the look my parents gave each other. They were communicating through expression, so I asked, "What?"

Mom looked at Dad and nodded her head. He went to the kitchen and brought back a plate of food. "Your mother thought you might want this."

Before me was a plate of human meat, seasoned with spices and blood. I looked at my dad and hesitated before grabbing the plate.

Mom nodded. "Go on. Try it. This man died at the hands of another human. We just ordered his meat."

It was almost like I had graduated not only from high school, but from the old version of Mia. As much as I hated to admit it, I wanted a taste after I ripped the mermaids' throats out.

I set it on my lap, using a fork and knife to cut off a piece. I took a deep breath, shoving my fork into the flesh. The smell was irresistible. It was soaked in juices and marinated enough to make my mouth water. My stomach grumbled, telling me it was time to take that bite. I had never done so willingly before.

I put the bite in my mouth before I changed my mind, chewing slowly to really savor the flavor. I continued to chew, nodding. Mom looked at me, lifting her eyebrows. "Well?"

Deep down, I knew without a doubt I was what I ate.

As I shoved another bite into my mouth, chewing it, I said, "I love it."

Dylan

PURE. METALLIC. SHIMMERED WHEN the light hit her just right.

Mia Dawson had always been the kind of girl that others ran from and that was solely because they were afraid of the boldness that came through her even when the darkness and misery tried to drag her down. She never let that happen, though.

She was a different kind of girl, forged by the unending heat of Florida summers but also the not so kind words Todd had thrown around in her absence.

How I missed that radiance she would carry with her.

The bright smiles and laughter that would light up anyone's day, but mostly mine. It had been seven years too long without any of it.

How did anyone forget someone so absolute?

They all forgot about her like she was just the unfiltered scraps, but she was so much more than that. She was the spirit molded from the world around her. She was ten times what they'd ever become. So authentic that you couldn't tell if she had been the before or the after. She was neither, yet both all at once.

She was *gold* in its raw form.

Olivia picked up the last twizzler, devouring it in seconds. "You gotta be faster if you want it. I don't mess around with my candy."

I rolled my eyes as I went up to my room to change my shirt.

Pulling my shirt off, I heard thumps coming from the room across from mine. I glanced out my window. The window across from mine—Mia's window—was open. Not all the way, but just enough for me to notice. Her pink curtains were drawn, but my eyesight didn't fail me now.

I opened my window and called out, "Mia? Mia, are you in there?"

No response. Maybe I'd been crazy. Maybe it was her parents cleaning out her room.

Why had they sent her away in the first place? I asked but they never gave me the real answer. Boarding school, sure. But why? She'd been a good kid.

After determining that she was not there, I closed my window and headed back downstairs. "Damnit, I forgot my shirt," I mumbled.

Olivia laughed as she handed me one from the clean clothes. "Don't hesitate to ask next time."

A loud bang ripped through the sky. A flash of lightning and the power went out. Great. Loved the storms around here. As long as it wasn't another hurricane.

I went over to the windows and looked up into the sky as the clouds darkened. "Get the candles out. It'll probably last all night," I told Oli. She didn't waste any seconds getting them out as well as a lighter. While she lit them, something caught my eye.

Outside. I saw Christian out in the rain as someone rummaged through the truck. I recognized the near-auburn hair almost immediately.

It was *her*.

"Oli, I'll be back later." I rushed outside before she could ask questions.

Seven years. *Seven years too long.*

"Got it! We can go now!" she yelled as I approached.

"Mia?" I asked.

She seemed to freeze where she was. Did she hate me? Did I do something wrong? No, that couldn't be.

Christian looked between us before grabbing the flashlight from Mia, saying, "I'll be inside." He left us alone.

When she faced me, she seemed a little taken back. "Hi, Dylan."

Mia still had the same facial structure so it was obvious that it couldn't be anyone else but her. Now—now she looked so grown up. She looked so much more like the adult version of the girl I once knew.

Still, she was golden.

I rubbed my neck. "I didn't realize you had come home."

Her voice was quiet. "I came home today. I haven't been home for long, really."

Inspecting the street and concluding that the whole block was experiencing this power outage, I smiled a little. "Well, since you are home and the power has brought us back to the dark ages, why don't we head inside?"

A smile formed. "Sure."

We headed inside and I almost debated turning around and running. But that wouldn't do any good. I needed to see her again. I needed to talk to her again and figure out if we were still best friends after all this time.

Once we made it to her room, I sat on the small chair in front of her childish vanity. "I see you grew but your room didn't," I said, laughing.

Her smile seemed to soften. "It has been a while."

Without thinking further, I asked, "Where were you for those years?"

Sure, her parents told me she went to boarding school, and sure I could have told her they told me that. But I wanted to hear her answer without any bias, or influence.

"I..." Her smile faded away, yet even through it all, her light shined bright. "I went to an academy."

Not a boarding school, but similar enough.

"Didn't picture you as the academic type." I studied a mini lipstick. This had to be far past expired by now.

"It was just a program. Supposed to help my future or something like that. An academy for girls. That's all." Girls? Her parents never mentioned she went to an all-girls school.

I asked, "You went to an all-girls school?"

As she nodded, she picked at her fingernails. Was she nervous, or lying? "I did."

Furrowing my brows, a thought occurred. "Why? I could never survive with only boys for seven years. You..." My face heated up as I realized the direction of this conversation. "You started to have crushes and date."

Mia didn't take it the way I expected. "That's true." She nodded.

Then I had to ask the question, out of curiosity. "Were you sneaking out to look at the boys or were you getting eye candy in class already?" I remembered she could take it the wrong way, and I didn't need to push her away, so I added, "but that's cool if you are! Olivia is into girls, too."

Olivia and Mia? I wasn't sure how I felt about that, but I supposed my feelings didn't matter all that much here.

She laughed with the shake of her head. She actually laughed at me. "No, Dylan. I like boys. I just didn't date any. But I'm home now and there's a possibility I could find someone here. Maybe. It is senior year. We should make the most of it."

She didn't date? Did that mean she'd never kissed anyone? She'd never been out on a date? Did she even have crushes? She said so, though. She said she could find someone here. As if anyone here was worthy to even touch someone as admirable as Mia.

"Fair," I said. I looked at her wall. "It's been so long that I'm surprised you're back."

"Why? Did you think I was not coming back?" Her tone had a hint of sarcasm in it.

If she'd been in my shoes, she'd understand that I had accepted she was never coming back. It was a cruel reality I was forced to live in.

"I assumed you were going to be at that school until you graduated. You'd come back here to see your family for the summer but forget about me. You'd leave again to go to college." I grabbed a loose thread from her blanket and wrapped it around my finger.

She shrugged so nonchalantly. "It's a seven-year program. Thankfully, I did find a friend there. The school wasn't all that bad." Was that friend of hers trustworthy? Did she take care of Mia, and support her in every situation? I hoped to hell she did.

My phone went off and I checked the notification. "Oh damn." It was one thing to hear about crimes, but murders? Murders right in our own area? On our beaches? It was terrifying.

"What is it?" she asked. Her voice sounded like chocolate that had been freshly melted. I wasn't sure why it did, but it was pleasant.

I showed her my screen as I shook my head. "They found a dead body tonight. A boy. Down by the ocean." I could only imagine the way his parents felt. His friends, too.

She seemed a little upset by it. "A dead body? Do they know what it looks like? How he died?" When I peered into her eyes, I noticed how sick she truly felt. Maybe it had been too much to show her. She had just returned home and here I was already warning her to run like hell before something happened to any of us.

"Nothing. It just says any information is going to be released at a later date. They haven't released any details other than that." I slipped my phone back into my pocket.

Her gaze moved out the window. "Do you think it was the storm? Or something else?" She leaned against the window with her hands against the windowsill.

"Something else? Like a shark, or a person? I think maybe he was swimming in the ocean and got caught in the storm. He drowned." I coughed a bit. Maybe that would ease her fears. The last thing I wanted was for someone so gleaming to be scared of something like this. She deserved to smile, didn't she? Of course. And this boy's death was merely an accident. It had to be.

"It's possible, sure." Something in her voice changed. More of like she wasn't terrified of the possibilities but rather interested in the case.

"I think I learned something new about you." I watched her.

"And what is that?" She looked back at me.

"Crime and mystery intrigue you."

She leaned deeper into the window. "You could say that." She pushed herself off and got the flashlight. "But I need answers."

I jumped to my feet as I figured out what her intentions were. "Whoa, whoa. You're not considering going to a crime scene, are you? In the middle of this storm?" Was she crazy? Maybe. But that hadn't changed much over seven years.

"Rain doesn't scare me, Dylan." And by the look on her face, she was telling the truth. She didn't appear to be scared of the weather. She wanted to solve a crime that wasn't even ours to solve. We were barely seniors in high school.

With a snicker, I said, "No, but lightning should."

"I'm not afraid of a little lightning. Besides, it's more likely to strike farther away from the storm. Not in it." Where did she get her facts from? She studied weather now?

She gave me a smile before disappearing into the hall. I quietly followed her downstairs and through the backyard. She went to close the gate, but I stuck my foot in to jam it. "You decided to come?" she asked.

"I can't let you go alone." I'd never allow that. No best friend would.

She hesitated for a moment. "If you follow me, we can't tell anyone about this."

"Aren't you about to turn eighteen?" She was. I knew that. I could never forget it. I could never forget her no matter how hard I tried. All those years apart and she was still my other half.

"You remember my birthday? After all these years?" She appeared so surprised by that. We had been best friends for most of our childhood. Not including those seven years she left me, sure. But we were inseparable at one point, and I wanted to get back there again.

I shrugged, smiling. "You think I would forget my best friend's birthday? Highly unlikely. Even if you were gone for so long. Now come, let's go see this crime scene." I pulled her flashlight from her fingers and decided to lead the way to the ocean. Not to assert my authority or say she couldn't do the job just as well or better, but to prove to her I was wholly in this even if I didn't want to be.

Simply because she *was*.

Simply because she was my best friend and I wanted to jumpstart that friendship once again.

When we approached the beach, we noticed the tape first. It didn't deter us from slipping underneath it. Nothing could. Not here. Not now.

Until Mia spotted the blood splattered across some rocks. "Dylan," her voice came out in a whisper. "I don't think the boy drowned."

My first thought was to shield her from such horrors. She didn't need to be exposed to something so grotesque.

"Mia, look at me," I said. When she did so, I kept my eyes focused only on her. "Maybe we shouldn't be involved in this."

"Maybe. But I feel an obligation to find his killer."

"Why?" I searched her eyes for the answers.

Unfortunately for me, I never got a single one.

Also by Monica Shantel

THE FEATHERS AND FLAMES TRILOGY

Beauty of a Crimson Soul

Beauty of a Burning Flame

Beauty of a Permanent Love

THE TO BELIEVE DUOLOGY

To Believe in Peter Pan

To Believe in the Demon King

STANDALONES

37 Nights

Acknowledgements

Thanks to my mom for always supporting my writing, even as a valid career. Thanks to my brother who's asked questions and made me think about my plots, and to the other family members who have picked up my books just to say they were proud of me.

To Ashly for always supporting me, and to my old best friend who was in my life for a time when I needed it. I appreciate the inspiration for this book when we used to pretend to be mermaids at the community pool.

And thank you to Samantha for pointing out the rights and wrongs of this book to help me make it the best it would be. This book needed all your help.

About the Author

Monica Shantel has always had an interest in artistic and creative hobbies of sorts, including but not limited to: drawing, crafting, graphic design, and painting. Although all she has is a high school diploma under her belt, she is not new to the writing community. At the age of twelve, she began building stories to escape reality and find hope in life once again. Her debut novel is Beauty of a Crimson Soul. Along the same genre, she writes dark tales of mythical romance which only add more to the growing fantasy worlds inside her head.

www.ingramcontent.com/pod-product-compliance
Lightning Source LLC
Chambersburg PA
CBHW020339310726
48979CB00015B/2437/J

9781960696007